COMPULSION

'Remove your dress, Mrs Penrose.'

Automatically her hands went to the buttons of the bodice and she began unfastening them. If she simply obeyed instructions, as she had been told to do, it seemed easier. Things would just happen without her making them happen. In a way, she would be innocent of anything that occurred.

Even so, she hesitated at the final button, realising that the bulge of her breasts in the black brassiere could be seen. It was now or never, she realised; now was her last chance to walk out of the door and tell the chauffeur to take her home . . .

Also available from Headline Delta

Bianca
Two Weeks in May
The Lusts of the Borgias
Love Italian Style
Ecstasy Italian Style
Rapture Italian Style
Amorous Liaisons
Lustful Liaisons
Eroticon Dreams
Eroticon Desires
The Sensual Mirror
French Frolics
Claudine
Wild Abandon
French Thrills
In the Mood
A Slave to Love
Amorous Appetites
The Blue Lantern
Sex and Mrs Saxon
Fondle on Top
Fondle in Flagrante
Fondle All Over
Kiss of Death
The Phallus of Osiris
High Jinks Hall
The Delicious Daughter
Three Women
Passion in Paradise
Ménage à Trois

Compulsion

Maria Caprio

HEADLINE DELTA

Copyright © 1994 Maria Caprio

The right of Maria Caprio to be identified as the Author
of the Work has been asserted by her in accordance with the
Copyright, Designs and Patents Act 1988.

First published in 1994
by HEADLINE BOOK PUBLISHING

A HEADLINE DELTA paperback

10 9 8 7 6 5 4 3 2

All rights reserved. No part of this publication may be
reproduced, stored in a retrieval system, or transmitted,
in any form or by any means without the prior written
permission of the publisher, nor be otherwise circulated
in any form of binding or cover other than that in which
it is published and without a similar condition being
imposed on the subsequent purchaser.

All characters in this publication are fictitious
and any resemblance to real persons, living or dead,
is purely coincidental.

ISBN 0 7472 4306 9

Phototypeset by Intype, London
Printed and bound in Great Britain by
Cox & Wyman Ltd, Reading, Berkshire

HEADLINE BOOK PUBLISHING
A division of Hodder Headline PLC
338 Euston Road
London NW1 3BH

Compulsion

Prologue

Amy's wrists were tied with the satin belt of a white negligee. Her arms were raised above her head and her bonds were attached to a chain that hung from a beam in the ceiling.

The beautiful blonde girl wore only white underwear and stockings; her shoes were spike-heeled for fashion rather than comfort.

'You can't do this,' she said. 'Let me go.'

The three men and a woman smiled and continued their preparations. Two of them dragged a mattress across the dusty floor towards her. They did not even answer.

This cannot be happening, she thought. Not in the middle of London.

But this was an isolated part of London, the warehouse studio of photographer Paul Belmont. He had been the unifying force during the three-day shoot for a lingerie spread for Vogue, of which she was the star model. But now he had gone and would not be back until the morning.

The crew had remained, ostensibly to carry on

working, but Amy had said one thing too many and they had turned upon her.

Julia, the elfin faced art director, had pointed an accusing finger, and said: 'That's it. Enough. We've had all we are going to take from you, you arrogant bitch.'

'You can't talk to me like that,' Amy had retorted. 'I'm the one that makes all this work. I'm the face that gives you a pay day.'

Rory, Belmont's muscular photographic assistant, stepped forward. 'You've got the beauty all right. It's a shame you don't have the sense to go with it.'

Amy had said: 'I'll have your job.'

Gavin, the electrician and engineer who built the photographic sets and never wore anything other than tight jeans and a heavy metal T-shirt, ran his eyes over her half-clothed body.

He said: 'It's a shame you don't know when to cover up. Julia got it only half right. You're a prick-teasing arrogant bitch.'

'You're out, too!' Amy had said, suddenly aware that she was still wearing the lingerie from the last shoot.

It had been her practice during the whole three days. Wearing flimsy clothing whilst being photographed was work and everyone should be professional enough to ignore the sexual connotations.

But when the camera was no longer looking, the assistants became human again and professionalism took second place to the surreptitious glances of admiration and lust that she enjoyed provoking.

COMPULSION

And then, even Broderick, the camp make-up artist, had joined in.

'You know what's wrong with her, don't you?' he had said. 'She is not known as the Ice Maiden for nothing. She needs a good fucking.'

His words had shaken her, and had charged the atmosphere in the large echoing studio with the sudden possibility of an outrageous act.

'Why not?' Rory had said, stroking the front of his Levi's. 'She won't tell anybody. It would ruin her reputation.'

Amy had then said the words that had triggered the action.

'You are all so pathetic,'

As she had tried to turn away and move from their threatening circle, Julia had grabbed her arm and spun her around. The negligee had opened, and someone had taken hold of the belt and pulled it free. Someone else had pulled the flimsy garment from her body.

'Tie her hands together,' Julia had ordered, suddenly taking charge.

Rory had grabbed her from behind, pulling her slim but curvaceous body against his so tightly that she could feel the bulge in his trousers pushing against her buttocks. Gavin tied the satin strip around her wrists and they had raised her arms and attached them to the chain.

And now they prepared.

'Let me go,' Amy said. 'Let me go now and I won't say anything. We can all just walk away.'

Rory stood in front of her, grinning. He opened his

shirt slowly, revealing a hairy chest.

'When we've finished, you won't be able to walk.'

'What are you going to do?' Her voice trembled.

'Everything,' he said.

The bra she wore was strapless and he reached behind her and unclipped it. It fell to the floor and her breasts were free and naked; they quivered in apprehension. He covered them with his hands.

'You are not so arrogant now,' he said.

Amy was helpless and frightened but inside she was seething with a previously untapped excitement. Her nipples hardened beneath his palms and he felt them rise and thumbed their peaks. She gasped.

'I think she's going to enjoy it,' he said, and laughed.

'No,' she said, but she knew the denial was a lie.

Julia said: 'I don't care if she enjoys it or not. But she is going to endure it.'

The young woman began to strip, pulling off her baggy sweater and jeans to reveal a slim, boyish body. She wore no bra and her breasts were small and bud-like; she stood before Amy naked except for black bikini briefs.

'Anybody going to join me?' Julia said.

Rory pulled off the shirt and pushed down his Levi's and boxer shorts. His erection was already big.

Gavin now stood before her and made no attempt to pull the T-shirt over his head. Instead, he gripped it in both hands and ripped it apart. He laughed as she shuddered, this time with anticipation. His jeans came down and he wore nothing beneath them. He stroked a large and angry penis.

'Broderick?' Julia said.

The make-up artist looked at the other two men and shrugged. He undressed with less enthusiasm and his physique was skinny compared to Gavin and Rory. His penis was tumescent but flaccid, and hung against his thigh.

Julia said: 'Go to it, boys. See if you can melt the Ice Maiden.'

Rory and Gavin approached Amy, one from the front, the other from behind. Her panties were pushed down until they hung around her thighs, and their hands were upon her and their bodies against her.

Their erections were hot and throbbing upon her nakedness and she closed her eyes as a mouth sucked upon a breast and fingers went between her legs, probing for entry into her vagina.

'No, no,' she whispered, as her body began to react against her wishes.

Julia spoke again, her voice harsh.

'Get her down here,' she said.

Amy's bound wrists were removed from the hook and she was laid upon the mattress. Her eyes remained closed as bodies and hands pressed against her. Her legs were spread, her vagina entered, first with fingers, then a tongue and finally a penis.

She was moved about the mattress at the whim of her captors, unable to resist. Her face was pressed between Julia's thighs and she had to suck and lick at a strange new taste and sensation, pricks were put in her mouth and finally, when she thought they had done everything they could, someone attempted to gain entry into her anus.

Amy cried out and opened her eyes wide.

Behind her, Broderick said: 'Hold her. Hold her.'

He entered while they held her, and she was sodomised in the grip of a circle of sweating bodies of mixed gender, oozing the smell of sex...

'Wake up,' her husband, Tarquin, said. 'We are almost there.'

Chapter 1

The drive from the main road was half a mile and Amy got her first sight of the house on the crest of a hill. It was floodlit against the backdrop of night – a surprisingly square edifice, with doric columns flanking the wide stone steps that led to the front door.

Crenellations around the top were highlighted by spotlights in the grounds and the shadows they cast hid the roof, except for a spired tower. It looked like a castle.

She stretched, still uncomfortable from the fantasy.

'I thought it would be bigger,' she said.

'It's big enough,' said Tarquin.

He headed down the hill, towards the row of limousines that were parked in line on the gravel frontage to the west of the house.

'How long is it since you were here?' she asked.

'Ten years.'

'How long since you have seen your father?'

'The same.'

'Was he that bad?'

'He was successful and, as he often told me, to be

successful you had to be ruthless. I was never ruthless and I never had his passions.'

'So you left. Was he disappointed?'

'Very much. He felt I had let him down. But he gave me an allowance and let me get on with my life.' He shrugged. 'So I went to Spain. I think he lives in hope that I will mature into his ways.' He smiled and patted her knee. 'For a time, I think he suspected I had no interest in women. It was a great relief when I called to tell him of our marriage.'

'I am looking forward to meeting him.'

'Be careful. Remember all I have told you about him.'

'Surely he cannot be that bad?'

'Just be careful.'

Tarquin parked the car at the end of the line of limousines and they climbed out. He straightened his dinner jacket and bow tie. Although it was summer, the air was cool.

'Perhaps you should have worn something else,' he said.

Amy followed the direction of his gaze and laughed. She wore a white silk shift with a back scooped to her waist, and no brassiere. The coolness had hardened her nipples, making them prominent against the thin material.

'You are a prude,' she said.

'You are naive,' he replied. 'Now, shall we join the party?'

The main door of the house was opened at their approach by a large, unsmiling man in a dark suit.

COMPULSION

Tarquin gave his name and they were admitted into a large hall from which a circular staircase ascended. Men in dinner suits and women in cocktail dresses stood in groups, glasses in their hands, and made inconsequential conversation.

Down a carpeted hall more people were coming and going between two rooms: from the left came the sound of music, from the right the clink of glasses and more conversation to the background tinkle of someone playing a piano.

Tarquin led the way into the room on the right and Amy noticed, without surprise, that men turned to look at her. She was aware of her beauty and used to turning heads. She smoothed the long, straight blonde hair from her face and smiled.

'There he is,' her husband said.

His father was unmistakable, even though she had not even seen a photograph, for he had the same grin as Tarquin, the same blue eyes. But Tarquin's grin was soft and often shy, and his eyes gentle and evasive. His father did not give the impression that he had ever been soft or evasive in his life.

He was sixty, of medium height and overweight without being fat. His head was bald except for white tufts of hair over each ear and round the back of his head. He was in the centre of a group listening to him talk. He was as comfortable with his obvious authority as Amy was with her beauty.

They approached and Amy made a comparison between father and son; one a businessman and a hedonist who had apparently achieved great success at both occupations, the other a slim artist with ideals.

Sir Alec saw them and broke off his conversation.

'Good God. I don't believe it,' he said.

He viewed Amy with open admiration.

'Father, this is my wife, Amy.'

'And she's far too good for you,' said Sir Alec.

Amy smiled.

'I have been looking forward to meeting you,' she said, and held out her hand.

Sir Alec took it in both of his and raised it to his mouth.

'I am absolutely delighted, my dear, to welcome you into the family.'

He kissed her fingers with his lips parted so that he left a moist patch upon her skin. When he lowered her hand, he did not let it go.

Tarquin said: 'I have warned her about you, father.'

'Good.' He nodded but ignored his son and kept staring at Amy. 'What did he say?'

'That you were sin incarnate.'

'Oh, but that's inaccurate. It also depends upon your definition of sin.'

'He was actually more specific, Sir Alec.' She glanced at the three or four people who were nearby and listening to the exchange. 'He said that you lived for sin, sex and seduction.'

Sir Alec laughed loudly.

'That's more like it. But, of course, it is a philosophy that Tarquin does not follow.'

'If he had, I would not have married him.'

'If *you* had,' Sir Alec said, with a sly smile, 'you

certainly would not have married him.'

The group of people laughed politely and Sir Alec, who was still holding her hand, nodded his appreciation and ushered Amy and Tarquin towards a quieter part of the room. When they were alone he appraised his son properly.

'It has been a long time,' he said.

'Ten years.'

He turned to Amy.

'Was he a virgin when you married?'

'Father!' Tarquin said.

Amy smiled the cool superior smile she had mastered as a safeguard against anything or anybody that she did not wish to be bothered by.

'That is none of your business, Sir Alec.'

'I knew he would be. I had my doubts about him, you know. I am amazed he got someone like you. What was it? Did you feel sorry for him?'

She smiled again. If the truth were known, she *had* felt sorry for Tarquin the first time they had met. He had appeared so helpless at coping with life.

'It was love, Sir Alec.'

'No such thing. Lust, I'll go along with. Friendship, I'll accept. Even companionship. But I don't believe in love.'

'Perhaps you're too old for love.'

Her smile remained in place and her lips twitched at the mention of his age.

Sir Alec frowned for an instant before he regained his humour.

'We'll see. Has he consummated it, yet? Or would

you like me to? Keep it in the family.'

'Oh, father.'

Tarquin's voice was tired and pained at his father's crass behaviour but Amy continued to smile. She raised the fingers that Sir Alec was still holding and removed them from his grip with her other hand.

'The consummation was beautiful,' she said. 'Your son is a wonderful lover.'

The older man stared at his son for a moment and shook his head in disbelief.

'How long have you been married?'

'Seventeen days,' she said.

'Give it time. Before long, you'll need diversions. Come to me. I'm full of them.'

She took hold of Tarquin's arm.

'We won't need diversions.'

'Everybody needs diversions.' He glanced again at his son. 'Are you making a living yet?'

'Of a sort.'

'What kind of answer is that?'

'We get by.'

'On the allowance I give you?'

'It helps of course.'

'Of course it does.' He looked at Amy. 'And what about you, Mrs Ramsden? Do you work?'

'I pose for Tarquin.'

'What a waste. He would be better off with a bowl of fruit. Why not pose for me?'

'Do you paint?'

'No, but I've got a box brownie.'

'Father!'

COMPULSION

He looked at his son.

'You have responsibilities now. You have a wife. Who knows, perhaps children someday, with the aid of a miracle. And you are trained for nothing but sitting on your arse in the sun, painting by numbers.'

'You are not being rational or fair, father.'

Sir Alec spoke to Amy.

'How about you, young lady? Do you do anything else, apart from look beautiful?'

'If necessary. The Sorbonne and a Swiss finishing school prepares you for anything.'

'But what specifically?'

'I am proficient in languages, skiing and planning dinner parties and I am computer literate. I also modelled for two years and could always model again.'

He dipped his head in recognition of her talents.

'I am impressed. Are you looking for a job?'

'That depends on the job.'

'You could work for me.'

Tarquin said: 'That is out of the question.'

Amy looked at him sweetly.

'Not necessarily, Tarquin.' She turned back to Sir Alec. 'Make me an offer.'

He grinned.

'That you can't refuse?'

'I can always refuse.'

Sir Alec laughed.

'I have heard that said before, but people do not usually refuse my offers. It's the way I make them.'

A distinguished man in his forties, who had approached discreetly, now touched Sir Alec's arm.

'It's time, Alec.'

'What? Oh, of course.' He smiled at his son and new daughter-in-law. 'Enjoy the party. I have business to attend to but I will see you later. I have put you in your old room, Tarquin, but I will see you before then.'

He nodded again, the smile turning inwards as if he had told himself a joke, and moved away with the other man.

Amy watched them approach a couple near the doorway, and when they eventually left the room the woman's companion went with them. The woman, in her thirties, was strikingly good-looking. Too good-looking to be left alone, she thought.

'Well,' Tarquin said. 'What do you think?'

'I think I am hungry,' Amy said. 'Let's eat.'

Chapter 2

Caroline Penrose sipped her glass of white wine and wondered how long her husband would be gone.

Fifteen minutes had already passed, although Sir Alec had promised the contracts would not take long. There were too many guests at the party for her to do anything other than wait where he had left her, in the hope that he would return soon.

'Beautiful women should never be left alone.'

For a moment, Caroline almost looked round to see whom the handsome young man in the elegantly cut dinner suit was addressing.

'I beg your pardon?'

'It is not safe. Someone may snatch you away.'

She laughed.

He looked perhaps twenty-two or twenty-three, even white teeth smiling from a suntanned face. His hair was thick and black and long to his shoulders, and he spoke English with a French accent. What was he doing talking to her? A woman of thirty-seven?

She smiled.

'I think I am perfectly safe,' she said.

'Not so. I have been watching. You have been alone too long. It is a crime you are alone. You are also bored, and that is dangerous. Your husband is foolish.'

'My husband has been called to a meeting with Sir Alec.'

'Ah, Sir Alec. Our host is always calling meetings, always making money.'

'Are you with the company?'

'Yes. I am Jean-Paul Marceau, from the Paris office.'

'I am Caroline Penrose. Perhaps you know my husband, Tom?'

'Only by name. We have never met. And if we did, I would tell him he is foolish to leave you alone, even though he has been called to a meeting with Sir Alec. Beautiful women should never be left waiting.'

'I am used to it.'

She blushed slightly at her small confession. But, for the last year, her whole life seemed to have been spent waiting while Tom got on with business and furthered his career.

'*Terrible*!' He said it the French way. 'But now you are alone no more. I shall not leave your side until you are claimed.'

Caroline laughed and discovered she had finished the glass of wine.

'You are very gallant. But really, you do not have to stay with me.'

He looked affronted.

'It is my honour and pleasure to be your escort until your husband returns. Please, let me get you more wine.'

It seemed churlish to refuse, although she rarely drank more than the two glasses and she had already consumed. Tom said she did not have the head for alcohol. But then, he said a lot of things about her, and not many of them were complimentary these days.

She accepted the wine and began to enjoy Jean-Paul's company. They laughed easily together so that she forgot the difference in their ages and lost count of the glasses of wine she drank. Besides, he had said she was beautiful and he made her feel beautiful.

Tom had not commented upon her appearance for a long time, except to criticise. He had not commented this evening upon the elegant black silk dress she had chosen with special care because they were visiting the home of his employer, Sir Alec Ramsden.

Caroline caught a glimpse of herself in a mirror behind the Frenchman: she was laughing and looked carefree and, if she did say so herself, she was very attractive, if not beautiful. Her shoulders were white, her cleavage tempting, her auburn hair rich.

'Your husband is taking too long, especially for business. Perhaps, my lady would like to dance?'

His invitation was so charming she could not refuse, and he led her from the hall where they had been talking into a room where the lights were low and couples danced to soft music.

He took her into his arms, holding her right hand against his shoulder, his right hand gently around her waist, and they joined the slow-moving throng. The record was by Smokey Robinson, the beat soft and insistent, the words a message of love and she enjoyed this stolen moment of flirtation before her husband arrived to take her back to boring reality.

By the time the second song had started, Jean-Paul had pulled her close enough for her to feel his body against her; a strong body, without excess weight, a slim waist and muscular thighs that brushed hers. His face was close, and she could smell a discreet cologne.

She smiled in satisfaction as she felt his erection pushing against her. It had been a long time since she had aroused a man this way, particularly one so young and good-looking. He must be fifteen years her junior, she thought. Even Tom did not react this way.

By the third song, she was feeling flushed with the atmosphere, the wine and his presence, and she caught her breath as his lips brushed her neck and the hand on her waist pulled her closer against the stiffness at his groin.

This was going too far, she thought, but she could not stop it until the song finished. His lips caressed her neck again and, emboldened by her acceptance of his actions, his tongue licked the lobe of her ear. Without being aware of what she was doing she reacted by pushing gently with her hips and he responded by moving his hardness discreetly against her.

The song finished and she broke away from him with relief.

'I need to go to the powder room,' she said, her voice a little hoarse from the encounter.

'But of course.' His smile was encompassing, his eyes full of her, and she was intensely flattered. 'Please, allow me?'

COMPULSION

He escorted her from the room, a hand on her hip in guidance and protection, and indicated the way she should go along the carpeted corridor.

At the door, he took her hand and kissed her lips.

'I will wait for madame,' he said.

'My husband will probably be looking for me,' she replied, with a touch of sadness in her voice.

'Then we will look for him together.'

In the powder room she assessed herself in the mirror. Her colour was a little high and her head a little woozy with the drink but, for tonight, she really did feel beautiful. She repaired her make-up, added a touch of perfume between her breasts and wondered if Tom would be waiting outside.

He was not. But Jean-Paul was, holding two glasses and a bottle of champagne, and wearing a large smile.

'You have added a sparkle to my evening. Now I will add a sparkle to yours before we find your husband.'

She laughed and accepted one of the glasses. He poured the wine and they toasted each other. They sat side by side, on a couch in the corridor.

'I have always thought English women were cold,' he said. 'Like ice. But you have made my visit *memorable.*' He said memorable the French way. 'I will remember our three dances. I will obtain the record and play the songs to help the memory, my beautiful Caroline Penrose.'

Her glass was surprisingly empty and she allowed it to be filled again, as they continued making deliciously, flirtatious small talk. At last she looked at her watch and was surprised to see her husband had been gone for an hour.

'I really must find him,' she said. 'The meeting must have finished ages ago. He will wonder where I am.'

'Of course.'

They got to their feet and she took a moment to correct her balance, after the champagne. They walked to the large, circular hall, glancing up the marble staircase, before returning to the room where canapés and drinks were being dispensed.

'This house has so many rooms,' Jean-Paul said. 'And Sir Alec's hospitality is so excellent. Your husband will be talking export orders with a colleague over brandy and will have forgotten the time.'

He smiled at her but she looked unsure.

'Okay,' he said. 'We will continue the search for your very foolish husband.'

They went to the cloakroom and disturbed a young couple in a passionate embrace. The Frenchman pulled the door closed with a smile although Caroline flushed at what she had seen.

'*Amour*,' he said.

The went into the room with low lights and soft music but it was difficult to penetrate the gloom.

'At least, let me beg one last dance,' he said.

She smiled and went into his arms again. He renewed the intimacies where they had left off and she was amazed that his erection was still there. The champagne and the strength of his arms made her forget, for a moment, that she was searching for her husband. She closed her eyes and let herself move against him. His tongue dipped into her ear and her breath escaped in a sigh against his neck.

'We should be looking,' she whispered.

'I am sorry,' he said, kissing her nose as they parted, and they crossed the room, but could still see no sign of him.

Perhaps, she thought, there is time for another dance. If Tom had got involved somewhere and forgotten her, then she was entitled to some innocent pleasure.

'Perhaps,' she said, about to give voice to the decision . . .

'Perhaps,' he said, at the same time, and they laughed.

He pointed behind her, to heavy drapes that covered the windows.

'They lead to a conservatory. If he had too much brandy, perhaps he is taking a rest?'

'Perhaps we will disturb another couple?'

They chuckled together, sharing memories already.

He parted the curtains and she stepped through. Glass doors were ahead of her and they stood together in the gap between curtains and glass, the music already deadened by the velvet, the only illumination that of the moon.

Jean-Paul opened the door silently and they entered the large conservatory and were surrounded by the smell of plants and nature. Her companion remained by the door and she went further into the room of glass and greenery, drawn by a sound of wheezing breath, as if someone was having a heart attack.

Caroline peeked around a bush. A man was lying back on a garden seat while a young woman knelt alongside, her face at his groin. She recognised other sounds she had been unable to hear before. The woman was fellating the man.

Behind her, she sensed the presence of Jean-Paul, who whispered in her ear: '*Amour!*'

The word made her smile nervously, for the sight of the couple had sent the flush of wine to her loins.

Respectable married women should not feel like this, she told herself. Respectable married women should not spy secretly upon the passion of another couple.

But she could not draw her eyes away. The woman held the man's penis at its base in the fingers of both hands and moved her head up and down with great concentration. Her mouth made slurping noises which, in the presence of the handsome young Frenchman, were far more embarrassing than the moonlit tableau the couple presented.

Jean-Paul moved close behind her and she could feel his erection against her buttocks. His hands held her hips and he moved himself gently against her while they watched and her breath caught in her throat. He became bolder and kissed her neck; his movements became more rhythmic, one hand strayed to her breasts, and still she could not draw her eyes away.

The man on the bench began to groan and the woman kneeling by his side sucked more loudly in encouragement. Suddenly he came, his hips shaking and his arms flopping, and all the time the woman kept her lips around his penis while he disgorged into her mouth.

Caroline finally found the energy to move away and they left the conservatory as silently as they had entered, going through the curtains.

In the darkened room, where the music gave them a reason not to talk, he immediately took her into his arms and they moved slowly to the dance once more. The pretence was gone and she could feel him burning against her.

'Shall we look some more?' he said. 'There are rooms down the corridor.'

'Yes,' she whispered. 'We should look some more.'

They left the music and he held her hand as they retraced their steps down the corridor, past the powder room, and round a corner to a part of the house not being used for the party. He opened a door and looked inside, then pushed it wider so she could enter.

It was a bedroom. The same heavy velvet curtains covered the windows. Jean-Paul pressed a switch and the bedside lights came on. The shades cast a warm pink glow upon the white coverlet.

He closed the door behind them and she heard a key turn in the lock.

'He is not here, either,' he said.

'No, he is not,' she said in a small voice, the panic beginning to rise at the situation she had walked into.

He stepped up behind her, his arms enclosing her. One hand pinioned her arms, the other caressed a breast. His erection pressed against her buttocks.

'You are so beautiful, my Caroline. No man should ever leave you alone.'

He kissed her neck, his mouth open, his tongue licking, and the pit of her stomach tingled at the same time as she wondered how she could get out of the room.

It was her fault. She had led Jean-Paul on and had agreed to come here, so how did she now tell him she had changed her mind? How did she tell him that it was a spur of the moment decision that she already regretted.

He turned her around and pushed her by the shoulders until her back was against the door.

'Jean-Paul...' she began to say.

'Caroline,' he said, as his mouth covered hers and his tongue dug deeply inside.

She was powerless against his weight and strength and he pulled at her skirt, lifting it and getting his hands beneath the silk onto her stockinged legs. His mouth still covered hers, allowing her no sound of protest, and when she struggled it was as if she was moving with passion.

His hands slid upwards, from stockings onto the flesh of her thighs. His upper body pinned her against the door while he held himself away from her hips so that the skirt could be pushed around her waist.

Oh God, what is happening? she thought, as one of his hands slid beneath her loose panties to cup a buttock and the other slipped between her legs into the curly forest at her vagina.

I did not want this to happen. This is a mistake, her mind screamed through the champagne and the rising turmoil of agitation in the pit of her stomach.

He parted the lips of her sex and inserted a gentle but demanding finger that only added to the heat of her excitement.

'No, no,' she tried to say, but his mouth still enclosed hers, his tongue wrestling her tongue, licking beneath her lips and around her teeth. Then his fingers found the bud of her clitoris.

The Frenchman worked the sensitive spot expertly and she gasped into his mouth. Now he moved his lips to her neck and his tongue delved into her ear and she could no longer say no because her excitement and the champagne had combined too well.

Caroline could not stop herself and gave way to the inevitability of his fingers. Her eyes stared blankly over his shoulder, which her hands gripped like claws. It had been a long time since Tom had given her an orgasm, a long time since he had had the time to show sexual interest in her.

'No, no,' she muttered, but it was no longer a plea for Jean-Paul to stop. She did not know why she said it; perhaps it was a plea for it not to end? And then it did end, as she rose to the peak of this wild, impetuous orgasm that was all the more intense because it was so sudden and unexpected.

He had two fingers inside her while his thumb played with her clitoris and she was shocked at the sound of squelching they made, shocked at being pinned against a door with her skirt around her waist. Suddenly she came and she could not control the noise she made as she gasped and groaned over his shoulder.

Her body sagged and he removed his hands from beneath the skirt and held her against him. For a moment, she wondered if she could now break free, already regretting what had occurred, wanting to escape the consequences and return to normality.

He was solicitous and gentle again, after the wildness of his attack, and when he led her to the bed she gratefully sat on the edge of the mattress to rest the weakness in her legs.

Perhaps, if she just rested for a moment, she could make an excuse to leave. He eased her backwards onto the bed and knelt on the floor by her knees. Perhaps he would understand?

But his hands pushed the skirt back up her legs and, even as she reached to restrain him, she knew it would be no good. He had provided her with an orgasm and would require one in return and, after all, she had led him on.

The skirt was bunched around her waist, her legs exposed in black stockings and suspender straps, the loose silk panties flimsy protection at her crotch. He parted her legs, his fingers moving like butterflies across the soft flesh of her inner thighs, tugging the panties to one side. A finger stroked her vagina and she felt its lips open.

Jean-Paul leaned forward and his tongue licked between the lips. A groan escaped her throat.

'No, please no,' she murmured, but she had said no before and come upon his fingers, so what was he to believe?

He delved more deeply with his tongue and embraced the lips of her vagina with his lips, moving them against it as if kissing her mouth, his tongue lapping at the juices that his ministrations released.

His mouth slid higher, until it concentrated upon the bud of her clitoris. He nibbled and sucked and flicked it with his tongue. Once more, she could not contain the groans. As he worked the bud with his mouth, his hands were busy also, two fingers and the thumb of his right hand delving deeply inside her to create even more wetness.

Oh my God, she thought, what will he think? That I'm a bitch on heat?

Then Caroline began to lose rational thought once more – her pulse rose with the pounding of her senses, her eyes closed, her head tilted back and she no longer attempted to control the noises that came from her throat, noises she had held in check through months of sexual abstinence.

Her orgasm was approaching again, urged on by the lips around her clitoris, the thumb that pushed into her vagina like a penis, and the wet fingers that were wickedly delving towards the furrow of her bottom.

No! Not that! That was too personal. No one had ever touched her there.

But was she saying it or only thinking it, and what did it matter now that the orgasm was its own animal and taking hold of her body from deep inside?

As she opened her mouth to welcome the ecstasy, the tip of his forefinger breached the tightness of her anus and she screamed in shock at the strange pangs of pleasure.

Perhaps it was the champagne, but she passed out for a few moments with the intensity of the experience. When her senses returned she had been moved to the centre of the bed and was lying face down.

Oh my God. It was not over; it was only just beginning. He had given her two orgasms. Would he expect two in return?

He was standing beside the bed, undressing, and she turned her head to look at him. His physique was perfect, the deep tan broken only by a white strip where he had worn bathing shorts. From the whiteness grew his penis: large, much larger than Tom's, and as dark as his tan. He was totally naked.

'You are so beautiful, Caroline. So passionate.' He smiled and stroked his erection. 'And you want this so much, *n'est ce pas*?'

She felt helpless as he unzipped the back of her dress and pulled it down her body. He dropped it on the floor and she remained still while he unclipped and removed her brassiere and, finally, tugged down the panties.

Caroline lay on her stomach, more naked than naked in only black stockings and suspender belt.

He knelt behind her, his legs straddling her thighs, and his hands caressed her back and the curve of her buttocks, which she had always thought were too full.

But Jean-Paul liked them and raked them with his fingernails, causing her to cry out, and slapped them, causing her to gasp with pain and try to move.

Her movement caused him to fall upon her, his mouth suckling the white flesh of her shoulders before he moved downwards into the small of her back, his tongue leaving wet trails across her skin.

His hands held her buttocks as his tongue slid into the furrow between them and, before she knew his intention, his face was buried between the globes of spread flesh as he licked at her anus.

Caroline felt totally powerless, events now beyond her control. She whimpered and twitched as his tongue licked at the secret place and gasped as the fingers of one hand slid beneath her and found her vagina and clitoris again.

This was totally new and depraved. Thank God it was with a total stranger whom she need never see again, in the anonymity of a strange room, but, oh God, she liked it. Her whimpers became more pronounced and she found, to her shame, that she was thrusting her bottom against his mouth and tongue.

Her arousal was complete once more, the tiredness and lethargy dropping away like the clothes she had worn. As if he sensed it, he moved above her, spread her legs and pushed his giant penis between her thighs. She held her breath and raised her buttocks as he guided it into her vagina. He slid it in slowly, a portion at a time to test her elasticity, but she was so wet with all he had done previously that she accommodated him without strain.

When it was in completely he lay upon her, his abdomen flattening the cushions of her buttocks. He supported his weight with his elbows and knees.

He twitched it inside her and she could not stop her reaction.

'You want it, Caroline? You want it?'

'Yes. I want it.'

'*Bon.*'

He began to move it in and out, slowly at first but then with more deliberation and pace and she groaned beneath him. He raised himself on his arms and she spread her legs more, gripping the edge of the mattress with her hands, raising her buttocks to his thrusts.

His size filled her more than she had been filled before, and she gloried in the squelching and the slap of flesh. This was something she had brought upon herself but her attitude had changed from endurance to enjoyment.

The Frenchman pounded in and out, his grunts combining with her groans and the smack of his thrusts against her bottom to fill the room with intimate sounds of sex. Once more, a hand slid beneath her and a finger nudged the bud of sensation and precipitated the approaching orgasm.

Caroline bucked beneath him as she came and he held himself rigidly within her.

They remained in the same position for a few moments afterwards, until he rolled from her and turned her onto her back.

'My passionate English rose,' he said, stroking her face. She caught his fingers in her mouth and tasted her own juices upon them. 'Do you want fucking again?'

His language shocked her, but his smile was the same and his fingers moved to touch her between her legs.

'Yes,' she whispered.

'Then you must tell me. Tell me what you want?'

She licked her lips, aroused by the word game he was playing, as she had been aroused by all he had done.

'I want fucking.'

'You are whispering, Caroline, I cannot hear you.'

'I want fucking.' Saying it louder aroused her more. 'I want fucking. Fuck me, Jean-Paul. Please fuck me!'

Still smiling, the Frenchman opened her legs and knelt between them. He inserted his penis again and, when it was fully inside, he raised her legs, putting one over each arm so that her body was doubled up on the bed for greater penetration.

'With pleasure,' he said.

This time he held nothing back and his assault made her cry out in time to the strokes of his penis. He was reaching so deep that it hurt, but the pain was a blur that mixed with the sensation of being taken so totally by a stranger.

He released her legs and she gratefully dropped them to the bed, spread wide as he continued his attack, his grunts becoming louder than her groans, and she sensed his own approaching climax.

The Frenchman held himself above her on stretched arms, beads of sweat upon his forehead, his mouth open and his eyes burning into hers.

Caroline curled her legs around his back, consumed by the madness of the occasion, and worked herself against his pelvis to achieve her own orgasm.

There it was, rising with his, and her eyes opened wider as they both recognised the approaching apocalypse.

'Fuck me, Jean-Paul,' she said, and the words were an added release. 'Fuck me. Fuck me. Fuck me . . .'

Her last words became a strangled gasp as he spasmed deeply inside her and twisted heavily against her, triggering her own climax. He seemed to pulse for ever and her eyelids fluttered closed. The tension left her body and was replaced by that floating aftermath of contentment that she had missed for so long.

Caroline must have drifted off to sleep for when she became aware of her surroundings again, the Frenchman was dressed and sitting on the side of the bed.

'It really is time for you to find your husband, Caroline. And time for me to leave.' He leaned over her and kissed her gently on the lips before standing up. '*Au revoir*, my passionate rose.'

He unlocked the door and paused.

'Perhaps it would be best, if you were to lock this after me, in case your husband is looking for you?'

She was suddenly aware that she was almost naked.

He smiled again and left the room. She climbed from the bed and staggered. The champagne had had some effect, but her legs ached from the intensity of the sexual encounter after such a long period of doing without.

COMPULSION

Caroline went to the door, locked it and leant against it, the enormity of what she had done seeping into her brain.

Tom must never find out that she had been unfaithful, even though it had all happened by accident; even though he was to blame for leaving her alone.

But, even in her anguish, she smiled at how handsome her lover had been, at how he had said she was beautiful, and at how fulfilling had been the sex.

Chapter 3

Amy and Tarquin had drunk champagne and danced, and she had been pleased at how she had made his trousers grow in the half-darkness amidst the other swaying bodies.

People stimulated him. Their proximity while he had been so close to her had aroused him. Amy had discovered this during their short pre-marital relationship. He enjoyed the semi-public occasion where he could touch and be touched with the possibility of being seen or discovered.

She had always liked being on show; it came naturally to her. When she modelled she had had no shyness to shed, as she found it perfectly normal that people would want to look at her, would want to focus their cameras upon her, to revolve their lives around her.

Her career could have been greater but she had become bored with the ease of her success, the campness of most her male colleagues, and the crudity of the men of power who thought they could buy her body.

Actually, apart from a brief affair with a television producer in her teens, she had kept her body to herself – until she met Tarquin in Spain.

His gentleness reminded her of the occasional gay companionship she had enjoyed on photographic shots. He was not grasping or obvious or demanding. She had volunteered to pose for him and had done so, naked, on three occasions before their relationship had become physical. As soon as it did, he had proposed marriage.

'I am thirty,' he had said, 'and I am aware of my shortcomings, but I believe I love you and that you return these feelings to me. I would be very grateful if you would be my wife.'

Amy, who was twenty-three, had never really known love before. She had been cocooned from it in her beauty and by stepping through career options that had come easily and which she seemed able to pick up and discard at will.

But Tarquin was sweet and she felt great tenderness for him. He had been a virgin and she agreed. It was only later that she had thought that a proposal that mentioned being grateful might be a little odd.

They had known each other three months and, although he had never instigated lovemaking, he had been willing to accede to her inclinations, even on those occasions when he had been unable to raise an erection because of worry or temperament. He had been happy to use his mouth to give her release rather than his penis, and she had reciprocated several times – until fellation and cunnilingus had become their normal sexual practice.

COMPULSION

But dancing in the dark had raised his erection through the stimulation of her body rather than her hands and mouth, and she had hopes of full intercourse – until Sir Alec stopped them as they left the diminishing throng to go to bed.

'I have been considering offering you a job,' he said, as they met at the foot of the circular staircase. 'Both of you.'

Tarquin said: 'I can hardly wait to hear it.'

'Now you have responsibilities, why not come back and work for me? You can paint in your spare time. The work will not be arduous. There will be plenty of time for painting.'

'I do not think so, father. I am used to the light in Spain. Light is everything to an artist and while I appreciate the offer, I could not possibly leave the Costa Brava for London.'

'That is what I thought you would say. But what about you, Amy? Do you want a job?'

'My place is with my husband.'

'You can see him weekends. I'll pay the fares. First class.'

She smiled, but it was a tired smile now, for she was sure the delay in getting to the bedroom had reduced her husband's libido.

'What is the job?'

'My private and personal secretary, with special responsibilities for cataloguing my library.'

'That sounds rather boring.'

'I would have thought challenging would be a better description. My library is not what you might think. I have some very rare editions and they need cataloguing. It could be fascinating.'

'I do not think so, Sir Alec.'

'I will pay you the same as I pay Tarquin. Plus travel expenses to Spain every weekend.' He grinned again. 'You can claim those even if you do not go. And any of the cars in the garage for your personal use.'

Amy's eyes widened.

'A generous offer.'

'There could be side benefits.'

'Such as?'

'We would have to discuss those separately.'

Tarquin said: 'You are being tiresome, father. Why not just double my allowance and let us return to Spain?'

'Because you do not deserve it. But Amy does.'

She was surprised at herself for even contemplating the ludicrous offer which, she suspected, masked his real intention of attempted seduction.

'Thank you, but no thank you, Sir Alec.'

'Sleep on it. I will see you in the morning.'

They continued upstairs and Tarquin led the way along a corridor on the west side of the house.

'Here we are.' He opened the door, reached in and switched on a light. 'My old room.'

It contained a double bed with a brass frame, dark wood furniture, a desk upon which sat a typewriter, an easel in a corner and paints and books stacked on shelves. A large box was at the foot of the bed, and he opened it and rummaged among toys until he produced a battered teddy bear.

'Bongo,' he explained, with a smile. 'When his leg

dropped off, nanny mended it with a piece of wood. He is the only teddy bear with a wooden leg in captivity.'

'Amazing.'

She turned to look at herself in a mirror. Her face was showing the slightest signs of fatigue that even youth could not hide. It had been a long day and an interesting night. She reached behind her and unfastened the button at the neck of her dress.

Unrestrained, the silk slipped from her shoulders and pooled at her feet. She continued to admire her perfect reflection of rising breasts, curved hips, flat stomach and long, shapely legs. She wore only the briefest of white silk panties and high-heeled shoes.

'Are you tired?' she asked Tarquin's image in the mirror.

She watched him looking at her body from behind and the joy of finding the teddy bear left his face. His gaze lifted to the mirror itself, and she smiled but he did not respond.

'No,' he said. 'I am not tired.'

He dropped Bongo the teddy bear on top of the box and stepped towards her. His arms came round her and she could feel him hard in his trousers against her bottom. She tilted herself against his bulge.

His hands held her breasts, manipulating them, pulling and tugging at them with more fire than ever before. She closed her eyes and lay her head backwards onto his shoulder. She gasped as his right hand went into her panties and his fingers curled through her blonde bush of hair and into the groove of her sex.

'Oh, please,' she whispered, as his fingers went inside her, finding the secretions that had been waiting hopefully.

She moved herself against his hand, seductively at first in case she scared him by being too demanding, and then, when he maintained the rhythm, she moved more strenuously until she was fucking herself upon his fingers.

Had she thought that? Had she thought such a word? Oh, but it was so good, after so much gentleness, to be so direct.

'Yes,' she said. 'Yes.'

Her breath began to shorten, and she came, rocking on his hand, held upright by the other hand that gripped a breast with possessive passion.

As she sagged, she felt his erection wane.

'Let's go to bed,' he said.

She turned in his arms and kissed him tenderly on the mouth.

'But what about you?'

He smiled.

'Let's go to bed.'

He turned the lights out and began to undress in the dark. She sat on the bed and when he sat beside her to remove his trousers, she slipped to the floor and reached towards his genitals. Instead of a half promise that she could rouse with her mouth, she encountered only stickiness around a limp penis.

Tarquin leaned over her and kissed her forehead.

'It was too intense,' he whispered. 'I could not wait.'

Amy helped him remove the rest of his clothes and

they slipped into bed together and she cuddled him until he went to sleep.

Sir Alec sat in an armchair in the next room, a video camera on a tripod by his shoulder, and watched the dim shadows of his son and daughter-in-law in bed through the mirror in which Amy had admired her reflection.

His son had married a beautiful and desirable young woman, of that there was no doubt, but he doubted he was capable of holding onto her.

He sipped the whisky in his hand and contemplated his plan of campaign. Tarquin obviously had a problem and was unable to satisfy her. Sir Alec believed it was his duty to help.

My God, but she was beautiful.

He turned in his chair, switched off the record button and pressed rewind. He would re-run the sequence once before he went downstairs to usher the last of his guests into the night.

Chapter 4

The ring of the telephone made Caroline Penrose jump. Ever since the previous night, she had been on edge. This morning she had felt tired, but also satisfied, and the tops of her legs still ached.

She had hardly dared to look Tom in the face at breakfast, but he had been distracted himself and had left for the office earlier than usual.

Caroline picked up the telephone and gave the number.

'Caroline? This is Jean-Paul.'

Oh my God, she thought. How should she react?

'What are you doing, calling me here?'

'I need to see you, Caroline. One last time before I return to Paris.'

'No. That can't be. Look, last night was wonderful, but it was a mistake.'

'One last time, Caroline. You must see me, so I can say goodbye. So I can give you a gift to remember me.'

His voice and the romantic words he used were melting her reticence.

'It is not possible, Jean-Paul.'

'Yes, it is. I am nearby but I do not want to come to your house. You must come to me. For a few moments only, but you must come.'

'Where are you?'

'I am at the railway station. It is only a few minutes away. Come here, to the station car park. I am in my car and I shall look for you. Be here quickly, or I will have no alternative but to come to you.'

'No. You can't do that. I'll come. I'll be there in ten minutes.'

'My English rose. Hurry, for I am impatient.'

She put the telephone down, ran into the hallway and stopped. She could not go like this? He had called her beautiful and last night, in a party atmosphere and wearing an elegant dress, she had been beautiful. What if he was disappointed when he saw her in the daylight?

Caroline ran upstairs and checked her make-up. At least she always made sure her make-up was in place every morning without fail, but her hair could do with brushing. And what should she wear?

Good God, she was only meeting him to say goodbye. It was not as if he was going to fling up her skirts in the car park and make love to her. Not at ten o'clock in the morning.

The thought that he might terrified her – as well as awakening a small twinge of desire – but instead of changing, she remained as she was, in cotton slacks, white socks and tennis shoes, and a white cotton sports shirt.

She drove to the station and into the car park, found a space and left her car. Where would he be?

As she walked slowly towards the exit, between the ranks of vehicles, a Rolls Royce approached from behind. The driver wore a peaked cap but she could not see into the back because the windows were of smoked glass and there was a partition between the driver and the rear seats.

The Rolls Royce slowed and stopped alongside her and the rear door was pushed open. She hesitated and looked inside. Sir Alec Ramsden smiled back.

'Mrs Penrose,' he said pleasantly.

'Sir Alec!'

Caroline was shocked and surprised.

'Please, get in.'

'Oh no, I can't.' She glanced over the top of the car in case the Frenchman was looking for her. 'I'm meeting someone.'

'Jean-Paul had to leave suddenly, my dear. Please, do get in.'

'Oh?'

She was taken aback that he knew she had come to meet Jean-Paul and at a loss about what else to do other than get into the Rolls Royce. After all, this was her husband's employer, upon whose wealth and business acumen she and Tom relied for their future. She got into the back of the car, sitting to his left.

The seats were soft leather and the fittings were luxurious. The chauffeur was hidden beyond a smoked glass screen.

Sir Alec wore a tan linen suit, cream shirt and bow tie. He leaned forward, pressed a button and said: 'Drive on, Charles.'

He sat back and smiled at her.

'Sorry to disappoint you, my dear.'

'No, really. You haven't.'

'It's not often I get the opportunity to talk to the wives of my executives. I have wanted to talk to you for some time.'

'Really?' She wondered why. The limousine left the station car park and was driving along the High Street. It was a peculiar sensation, being able to see out without passers-by being able to see in. 'Where are we going?'

'Just for a little drive, my dear.' He held up a finger. 'And some entertainment.'

He slid back a panel on the arm-rest against the door on his side of the car, revealing a series of electrical control buttons. His fingers pressed one button and a panel in front of them slid sideways. Behind it was a television screen. A second button switched it on; the screen was black and speckled with interference. A third button activated a video and, after two or three flickering shots of a darkened room, it became steady and focused.

Caroline watched with fascination. The room looked familiar but she did not know why. And then she recognised the two people standing by the door.

Oh my God! It was her and Jean-Paul, the night before.

She was speechless as she watched the Frenchman lean her against the door as he pushed up her skirts and his hands got to work. This could not be happening. It was a dream, a nightmare. This was awful.

Caroline felt physically sick as she thought of the

possible consequences of the previous evening's brief fling and of the embarrassment at sitting alongside another man while it was screened on television.

'Please. Turn it off.'

'Oh no, my dear Mrs Penrose. I think it is very good. A little dark in places, but it certainly captures the mood of the occasion, don't you think?'

The camera had zoomed in on her face as she approached orgasm; even the sounds had been picked up.

She closed her eyes and clenched her fists.

'Please. I can't look at it.'

'But you must, Mrs Penrose. You were not so bashful last night.'

'Last night I had been drinking. It was a dreadful mistake. Things got out of hand, things happened that I did not want to happen but I couldn't stop them.'

'Of course.'

He smiled and turned the sound up as she orgasmed on screen for the first time.

She opened her eyes and looked into his face. He was smiling, almost benevolently.

'How did this happen?'

'You mean the video?'

'Yes.'

'You may or may not know, but I have the reputation for eroticism. I count myself an expert.' His smile became a grin. 'My enemies, however, call me a dirty old man. That room is specially equipped with cameras behind every mirror, microphones in all strategic positions. I enjoy watching house guests, or even party guests.'

'My husband must not see it.'

'You do not think he would understand?'

'Good God, no.'

'But what am I to do with such evidence of infidelity? As his employer and friend it should be my duty to give him a copy personally.'

'No! Please, no. I'll do ...'

'Anything?'

He was still smiling benevolently.

'It would break our marriage.'

'And that would upset you?'

'We have a good marriage. We love each other.'

'And yet, I get the impression, particularly after watching this,' he nodded to the screen, 'that it is a marriage that is lacking in love of a physical kind.'

Caroline stole a glance at the screen and saw that she was now lying on the bed, her legs spread, with Jean-Paul kneeling between them, his mouth busy at the juncture of her thighs.

Despite the circumstances, she squeezed her thighs together at the sight and the memory.

Sir Alec said: 'Look at yourself, Mrs Penrose. You are a beautiful woman in the grip of glorious passion. Not love, that feeble word and concept, but passion, lust, desire. You have allowed yourself to be taken by a stranger in a strange house. There is no one to judge you, to blame you. You have only yourself to consider and you have opted for ecstasy.'

On the screen, Caroline came for the second time.

'Look how you affected that young Frenchman, how you made his blood boil, how his sap rose at the touch of your hand.'

Her eyes were glued to the screen now and she remembered the passion and the lust as Sir Alec had described it. For that is what it had been; uncomplicated lust that should have had no repercussions.

Sir Alec picked up her right hand and squeezed it comfortingly.

'Don't worry,' he said. 'This can be our secret. I would not like to be the cause of a marriage failure. But look, Mrs Penrose. Look at the excitement in your face. Listen to the desire in your voice. Remember how completely you gave yourself and how completely he gave you satisfaction.'

She remembered, and the embarrassment and being forced to watch herself caused her emotions to mix strangely.

'Feel how your presence can arouse a man, Mrs Penrose.'

He placed her hand upon the front of his trousers and she could feel his erection beneath the linen.

'Feel your power, my dear, pulsing at the touch of your hand.'

Her eyes remained on the screen, but her mouth fell open in shock as he spread her fingers around his erection and held them in place. Slowly, he moved himself against her hand and she whimpered in her throat.

This could not be happening. The morning had been so ordinary: Tom had hardly spoken at breakfast, which was regrettably normal these days, and had left for the office, and the cleaner had arrived. She was supposed to be meeting Marjorie Lawson for lunch at twelve-thirty.

Yet here she was, in the back of a Rolls Royce, driving through the leafy suburbs of the place she called home, watching herself in pornographic antics on a television screen while allowing a man old enough to be her father to masturbate against her fingers.

'No,' she said, and tried to withdraw her hand, but he held it tight.

'Dear Mrs Penrose, forget the social niceties. Social niceties are boring; a straightjacket for the middle classes. But release the straightjacket and you find a writhing mass of unspoken and unspeakable desires. I have just thrown your straightjacket away, my dear. Look at the screen, at that woman of lust, who last night rediscovered the animal delights of sex without reason or complication. Become her again, Mrs Penrose. Feel your power.'

Caroline no longer tired to remove her hand and he continued moving himself against it. She watched the screen with the captivated horror of a victim hypnotized by fear. But of what was she afraid?

Sir Alec groaned beside her and, without thinking, her fingers gripped his erection applying pressure in response to the noise he had made.

Oh my God, what was happening to her?

'The lust in your face, my dear. See the lust in your face. Remember the fierceness of his assault. Remember the power of his thrust.'

Her mouth was dry. She licked her lips and this unreal dream continued, within the shaded interior of a limousine that drifted through reality, while she watched herself writhe beneath the muscular young body of a man she had met only thirty minutes before.

Sir Alec removed her hand for a moment but she was too involved in what was happening upon the screen to notice – until he put it back. He had unfastened his trousers and now placed her fingers around his naked penis.

Her initial reaction was to relinquish her grip, but he had anticipated this and held her hand firm beneath his until she got used to the heat of his weapon in her palm.

'Such a touch, Mrs Penrose. Such power to arouse.'

He moved his penis within the folds of her fingers and hand and she felt its vibrations and the way it throbbed. If she did not look at it, it was not happening, she told herself, so she kept on looking at the screen.

His penis was wide and short and hard as iron within its lubricated sheath of skin. It burned her hand. Without really being aware of what she did, she began to move her hand upon it, becoming bolder as she watched the screen.

'Mrs Penrose,' he said. 'Beautiful Mrs Penrose. Listen to your desire.'

He turned up the sound again as she whispered to the Frenchman: 'Fuck me.' Then in a louder voice, she said: 'I want fucking. Fuck me, Jean-Paul. Please fuck me.'

'And he did, didn't he, Mrs Penrose?' Sir Alec said,

in a low voice, full of the tension of his own pleasure.
'He did. Look at him fucking you.'

Caroline looked and remembered. She could feel the wetness between her legs and the twist of desire in the pit of her stomach. Her hand moved of its own accord, pulling and caressing his stiffness, running her hand up to the circumcised head to run its oily surface in her soft palm.

His breath was getting shorter and she had a fleeting thought that she must be mad, but he had the tape and he could give it to her husband if she did not do what he wanted, so she maintained the rhythm of her right hand.

'Look, Mrs Penrose, look. And listen to your lust!'

On screen she was climbing to her final orgasm.

'Fuck me, Jean-Paul,' she said. 'Fuck me, fuck me, fuck me.'

As she orgasmed on screen, her hand involuntarily gripped the base of Sir Alec's penis. He gasped with deep satisfaction and came. His weapon pulsed and shook and his hips twitched. She felt a spot of hot sperm land on her wrist and then more ran down the shaft and over her fingers.

Caroline had not realised she had been sitting on the edge of the seat and now the tension had been released she fell back into its softness.

Sir Alec handed her a tissue, switched off the video and television, and wiped himself.

'Thank you, Mrs Penrose. A delightful interlude that we must repeat.' He pressed the intercom button once more and said: 'Return to the station, Charles.'

COMPULSION

Caroline looked out of the window. Girls were playing netball in the grounds of a school. A young woman, whom she recognised from frequenting the same shops, walked towards them pushing a pram. They passed her, the woman giving the darkened windows of the Rolls Royce a quizzical glance.

If she only knew, Caroline thought.

If Tom were to find out?

'You won't show the video to Tom, will you?'

She dare not look directly at her husband's employer.

'Probably not. I would not wish to cause you any grief, my dear. Especially as I believe you have marvellous potential.'

Now she looked at him suspiciously.

'Potential for what?'

'Dealing with people. I wish to offer you a commission on behalf of the company.'

'What do you mean?'

He smiled enigmatically.

'I believe that you may have a future with the company. You have special qualities and I am an expert at bringing out the best of people's special qualities.'

'I do not want a future with the company.'

His smile was still benevolent as he dismissed her statement.

'Oh, but it will be an offer you cannot refuse, my dear Mrs Penrose.'

He looked out of the window and her eyes followed his gaze. They were re-entering the station car park.

He said: 'I shall send a car for you tomorrow.'
'But—'
'No buts, my dear. It is decided. Tomorrow at ten. And do wear something more becoming. I have two pet hates with the clothes that women wear: trousers – of any kind – and tights.'

The car stopped and he pushed the door open. Her own car was nearby.

Hesitantly, Caroline got out of the Rolls Royce.

'I do not want a job, Sir Alec.'

'It will do you good, my dear. You will see. Tomorrow at ten.'

He smiled, pulled the door closed and the limousine purred away, leaving the car park and disappearing in the traffic of the High Street.

Caroline took a deep breath. It was a hot day. Perhaps she had fainted and imagined everything that had happened. Except that she was wet between her legs and wished Tom was at home instead of at the office. She also had the tissue in her hand – sticky with Sir Alec's sperm.

Good God. What on earth had she got herself into?

Chapter 5

Amy was in the library reading the titles of leather-bound volumes of the classics when Sir Alec got back to the house.

'Where is your husband?' he asked.

'He took his sketchpad down to the lake.'

'Then he is very foolish. This is much more beauty to sketch here.'

She responded to his flattery with a tired smile.

Amy wore a cream pleated miniskirt, a floral crossover blouse in matching pastel shades and flat shoes. She wore no brassiere and her breasts moved delightfully within the material.

Sir Alec walked across the room to stand alongside her.

'Are you looking for anything special?' he asked, as she leaned forward to inspect a title on a lower shelf.

'No. Are you?'

She turned her head to look up at him but did not attempt to cover herself, although she knew the front of her blouse was hanging open and that he could see her left breast.

Maria Caprio

Sir Alec smiled.

'Charles Dickens is very good if you have the patience,' he said. 'But my private collection is more spicy.'

Amy stood up and looked at him.

'You have a private collection?'

'Of course. Books, magazines, photographs, videos, tapes. But I need them cataloguing. This is what I want you to do.'

'I thought the job you offered was as a private and personal secretary?'

'The material I am talking about is *very* private and personal.'

She had assumed that what he had been carrying was a book but when he held it up she saw that it was a video cassette.

Amy walked away. 'You are very predictable, Sir Alec.'

'Why not call me daddy?'

'To feed your fantasy?'

'Why not? It is a harmless fantasy.'

'You are not as young as you once were. It might prove a fatal one.'

'Ah yes, but what a way to go!'

The sound of a key in a lock made her turn round. He was opening a small door in the corner of the room. He reached inside and switched on a light before bending down to go through the stone archway. He walked down some steps and disappeared. He returned a few moments later, without the tape, switched off the light and closed the door.

He beamed at her.

'My private collection,' he explained.

Amy said: 'Sir Alec, I am your son's wife and I intend to remain faithful to him. I do not intend to become part of your private collection.'

'Of course not.' He continued smiling. 'But what about the job? The terms are attractive and it may broaden your outlook on life.'

'I am happy with the outlook on life I already have.'

'Surely not. Where is the adventure in that? I have tried most things, but I am still experimenting, still looking for that little extra. If you do not have a pot of gold to chase, life is boring. And it should never be boring. It should be challenging.'

'My life has its own challenges.'

'You mean Tarquin?'

She frowned.

'No. I do not mean Tarquin.'

'Ah, well.' He shrugged. 'I leave it to you. Return to Spain with my son if you wish, but I hope you seriously consider the position that remains open to you. I feel it would be far more rewarding. And now, if you will excuse me, I have business to attend to. I will see you at lunch.'

He left the library.

After he had gone, Amy walked to the window and looked through the leaded panes across the lawn towards the lake where her husband sat on a bench, sketching.

Tarquin had got up early and slipped out of bed before she awoke. When she had sleepily, and hopefully, reached for him, she had discovered he was missing. She was in the bathroom when he returned to the room, fully dressed and preparing to go out for his artistic walk. He had hesitated at the sight of her naked and damp from the shower and, for a moment, she had thought that he might be tempted, but instead he had made an excuse and left.

If the initial surge of sexual activity that had followed their wedding day had already died, what would be waiting for her back in Spain?

Amy knew the basics of sex but was aware that, despite her looks and her body, she was relatively unskilled in the erotic arts. A gentle husband with whom to discover the full delights of sexual activity had seemed an attractive proposition when she had first met Tarquin, but he was proving to be a shade *too* gentle.

She glanced down the room, towards the door behind which she presumed Sir Alec kept his private collection. What on earth could be in it? His hints had whetted her appetite and curiosity.

The key! Sir Alec had left the key in the lock. Perhaps their conversation had caused him to forget?

Amy went to the door, glanced back across the empty book-lined room, and tried the handle. It turned and the door opened inwards. She pushed it fully open, but the light was dim and she could not see a great deal apart from the fact that she had to descend three steps to enter the room.

She switched on the electric light and walked down the steps. The only natural illumination came from a row of small windows near the ceiling. Two walls were lined with shelves that contained books, magazines, boxes and videos. Against another wall stood a giant television set and a video machine.

There were two armchairs and a settee in soft leather, a heavy oak table and two upright chairs, thick rugs scattered upon the hard-cord fitted carpet, several mirrors and a peculiar box-like contraption against another wall, which Amy inspected.

Surely, it could not be? But, yes, it was unmistakeable. Two doors into two tiny rooms, separated by a grill at waist height. Two bench seats and two cushioned stools for kneeling upon.

It was a confessional box.

Amy laughed at such an oddity, went inside and closed the door. A dim light came on automatically. She sat on the bench seat and wondered what she should confess. That she was beautiful? There was no point denying the fact, after all, and she wondered wistfully to herself if it had been a blessing or a hindrance.

She smiled to herself, a sad smile that she turned into a defiant smile. She was what she was and there could be no changing that. And she certainly preferred to be of fair countenance rather than have a deformity or a hindrance to the easy lifestyle to which she had always been accustomed.

The peacefulness of the box relaxed her and made her philosophical. She knelt upon the cushioned stool, joined her hands together and stared at the grill in imitation of religion.

'But I have no sins,' she said softly to herself, and, as an afterthought, she added with a wry smile: 'How boring.'

Amy left the confessional and looked at the spines of the books on the shelves. The titles and the authors meant nothing to her. She moved on to a section where magazines lay stacked haphazardly. Some were very old, others in mint condition.

Pornographic magazines were not new to her; the television producer had had a collection that he had insisted on showing her.

She flipped open one that had German captions beneath photographs of a man and a woman copulating. The brief surge of anticipation died as she turned the pages. The photographs appeared staged and were without spontaneity or excitement.

Other magazines contained photographs of different combinations of people engaged in sexual activity. There was group sex, swopping couples, one woman and four men, and love solely between women.

Next to the magazines were cardboard boxes. She took one from the shelf, placed it on the floor, and removed the lid. Lying inside were audio cassette tapes in clear plastic containers. She picked one up and read the handwritten label through the plastic.

It said: Confession – Laura.

Confession?

She looked back at the confessional box.

Surely not?

But in this most peculiar house of her most peculiar father-in-law, everything appeared to be possible.

COMPULSION

The anticipation surged back as she wondered what might be on the tape. Was it an actual confession to a priest, or would it more likely be part of some ritual or game devised by the notorious Sir Alec?

Amy glanced around the room and saw a cassette deck alongside the television and video. She put the lid back on the box, the box back on the shelf and took Laura's confession to the tape player. On top of the VCR, she now noticed, was the video cassette Sir Alec had been carrying. She picked it up.

The label on the side of the tape said: Caroline – 1.

Another mystery that caused butterflies to flutter in her stomach. Dare she play the two tapes and, if she did, which one first?

A noise from the other room startled her and she ran to the steps and looked through the doorway. Greta, the young Swiss maid who had served breakfast, was replacing books on a shelf. Overcome by guilt, Amy climbed the steps from the room, switched off the light and closed and locked the door.

Greta said, in her delightful accent: 'I did not mean to disturb you, madam.'

'That's all right, Greta. You did not disturb me.' She handed the key to the room of the private collection to the maid. 'Will you give this to Sir Alec? I believe he left it behind by mistake.'

'Of course, madam.'

Amy left the library and climbed the staircase. She wondered about the staff of the house, and how much they knew. Sir Alec had four permanent members of staff: Charles the chauffeur, Rupert the butler, a cook whose name she had no desire to know, and Greta the maid.

Greta was possibly still a teenager, certainly no more than in her early twenties, whose home was in Geneva, according to her father-in-law. She was an attractive girl, with short, brown hair, who wore a uniform that had a distinct continental flavour: a dark blue, cotton dress with a pleated skirt, blue knee socks and flat shoes.

Was she as innocent as she looked, or was she aware of the games being played behind the locked doors of this house of surprises?

Amy was at the top of the stairs before she realised she still clutched the two tapes.

It was too late to go back now. Her heart surged. Besides, she was bursting with curiosity to see and hear what they contained.

She reached the bedroom and closed the door. From the window, she could see the lake. Tarquin was still communing with nature and his sketchpad. But she had the urge to commune with something much more basic.

The room had a sound and vision system discreetly located in cupboards alongside the dressing table. Again, Amy was torn between which to play first. She opted for the video and slotted it into the VCR, using the remote controls to switch on the television set and activate the video recorder.

Amy backed to the bed as the screen flickered, showing a darkened room. A man and woman were near the door. They were embracing. The man became demanding and the couple became locked in a passionate exchange and the woman's skirts were pulled high, abruptly and without ceremony.

The blonde girl sank back on the bed to watch, utterly gripped by the sexual drama unfolding before her. This was no staged scenario being played by actors. Here were two real people involved in a real sexual encounter. Two people who did not know they were being spied upon.

Being a voyeur gave her a ripple of wicked pleasure as the camera focused on the woman's face and Amy recognised her from the party the previous night. So this was Caroline? Recognizing her provided another spasm of delight, as if being able to place the woman in polite society as well as watching her in a bedroom made it even more naughty.

The man was very demanding, the woman reluctant. It was almost rape. Amy licked her lips and groaned at the thought of her eternal fantasy. Her hand slid beneath her skirt and she stroked herself through the silk briefs.

For a moment she wondered what she was doing, then realised false modesty was unnecessary after so much frustration and with such a stimulus as the action on the screen. She pushed the panties down her thighs and over her knees and kicked them off. Her fingers then returned to her vagina, which was already wet.

The relief of utterly letting go was immense and she opened her thighs and plied herself with both hands, pushing the fingers of one inside herself while she rubbed her clitoris with two fingers of the other hand.

Her orgasm was swift and intense and made her cry out. Her body shook and tensed around those magic fingers. And, as soon as she had relaxed backwards against the pillows and the screen came back into focus, she began again, her fingers slurping in and out of herself, her gasps more frequent, and she came again and again as the man and the woman sweated and orgasmed on screen.

Sir Alec sat in the armchair in the room next door, the video camera recording all that occurred through the two-way mirror on the wall.

My God, but she was a beauty.

He had watched her lie on the bed, watched her hand go beneath that delightfully short and pleated skirt, and watched her lift herself to eventually fling off the cream panties.

He had watched and admired the dexterity of her fingers and the delicious curve of her buttocks as her hips rose and thrust. He had listened to her moans and cries and had stroked himself through his trousers but had refrained from masturbation.

The journey, as he was fond of quoting, could often be more pleasurable than the arrival.

Sir Alec enjoyed maintaining his libido at a high level through excitement and incitement. The games he played were amazingly fulfilling in themselves, and he saved his orgasms for special occasions.

Caroline Penrose had been a special occasion. She

had not known why she had allowed what had happened to happen. He had not issued a direct threat to blackmail her into submission, although she could pretend to herself that that had been the implication.

But somehow, he did not think Mrs Penrose was a woman who would need to provide herself with justifications or excuses; not when she had finally broken free from convention, as he was sure she would.

She just needed a little push in the right direction. A little guidance from an expert. He smiled at the memory of her touch. He would have been content to have held her hand upon him, to add credence to the pretence of justification, but that had not been necessary.

Mrs Penrose's instincts had got the better of her and she had taken the matter into her own hands, so to speak, with a beautiful touch.

Her husband was a lucky man; it was a shame he did not appreciate her. But Sir Alec did.

On the other side of the mirror, his daughter-in-law came for the fourth time as the video ended. She lay supine for a moment as she recovered, and Sir Alec looked at his watch. It was almost time for lunch.

But Amy was not hungry, at least, not for food. She switched off the video and slotted the audio tape into the cassette deck. Now she unfastened the waistband of her skirt and slipped it off. The blouse ended halfway down her buttocks, and Sir Alec had a delightful view of her posterior as she glanced through the window, presumably to check on Tarquin.

Her legs really were perfection and that little bush of golden hair, slicked and wet now around the greedy mouth of her vagina, was good enough to eat. She switched on the audio tape and climbed upon the bed to listen.

A young woman's voice said: 'My name is Laura.'

Ah, Laura. Sir Alec remembered her well. Another delightful creature who had, eventually, entered fully in to the spirit of the great game of lust and fulfillment.

He stood up and smiled at the sight of Amy in the other room. Her fingers dipped into the wet valley between her legs as she listened to Laura's confession, and the video camera filmed on.

Sir Alec blew her a kiss goodbye and left for lunch.

Chapter 6

Laura's Confession
My name is Laura and this is my confession. It happened when I was sixteen years old.

I was a slim girl, with good legs, a firm bottom and a very large bust. My bust embarrassed me because it was so large, although it made me popular with boys who all seemed to want to take me out. Even so, I was careful with boyfriends and I had been going steady with Jamie for six months. I was confident enough of the relationship that I had allowed Jamie to make love to me and he had taken my virginity.

Afterwards, his interest seemed to wane. He could be passionate when he wanted sex, but then for days afterwards he would be indifferent to me. It made me want to please him all the more to keep his affection.

Jamie was two years older than me and had had previous sexual relations with other girlfriends. I thought him mature and sophisticated. He was in the sixth form and was hoping to go to university, while I was still only in the fifth form.

The day I am going to tell you about was in the

Maria Caprio

early summer. We both had free time from normal school work to study for examinations. My parents were both at work and Jamie and I were supposed to be studying at my home. We had the house to ourselves. Naturally, we had more than French and English on our minds.

It was a hot day and Jamie wore thin shorts and a T-shirt. I also wore a T-shirt with skimpy shorts. Jamie told me to take off my bra because he liked to watch the movement of my breasts beneath the cotton.

He had brought a large bottle of wine, and we played music and drank wine and lay on towels in the back garden, which was secluded from any neighbours.

We kissed and he felt my breasts. Then he pushed up the T-shirt and sucked my nipples, making them erect. He pushed his hand inside my shorts and his fingers went inside me and he rubbed me until I was hot and flustered and wanted to come. He was big in his shorts, and then he did what he enjoyed most of all: he put his prick between my breasts and rubbed himself against me.

Eventually, we got tired of the sun and went inside to lay on my parents' bed. There our activity progressed further. He pulled my shorts down to my knees and slid down my body. He sucked at my vagina until I was on the brink of orgasm but, as I neared the edge, he stopped.

He rolled me onto my tummy and lay upon my back, rubbing his prick between the cleft of my bottom until he made it wet. Then he pushed my legs apart and slipped it between my thighs and did it there as well, the tip of his prick nudging against my vagina so that I kept arching my bottom in an attempt to enhance the sensation.

At last, he inserted it inside me and lay flat upon me for a long time, so that he did not come straight away. Then he fucked me, his hands beneath me, grabbing at my breasts, and again he took me close to the brink of orgasm without letting either of us go over the edge.

We drank more wine and kissed again. He pushed my head down and I took his prick in my mouth and sucked it, as he had taught me, and knelt down so that my breasts hung over his genitals so that he could reach down and feel them or push himself up against them or simply watch their pendulous sway.

Still, he did not come and still he did not allow me to come.

We had been involved in this activity for more than an hour and were both heavy with passion, when the front door bell rang.

At first I was worried but I realised it could not be my parents, so we slipped our clothes back on and went downstairs. It was Rick, a sixth form friend of Jamie's. He had a bottle of wine and, like us, was in shorts and T-shirt.

'I need a friend,' he said. 'My girlfriend's ditched me.'

We had no choice but to invite him in. He was Jamie's best friend and a sports hero at school. I was self-conscious about the way my unfettered breasts moved beneath my T-shirt but I knew all my friends would have been jealous to have been in his company.

Jamie poured more wine and we sat around on the grass in the back garden drinking. Rick rolled a cigarette that had an unmistakable smell. I had tried it once before and it had made me feel pleasantly dizzy. As I was already a little dizzy from the wine, I accepted my turn at drawing in the smoke and holding it deep inside me until its buzz tingled through my body. What a story I would have to tell my friends.

Rick said: 'I'm going to miss that girl.'

Jamie said: 'You're better off without her. The trouble with her is that she was just a girl. What you want is a real woman, like Laura.'

He stroked my hair and I leaned my head against his hand and smiled, pleased with the compliment and the wine and the cigarette.

'You are lucky,' Rick said to Jamie, and he looked at me. 'Laura is beautiful.' His eyes were on my breasts. 'Really beautiful.'

'And a sex machine,' Jamie said, pulling my head round and kissing me open-mouthed upon my lips.

My mouth responded automatically and our tongues flicked against each other and his hands groped my breasts. After all, I was a beautiful woman and a sex machine.

But when Jamie's hand began to push beneath my T-shirt, I leaned away, even more flushed than before and glanced at Rick. He smiled and got up.

'I need some ice,' he said.

He went into the house and Jamie pulled me to him again. We kissed and he eased me backwards until I was lying on a towel and he was half over me. His knee was between my thighs and his hand beneath my T-shirt, feeling the soft flesh. I could not help but begin to breath faster.

If only Rick wasn't here, I thought.

Rick came back and I pushed Jamie's hand away. As my boyfriend sat up, Rick threw a jug of water over us.

Jamie got splashed but most of it went on me.

'You bastard,' Jamie said, laughing. After a moment I laughed as well.

'I thought you needed cooling down,' he said.

It was not a very original line but in my intoxicated state I thought it was hilarious. I thought it even more amusing when Jamie turned on the garden hose and soaked Rick. As they fought over the hose it was turned onto me and I got soaked as well. We were all laughing so much I didn't care that the T-shirt had become transparent and was stuck like a second skin over my large breasts, with my erect nipples threatening to pierce it.

'We're going to have to change,' Jamie said, and we all went into the house.

The two boys stripped off their shirts and I could not help but notice the way their chests were heaving from their exertions.

'Towels?' Rick asked.

'Upstairs,' I said.

I climbed the stairs with Jamie's hands holding my

hips, still giggling, still affected by the sun, the wine, the passion and the cigarette, but still without an inkling of what was to come. The cupboard at the top of the stairs next to the bathroom held dry towels. I gave one to Jamie and threw another to Rick who was waiting in the hallway below.

Jamie kissed me on the neck and I took my towel and went into my bedroom, where I began to dry my legs and arms. The door opened and Jamie and Rick came in.

'Do you need any help?' Jamie said.

'No thank you. I can manage.'

I suddenly felt threatened by the presence of these two bare-chested young men in my bedroom, even though they were both smiling in good humour.

'Come here, Laura. I'll help,' Jamie said.

He dried my neck and I could hardly object. Besides, I liked his touch. He moved behind me and kissed me on the back of the neck again. Rick just stood and watched.

Jamie dropped the towel and began to lift my T-shirt. I held it in place; I could not take my eyes from Rick.

'Come on, Laura. It's soaking.' He chuckled, but his voice was too heavy for laughter. 'We've taken our shirts off.'

He pulled the T-shirt higher and I did not know how to stop him without looking young and immature. It had reached my breasts and I raised my towel to cover myself.

Jamie whispered: 'You are beautiful, Laura. You

should be proud of your body.'

He kissed my neck and licked my ear and one of his hands slid over a breast and tweaked the nipple. My eyes half closed and I could not understand my feelings.

'Show Rick your breasts, Laura. Let him see how beautiful you are.' He then directed his comments to his friend. 'She has a fantastic body, Rick.'

He tugged the towel from my hand, pulled the T-shirt up and, momentarily, I could not see because the material was about my head. I felt so vulnerable at that moment that I could have orgasmed.

The T-shirt came loose and was thrown on the floor.

'Aren't they beautiful, Rick?'

Jamie reached round from behind me and held my breasts as if offering fruit. I could feel his prick, rock hard in his shorts, pushing against my bottom.

'Incredible,' Rick said.

His eyes were fixed on my bosom and I flushed even more, my eyes dropping to his shorts where there was a noticeable bulge.

He stepped closer and, before I could raise my hands in protest, Jamie took hold of my arms and pulled them behind my back in a gentle but firm grip.

Rick took hold of my breasts and felt them. Gently at first, experimentally. He weighed them in his hands, squeezed them to test their firmness, and let his fingers wallow in their softness.

'Incredible,' he said again, and kissed me, his tongue digging deep inside my mouth.

Surely now, I thought, Jamie would ask him to leave

so that we could be alone. After all, I was *his* girlfriend. Surely, this was as far as he would allow him to go.

Rick was so close that I could feel his prick too, pushing against my stomach. He continued to kiss me on the mouth as Jamie licked my neck and ear.

My senses were in turmoil. This was not natural. Perhaps they had been affected by the alcohol and cigarette. Perhaps they would suddenly realise what they were doing and stop in embarrassment.

Jamie was pulling me backwards to the bed but I resisted and instead of lying down on it, I sat upon its edge. They stood on either side of me. Jamie smiled and stroked my face.

'You are so good, Laura. You read minds.'

He pushed down his shorts and, to my shock, released his prick. It was huge and swaying a few inches from my face, so close I could see the throb of the veins.

'This is my favourite,' he said to Rick. 'And she is so good at it. Aren't you, Laura?'

It was as if he thought I had sat down on purpose to allow him to do this. Again I felt trapped by circumstances and afraid that I would look a fool to refuse.

He crouched slightly and pushed his prick between my breasts, holding them on either side to envelope it with soft flesh. He moved in the familiar movement that had been so private until now. He moaned loudly.

Then his fingers were in my hair and moving my head.

'In your mouth, Laura. In your mouth!'

He dipped my head, straightened his legs and pushed his prick inside my mouth. His hands held my head as he thrust in and out, his moans became even more pronounced.

Abruptly, short of his orgasm, he stopped and withdrew and fell to his knees beside me. He kissed me deeply, his hands tender about my face.

'God, I love you, Laura. You are amazing. So amazing.'

He pushed me backwards onto the bed and this time I had no resistance left. I was flat on my back on the mattress with my feet still on the floor. He licked and kissed down my body, past my breasts to my tummy. His fingers tugged at the waistband of my shorts and panties and he pulled them down together, over my bottom and down my legs. As he pulled them from my feet, his mouth went between my legs.

My vagina was still wet and open from our earlier passion and he licked down the hot crease, causing me to cry out despite myself. He consumed my slit with his mouth and, as my eyes opened wide at the pleasure he was releasing, I found I was staring at Rick, who was now naked and masturbating as he watched.

What was happening? I wondered. Then, all the tensions of being so close so many times before combined to break the barrier and I came, loudly, my mouth open, my eyes wide and fixed on Rick.

'Did you enjoy that, Laura?' Jamie said, as he crawled up the bed to lie alongside me. 'Did you?'

'Yes,' I whispered.

'Good. Do you want to come again?'

'Yes,' I said, for I was on fire.

Perhaps it would be all right for Rick to watch, I thought.

Jamie pulled me higher onto the bed and straddled my body, pushing his prick between my breasts again. After a few strokes, he moved higher still and I opened my mouth and accepted it.

I gulped in surprise when, as I was sucking, another mouth descended onto my vagina. Rick was no longer watching but participating, and my mouth was occupied so I could not voice an objection.

Jamie's stomach was against my face and the smell of his lust was in my nostrils. His prick made squelching noises as it moved in and out of my mouth and, in normal circumstances, I would have been extremely aroused.

But these circumstances were far from normal and Rick's mouth between my legs was frightening and exciting at the same time, and I could not contain my feelings as I felt another orgasm begin to build.

In an effort to stop it and free myself from the degeneracy of allowing myself to come on another boy's mouth, I heaved my hips and moved my head from side to side, but I could not prevent it happening.

I came, my mouth opened to yell, and Jamie finally lifted himself clear as he sensed what was happening. As the turmoil subsided and the waves of orgasm retreated and I regained my senses, I saw that both of them were lying by me, one on either side.

Jamie stroked my face again.

COMPULSION

'You are marvellous, Laura. So wild and sexy. Look how big you have made Rick. Time for you to pay him back.' He leaned over and kissed me. 'Do what you do best, Laura. Do it to him with your breasts.'

They had mistaken my struggles for passion and expected more. I felt obliged to do as they asked because they had given me two orgasms. Perhaps this was not degeneracy, after all. Perhaps this was sophistication.

Rick moved to the top of the bed and lay back and Jamie rolled me onto my tummy between his legs.

'You won't tell anybody, will you?' I said, with a sudden fear of what others might think.

Rick said: 'Of course not, Laura. This is just us, just the three of us. Our secret.'

Jamie crouched alongside and moved me into position and I knelt over Rick, allowing my breasts to hang above his erection. They swung and, when I glanced up, I saw the desire in his eyes and it made me excited. I moved my breasts so that they brushed the tip of his prick and he groaned loudly.

The more I did it, the more he groaned and I lowered myself slowly upon him, crushing his prick with my breasts, trapping it into the tunnel between the mounds, and he heaved against them, almost without control.

I realised with sudden insight what power I had over him and Jamie, too, for that matter. Then he pulled my head down and I took his prick inside my mouth and began to suck.

Behind me, Jamie knelt between my legs and

stroked his erection along the exposed groove of my vagina, causing me to tremble and moan. I wanted him inside me more than anything and I no longer understood or cared about what was happening or my doubts and guilts, and I moved my buttocks to entice him to enter.

He did so, with a long, slow thrust that caused me to momentarily remove the prick from my mouth and gasp in pleasure. Then, as I got used to him moving it in and out, I dipped my head again and sucked as Jamie had taught me, now eager to display my skills.

Neither of them took long to come. Jamie was first; I could tell he was getting close from the trembling of his thighs as he slapped against me from behind.

Rick could tell, too.

'Wait,' he said.

'I can't.'

Rick thrust faster in and out of my mouth and I gripped the base of his prick to hold it steady, which was more good luck than skill, for I now know that pressure on the base of the penis enhances the orgasm and the pleasure.

But Jamie could not wait and he came inside me with a great final thrust, his hands grabbing at my breasts as if they could save him from drowning in the intensity of the climax.

As he rolled from my back, Rick sat half upright – as if all the pleasure muscles of his body had contracted in his genitals – and he came violently in my mouth.

His prick jumped and lurched and his sperm was

so copious that I had difficulty in containing it. I swallowed and gulped but there was so much that some escaped and dribbled from my lips and down my chin.

They eventually staggered to their feet and went for the wine and another cigarette, then came back to start all over again. But I no longer needed any stimulation other than sex. I had gone over the edge, as if on one long orgasmic trip, and was prepared for anything they wanted to do that afternoon.

They fucked me together, they fucked me separately. They fucked me all afternoon long.

We repeated the threesome the next day, and again one day the following week, but then, as their appetites became sated, I discovered they had dropped hints of our escapades to other young men at school and, for a time, I became the victim of scandalous gossip.

I dropped both Jamie and Rick and became respectable, as if to deny their boastings with new found virtue. Their treachery upset me and made me wary of men for a long time. It also made me deny the incredible pleasure I had achieved during those three afternoons of sex – none more so than on that first occasion, when everything had unfolded almost as a dream over which I had no control.

That is my confession and I am grateful to have been prompted to remember it and allowed to divulge it.

Chapter 7

Amy was carried away with Laura's story of teenage lust, which seemed so much more personal than the video she had watched. When it finished, she rewound the tape and played it again, lying back on the bed, her fingers working frantically between her legs.

If only Tarquin was here to help; if only he had an erection as big as those of Jamie and Rick. How she would enjoy it. But all she had were her fingers, which were poor substitutes, even when she inserted two into the hot wetness.

She made them squelch because the sound was vulgar and she widened her legs so that she could push three fingers inside. It helped that her hands were slim and elegant, but she had to be careful of her long fingernails and was unable to thrust as wildly as she would have liked in emulation of the two teenage boys.

Even so, her limbs twitched upon the bed and her left hand gripped at the coverlet as small spasms of passion hinted at greater ones ahead. Then her fingers touched upon something hard and long and round.

Amy removed the fingers from her vagina and picked up the penis-shaped object which was attached to something soft and furry. It was the wooden leg of Tarquin's teddy bear and she shuddered with delicious, naughty delight.

She held the stuffed bear above her face and licked its button snout with the tip of her delicate pink tongue.

'Little bear,' she whispered, her hips already moving in anticipation, 'would you like to fuck me?'

Amy pushed Bongo between her legs and rubbed his face into the wetness of her vagina, squirming against the fur and the protuberance of its snout.

Then she waited for Laura's account of her adventures to reach a crucial stage – where Jamie was poised to enter her from behind – and, as Laura described the thrust of the teenage boy, Amy thrust Bongo's smooth wooden leg inside herself.

It was a substantial length of wood and it made her groan loudly.

As Laura continued her tale, Amy pushed and pulled the wooden leg in and out of herself, her membranes pulsing around it as it entered, grasping at it as it slid out, reluctant to let it leave. The other leg, the soft fur-covered leg, was trapped beneath her, providing another naughty sensation on her bottom.

The timing and her rhythm were perfect for the final orgasm as Laura reached the crucial double coming of Jamie and Rick. Her right hand manoeuvred the wooden leg while the fingers of her left hand played with her clitoris.

It was on its way... it could not be denied... the sensation was building until there was no longer room for any more sensation... she had reached the top and was going over.

Nothing could stop it, not even when the door opened at that precise moment and Tarquin walked in.

The noise that escaped her throat was strangled and hardly human and her body convulsed around the teddy bear as she shook helplessly. She stared at her husband who stared back in amazement.

Amy felt the sensations ebbing away and collapsed upon the bed weakened by the number of orgasms she had given herself.

Tarquin said: 'What on earth...?'

And then he saw what lay between her legs.

Amy withdrew the wooden leg, raised the teddy bear to her face and kissed him on the snout.

'He is such a good little bear,' she said.

'Bongo!'

Tarquin snatched the teddy bear and looked at it in horror. The wooden leg was slick and wet, its snout was sticky with white juices and even the fur on its other leg was ruffled and damp.

Her husband turned away without a word, went into the adjoining bathroom and slammed and locked the door.

Amy recovered sufficiently to sit up. She was glad she'd had the wit to make the final gesture of kissing the bear, even though she preferred not to dwell upon the future of her marriage.

She swung her legs over the edge of the bed and onto the floor and felt weak and very hungry. Her clothes lay scattered about the room. She gathered them up and dressed and checked her appearance in the mirror.

Her face was a little flushed but nothing more. Her features were still beautiful, her bland expression hiding anything inside.

At the door she hesitated. It was a nuisance that Tarquin had locked himself in the bathroom because she could smell herself on her fingers. Her vaginal area was also aromatic. Still, she was too hungry to worry and she quite liked the smell of sex.

Amy left the room and descended the staircase to join Sir Alec at lunch.

In the bathroom, Tarquin sat upon the floor. Tears were in his eyes and he stroked Bongo's head and kissed his snout.

The snout tasted of his wife and he pulled a face in disgust, then licked his lips. He kissed the snout again. The next time he licked it, experimentally.

'Oh Bongo, what has she done to you?' he murmured, inspecting the wooden leg. 'You poor thing. Never mind. I will make you clean.

He put the wooden leg into his mouth and began to suck and lick.

Sir Alec had finished his lunch and was drinking coffee and reading *The Financial Times*.

He waited until Amy was halfway through her omelette before he spoke.

COMPULSION

'There has been a cable for Tarquin.'
'Really?'
Amy was more interested in eating than cables.
'It's from Spain. He has been offered a show by an art house in Barcelona.'
She paused between mouthfuls to stare across the table at her bald-headed father-in-law.
'A show?'
'Yes. That is what artists have, is it not?'
'Yes.' She shook her head. 'I didn't think he had gained that sort of attention.'
'It would appear so.'
She resumed eating until another thought struck her.
'If the cable was for Tarquin, how have you read it?'
'I read anything that comes to this house. Didn't he mention it? I gave it to him when he came in. Where is he, by the way?
'He went straight into the bathroom. He mentioned nothing about a show.'
'The cable was explicit. If he wants it, he will have to return to Spain immediately. I suppose these things take time to organise?'
'I suppose they do?'
'Will you go with him?'
Amy avoided the question by putting another forkful of omelette into her mouth. Her fingers were still aromatic.
'Will you?' he asked again.
'I do not know. I had not planned on going back so soon.'
'The offer still stands.'

She inclined her head to acknowledge what he said.

As she finished the food, Tarquin entered. He was flushed and avoided looking directly at Amy.

'I have been offered a show at the House of Benitez. It is a small house, but one with an excellent reputation.'

'Oh, congratulations, darling.'

Amy beamed at him, as if the news was new.

He responded with a weak smile.

'They want me to go and see them as soon as possible.'

'Then you must.' She stopped herself from gushing too much about his need to leave. 'If you think it's worth it.'

'Oh yes, it is worth it.' He shook his head absently for a moment. 'There is just so much to do. It is rather unexpected.'

Amy said: 'Is it what you want?'

'I want it very much.'

'Then you must go.'

'What about you, Amy?'

'I . . .' She shrugged. 'I will be in the way if I come with you. At least for the first week, until you have things planned. I shall remain here until you tell me all is ready.'

'It could take a long time.'

He did not sound distressed that they might be parted for a long time.

'Well, you know best, Tarquin' She smiled sweetly. 'I am happy to be advised by you as to when is the correct time for me to join you.'

Sir Alec said: 'There is a flight this evening from Heathrow.'

Tarquin gave him a sardonic smile.

'Thank you, father, for your concern as to my travel arrangements.' He looked at Amy with a hint of concern. 'Are you sure you will be all right in this house?'

'Tarquin, I am an adult and a married woman. What on earth can befall me here?'

He looked again at his father, who raised his *Financial Times* and continued to read.

'Then I shall pack.'

'Do you want me to help?'

'No, that will not be necessary.'

'As you wish.'

'Yes.' He glanced over at his father again. 'As I wish.'

Tarquin left the room and Amy poured herself some coffee.

She said: 'Did you arrange this showing?'

Sir Alec put the newspaper down onto his lap.

'Of course.'

'Does he know?'

'He might suspect, but he does not know. Besides, ego is involved. He wants to believe that his art has been recognised. He does not want to know how much I paid to the House of Benitez to stage it.'

'Why?'

'Why what?'

'Why arrange for the show?'

'Because that is what he wants. He might not be my idea of an ideal son but he is still my son. It is a helping hand in his chosen way of life. The House is good. Who knows, he may be discovered?'

Amy stared at him – a hint of iron in the bland expression.

'Is it to send him away?'

Sir Alec shrugged.

'Is it to keep me here?'

'That is your choice, my dear.' He smiled. 'I am delighted you have decided to stay, at least for a while. I would be more delighted if you accepted the job I offered. I have an awful lot of items that need putting in order.'

'I am still considering the offer.' She shrugged. 'Perhaps I will. Life could be tedious around here without something to do.'

His smile became a grin.

'There will always be something to do, my dear. And none of it will be tedious.'

Chapter 8

Caroline Penrose broke her luncheon engagement and sat around the house all afternoon, her emotions in confusion.

How had she done what she had done?

Last night and this morning?

Good God, what was happening to her?

There were plenty of questions but few answers.

In mid-afternoon she found herself lying on the bed, staring at the ceiling – remembering. Pictures slid into her mind unbidden, visions of what she had done, visions of her image on the television screen in the Rolls Royce, visions of her hand moving of its own accord in the lap of Sir Alec Ramsden.

She raised the hand to her face. Looking at it, she remembered again the feeling of his sperm running over her fingers, and the noises he made when he came.

This was a giant of industry, a wealthy tycoon with business interests around the world, a man on familiar terms with the Prime Minister. And she had held him in her hand and milked him like a teenager.

The thought revived more memories, from long ago in her own teenage days, when sex had always been passionate and exciting, whether it had been a stolen kiss, or allowing a boy a first grope beneath her blouse, or feeling his urgency in his trousers.

Back then, their erections had begged to be handled. It had been the centre of any young man's universe, and they had been so grateful if she had deigned to touch them, even briefly. On occasions it had only needed to be briefly, before their passion had burst its barriers and they had come in their underpants.

These were thoughts not meant for a sunny afternoon in suburbia, she told herself. These were thoughts that should only be paraded late at night in the arms of her husband, and then secretly and to herself.

But surely that, too, was not right. She and Tom should not need secret memories to maintain passion. And yet, how long had it been since they had last been fired by each other's bodies? When they first met, they had indulged in marathon sex sessions, during which they had tried everything. But now? Tom was always so tired.

Perhaps she was partly to blame. Perhaps she should make more of an effort. How long had it been since she had dressed up for him?

It was the excuse she needed, for her own sexual needs were still aching to be relieved.

Caroline now moved with purpose. She prepared a salad, put two steaks ready for the grill, got a bottle

COMPULSION

of red wine from the garage and put a bottle of white in the refrigerator. She ran a bath and luxuriated in the perfumed bubbles, allowing her hands to linger longer than they should on the intimate parts of her body as she washed.

The temptation was there to use her fingers, but she had denied herself for years, deciding it was not quite right – particularly for the well-educated and properly brought-up wife of an upwardly mobile executive.

In the bedroom, she could not stop her imagination flirting with the possibilities of the night ahead as she deliberately chose her most outrageous underwear: a scarlet silk basque with underwired half cups over which her ample breasts bulged, a scarlet silk thong and black stockings.

My God, she thought when she looked at herself in the mirror, perhaps I have gone too far.

She had worn the basque only once, on a weekend away two years before, and it had sent Tom wild. Had she put on extra weight since then, she wondered?

Her breasts were full and the curve of her thighs fuller. She angled for a rear view of herself and caught her breath. Her bottom was larger than she would have wished, but not by much, and in the past it had been Tom's favourite part of her anatomy. Her gaze roamed its majestic curves and the only term that came to mind was lush.

Dressing this way heightened her feeling of sexuality. Butterflies were loose in the pit of her stomach again, as they had been the night before when she had watched the couple in the conservatory, as they had been when the Frenchman had led her into the darkened room and started his seduction, as they had been when Sir Alec Ramsden had wrapped her fingers around his penis in the back of his limousine.

Hurry home, Tom, she said to herself. Dinner is waiting.

Caroline put on a black silk dress that made her look almost respectable, except for the way the material clung to the outline of her underwear and the straps of the suspenders.

She wondered if he would even get through the first course before they had sex?

Half an hour before he was due home, the table was set, the bottle of red uncorked and her excitement was higher still. She tried to watch television and failed, so she switched on the radio. Its mundaneness annoyed her so she played a record. Almost by accident, she found she had chosen music by Smokey Robinson; the music that had been playing the previous evening.

It was six-thirty and he was due home, but where was he?

By seven, he still had not arrived and she telephoned the office – something he had asked her not to do. Telephoning the office to ask his whereabouts made him look as if he was not capable of managing his private affairs, never mind his company duties, he had said.

There was no reply. Perhaps he was on the way?

The telephone rang at seven-twenty.

'Hello, dear. I'm sorry, I've been delayed.'
'But where are you?'
'I'm at the office. Something dropped onto the desk ten minutes before I was due to leave and I haven't had a minute since.'
'When will you be home?'
'Not till late, I'm afraid. Don't wait up.'

Caroline sat at the dinner table and poured herself a glass of red wine. When she had finished it, she poured herself another.

When she had telephoned the office there had been no reply, and yet he had said he had been there all the time. He said he was still there.

She picked up the bottle of wine and her glass, and took them to the bedroom. She stood in front of the mirror and thought how foolish she looked, flushing with embarrassment at the preparations she had made and the sexual situations she had envisaged. Suddenly she felt middle-aged. But Jean-Paul had said she was beautiful.

But that, too, had probably been a set up, contrived by Sir Alec Ramsden. Jean-Paul had probably been paid to tell her she was beautiful and to seduce her.

She sighed.

But he had done it so well.

Caroline removed the dress and continued to stare at her image in the scarlet underwear. Did she look foolish or desirable? She did not know.

But even if Jean-Paul had been paid, and even if Sir Alec had set up the whole situation to ensare her, then Sir Alec must think she was attractive. To have gone to all that trouble must mean that the tycoon himself found her desirable.

She shook her heard. The events of the previous night and that morning were not adding up because they were outside her normal sphere of life. At least the wine made sense so she drank another glass and took off the underwear.

Perhaps she would wear it when she went to see Sir Alec, for she had decided – with a little help from the glasses of wine she had drunk – that when the car arrived for her, she would indeed go.

Her recent experiences might be outside her normal sphere of life, but her normal sphere of life was so utterly boring that almost anything would be worth trying to escape its monotony.

Tarquin prepared to leave the house at eight. He was driving himself to Heathrow in the hire car in which he and Amy had arrived the previous evening.

Sir Alec was in the hall as he came downstairs.

'I hope it goes well for you.'

'Since when have you been interested?'

'You misjudge me, Tarquin. But then, you never tried to understand me.'

'Nor you, me.'

'Perhaps I understand you more than you think?'

Tarquin shrugged.

'Have you seen Amy?' he asked.

'She was in the swimming pool. I am going that way. I will tell her you are ready to leave.'

As Sir Alec turned, Tarquin said: 'Father, do not forget that Amy is my wife.'

COMPULSION

His father grinned.

'Of course not. And don't you forget, if there is anything you need for this exhibition, call me.'

'This sudden concern is discomforting.'

'Amy told me how important the exhibition could be. I want to see you do well.'

'I would prefer to do well by my own merit.'

'As you wish. I shall tell Amy you are leaving.'

He left the room and a few moments later Amy entered the hall, wearing a one-piece black swimsuit that was high cut at the sides. The design made her legs look even longer and emphasised the roundness of her buttocks. She was drying her hair with a towel.

'I hardly think that is a fit way to dress around the house.'

Her eyes widened at his admonishment.

'I have been swimming.'

'You could have worn a robe.'

'I am hot and I did not have one with me.'

'What will the servants think?'

'I do not care what the servants think, and neither do you. You care what your father may think.'

Tarquin was having difficulty looking her in the eye. They both remembered how he had found her at lunchtime.

'I have warned you about him. He is a dangerous man. This house can be unhealthy in the ... temptations it can provide. I am only worried about your safety.'

'I will be all right, Tarquin. Besides, a little danger may be amusing.'

'What do you mean by that?'

'Nothing. I am just teasing.'
'Have you accepted the job?'
'I have not decided.'
'It will not be as straightforward as it seems.'
She shrugged.
'Neither is life.'

Tarquin sighed in exasperation and picked up a small leather grip.

'I have to go.'

Amy smiled sweetly at him, with genuine affection. He seemed so helpless at times. She kissed his cheek but he still avoided direct eye contact.

'Take care,' she said. 'Let me know the progress of the show.'

'I will.' He stared into her eyes for the first time. 'You take care.'

He left and Amy walked back to the pool at the rear of the house. Being on her own in a place of such unhealthy temptations suddenly filled her with a wonderful sense of freedom.

The pool was built out from the house beneath a glass extension. A waterfall ran into it over scenic rocks and imitation hothouse foliage gave it a jungle appearance. To one side, a large jacuzzi bubbled invitingly. The glass panels of the extension that served to seal in the temperature during the winter, had now been slid open to take advantage of the summer night.

Amy was alone. She dropped the towel and dived into the water, swimming to the other side of the pool near the waterfall. The water gave her a weightlessness that added to the illusion of freedom. It bubbled

COMPULSION

from a vent beneath the surface, like a miniature jacuzzi, and she pushed her hips forward so that the oscillations were directed towards the juncture of her thighs.

She slipped her arms from the swimsuit and pushed it down her body, bringing her legs up and making a slow roll in the pool as she pulled it from her feet.

Now she was totally free and totally naked. She allowed the swimsuit to float away and resumed her position, letting the vibrating bubbles caress her pubic area. Her vagina twitched in response and her stomach began its own oscillations. Slyly, she slid a hand between her legs to roll the bud of her clitoris beneath her finger.

Her eyes closed and she moved her hips slowly beneath the water.

'Is it warm enough?'

Sir Alec's voice, from the other side of the plastic leaves of a trailing vine, was a shock.

'How long have you been there?'

'Just arrived, my dear. To remind you that supper will be served in twenty minutes.'

Amy felt the flush on her face and recognised the interest on her father-in-law's.

'I will be there,' she said.

She pushed herself away from the side of the pool with her feet, deliberately raising her hips onto the level of the water and she swam on her back. She knew that her pert breasts and blonde pubic patch were now on show but she wanted to give him something to really look at.

Maria Caprio

Her swimsuit was alongside her and she grabbed it in one hand as she swam to the other side of the pool, aware that Sir Alec was watching her, every stroke of the way.

When she reached the other side, she hauled herself out of the water, making no attempt to cover herself, so that he got the back view of her buttocks as well. She picked up the towel and dabbed her face dry, before wrapping it around her like a sarong to walk through the house and upstairs to her room.

Once behind the locked door, she acknowledged that the jacuzzi in her stomach had become even more agitated by her blatant displaying of her body. She longed to submerge herself in solitary sex, and yet she resisted.

The audio and video tapes were still in the cupboard where she had left them, but Bongo the teddy bear was missing. Tarquin had rescued him from further abuse by taking him to Spain – but she was sure she would be able to find alternatives.

Amy pushed her hair back and stared at her reflection in the mirror, noting the high colour in her cheeks. She knew Sir Alec played games and was beginning to enjoy playing her own. The tapes would be saved until after dinner, when she would enjoy them at her leisure, long into the night. But before then, she had more games to play.

She piled her blonde hair on her head for added height and put on a black silk minidress and delicate black spike-heeled shoes. Amy wore no underwear and the curves of her body, accentuated by walking

COMPULSION

on her toes in the extremely high heels, shimmered beneath the almost transparent material. One final touch was a string of pearls around her neck, for sophistication.

How would Sir Alec's appetite be, when faced with such a dish, she wondered wickedly?

Rupert, the butler, dropped a spoon when she entered the dining room and her father-in-law's grin became so wide she thought his face might split in two halves.

'You are absolutely beautiful, my dear,' he said.

'Thank you.'

Her smile was both condescending and gracious.

They ate in silence, although his eyes never left her, and the attention and obvious desire in his face was added torture to the gorgeous feelings of lust in her loins.

When they had finished, she fanned the blooms in her cheeks and wondered if he could guess why her colour was so high?

'It is very hot this evening.'

'Yes. I am feeling it myself. Why don't we take coffee on the terrace?'

'Why not?'

Sir Alec was the perfect host as he escorted her through the french windows and onto a sheltered terrace with a view down to the lake. He held the padded whicker chair for her while she sat down, before choosing one that faced her at an oblique angle, so that he could admire her legs.

Rupert served the coffee on a sturdy glass-topped

cane table that was between them.

'Have you made a decision yet?' Sir Alec asked.

'Yes.'

She smiled and opened her legs a fraction, allowing the evening breeze to funnel beneath the short skirt and caress her vulva.

He looked at her thighs, most of which were exposed.

'Are you going to toy with me?' he said.

'What do you mean?'

'By not telling me whether you have accepted the job or not?'

'I accept it.'

His grin widened again and he now looked into her face.

'Well done, my dear. You will not regret it. Tomorrow, I will give you a key to the private library and explain some of my work and what you will be required to do.'

'Nothing too arduous, I hope?'

'Not arduous, but it could be time-consuming if you become seduced.'

'Seduced?'

She crossed her legs. Her vagina, which had been in a state of dampness for most of the afternoon, was becoming more excited, and she pressed the open lips of her labia together. The sensation of even such a small movement almost her her gasp.

He said: 'Seduced by the material you will handle. To an enquiring mind, it can be fascinating. You may want to watch every video, listen to every cassette, read every book, study every picture.'

'You make it sound as if it could be a job for life?'

His smile was more thoughtful.

'Perhaps it is.'

Amy could not resist moving her thighs together to give herself a little friction. The small moan that did escape, she muffled in her throat. She could not take much more of this, she thought. Soon, she would have to escape to her room and the video of the beautiful woman from the party and the haunting voice of Laura remembering innocence lost.

They drank coffee and exchanged light conversation that frequently could have had a double meaning, if either of them had acknowledged the fact. They did not, for that was not how the game was played. To heighten her pleasure, it had to be played at a distance.

At last, she made her excuses to leave and realised she was so wet with desire that she had stained the front of the silk dress. It was only a small stain, but noticeable nonetheless.

'Good night, Amy.'

Sir Alec got up from his chair and waited for her to rise. Amy did so, restraining her natural inclination to cover the stain with her hands. Perhaps he would not notice it anyway, and if he did, it would be another small goad to his own desire, which she was determined would remain unfulfilled.

'Good night, Sir Alec.'

He kissed her fingers, holding them a mite too long, and allowed his tongue to trail over the tips.

'I am sorry you will have to sleep alone.'

She retrieved her hand.

'It will be no hardship.'

'And do not stay up too late watching television,' he warned with a smile. 'You have a busy day ahead of you tomorrow.'

'Thank you for your concern, but as a model I am used to keeping a tight grip on my affairs. I always come on time.'

'Delighted to hear it.' He rewarded her with a slight bow as she passed him, allowing him to stare at the stain on the black silk. 'I think we will both find this collaboration exceedingly satisfying, my dear.'

'I already have, Sir Alec,' she said, and walked into the house.

By the time she reached the bedroom, she was almost passing out with desire, but the torture was delicious and she delayed it further.

Amy stripped off the black silk dress and stood in front of the mirror. Her breasts heaved and her hips made small undulating movements of their own accord, as if her loins were possessed. The colour in her cheeks was high.

Wearing only the pearls and the spike-heeled shoes, she approached the mirror and pressed herself against it. Her breasts were flattened against the cool glass and her hips rubbed across its surface.

Perhaps she was narcissistic but she had never believed in false modesty. She knew she was beautiful and desirable. If she met another woman as beautiful as herself, she would want nothing better than to

COMPULSION

take her to bed and made love to her. Like the woman in the video, the woman called Caroline.

Amy closed her eyes as she imagined making love to Caroline and getting her hands on the flesh of her bosom and buttocks. The Frenchman could stay, too, and they could all do disgusting things together, things she had never done before, things she had never admitted that she wanted to do, or had even contemplated before in detail.

When she moved away from the mirror, her open vagina had left smear marks on the glass. She knelt before it and delicately licked them off.

Now she was ready for Caroline and had already logged in her mind those sections of the video she would repeat or play in slow motion. Later, it would be Laura's turn and she would welcome her voice into her mind, creating images of virile boys whose erections never went soft.

Chapter 9

The orgasms she had administered to herself the night before made Amy lethargic in the morning. However, she was still on time for breakfast, looking fresh and extremely young with her hair in pigtails.

She wore white socks, tennis shoes and a white brushed cotton dress that was tight over her hips, and which reached to mid-thigh.

After staining her dress the night before, she now wore a white cotton thong. She had appraised her appearance in the mirror and thought it fetching. The waistband of the thong and the start of the strap that went between her buttocks could be seen through the cotton. Another goad for Sir Alec.

They exchanged pleasantries over cornflakes and toast. When they had finished, he led her through the main library to the small door that led to the private section.

He unlocked the door and handed her the key.

'We are the only two people with keys for this room and you must keep it locked at all times,' he said, with almost mock gravity.

Maria Caprio

They entered and her heart fluttered at the potential on the shelves inside. If the rest of the contents matched the cassettes she had already played, she would happily spend the rest of the summer here.

Sir Alec closed the door behind them and locked it again.

Now her heart fluttered for different reasons. Surely her father-in-law was not contemplating rape? He seemed to read her mind and smiled.

'Do not worry, my dear. I do not intend to attack you. You are beautiful, and I am madly attracted to you: any man would be. But you are safe with me, at least from physical assault. It has never been my style to force myself upon anyone, although there is nothing more that I enjoy than compulsion.'

'You are talking in riddles, Sir Alec.'

'Then perhaps it is time I explained.'

He indicated the armchairs and settee; she chose an armchair and he took the other one, which was opposite and which again provided him with a view of her legs. She crossed them carelessly on purpose.

'I enjoy sex,' he said. 'Unadulterated sex. And I enjoy nothing more than releasing the inhibitions of men and women who have forgotten how to enjoy sex. I call my hobby, compulsion.

'Once I have picked my subject, I place them in a set of circumstances in which they feel compelled to respond as I wish them to respond. Let me give you an example.

'At the party the other night was one of my executives and his wife. He is extremely competent at his job, but his desire for progress within the company has made him play power games among his peers. Power has replaced sex for him, unless he can relate the sex to power.

'He is having an affair with a female junior executive. She is responding to his position of superiority in the company, rather than because she is attracted to him. He is aware of this, but it gives him pleasure to think that he can use his position to impose his will upon a woman colleague. It gives him pleasure knowing that she will copulate with him in the hope that it will further her career.

'As a consequence, he has lost sight of the fact that his own wife is a beautiful woman who needs sexual attention. His wife is faithful and has not sought solace elsewhere. Consequently, her needs have remained unfulfilled.

'At the party I decided to take a hand. I introduced the executive to a woman whom I said was a senior vice president from one of our United States conglomorates. I stressed her power and influence, before leaving them alone together, to see if she could seduce him. She was older than him and rather plain. Of course, she succeeded.

'He was aroused by another variation of the power concept and was a willing partner in a very lustful encounter. She used him, just as he had used the junior executive, and he followed her directions with enthusiasm.'

He nodded to the shelves.

'The tape is on there.' He smiled. 'There are certain

rooms that are especially adapted for hidden cameras.'

'How naughty.'

'How exciting.'

'This woman who seduced the man. Is she really a senior vice president?'

'No. But she is an old friend with whom I have shared games before.'

'And the wife?'

'Ah, the wife. Mrs Caroline Penrose. I arranged for Mrs Penrose to be seduced by a very handsome young Frenchman.'

'Was that not a cruel thing to do?'

'Certainly not.'

'Even though you were tampering with her emotions? Her marriage?'

'Her marriage is in a parlous state. The way her husband is behaving, it is doubtful it if will survive. I am providing her with options and, possibly, the armoury to fight back and save her marriage, if she wants to. As for the seduction by my Frenchman, she could always have said no. She chose not to and she enjoyed herself tremendously.'

'It sounds as if you are playing at God.'

'I am playing at life and the core of life is the sex drive. Too many people keep it subdued when it needs to be freed and unfettered.'

Amy said: 'You think Mrs Penrose has subdued her sex drive?'

'Yes.'

'And it is your intention to help her break free of inhibition?'

'Yes.'

'How?'

'The seduction was the start. If she had not responded, I would not have proceeded.'

'Even though she may have been influenced by wine and flattery? Even though your Frenchman may have forced himself upon her?'

Amy realised she might be saying too much that could indicate to Sir Alec that she had actually seen the video.

'There was no rape, there was sexual persuasion. Mrs Penrose wanted to be seduced. Possibly she would have preferred her husband to have been the seducer, but a handsome Frenchman was an acceptable alternative.'

She had to agree with him. Caroline Penrose had shown some reluctance at first, but it had been the kind of reluctance open to persuasion, and when she had let herself go there was no mistaking the fervour of her response.

'You said you had proceeded with her course in freedom?'

'That is correct. I saw her yesterday and gave her the reason she needed for the experiment to continue.'

'What reason?'

'I showed her the video tape of her encounter with the Frenchman.'

'You blackmailed her?'

'No. I showed her the film. She asked me not to give it to her husband, which is a natural response. Such a film presented in evidence to a divorce judge would mitigate in her husband's favour. It was also a middle-class response at not wanting to be embarrassed. A response that reflects social convention. But what happened then went totally against social convention.'

'What happened?'

'Mrs Penrose masturbated me in the back of my car.'

Amy was shocked at the unexpectedness of what he said. She was also instantly aroused, after all his words of justification.

'Because you threatened to give the video to her husband?'

'No. I issued no threat, but I left the possibility there so that she could use it as justification for doing something totally against her normal pattern of behaviour.'

'You draw a fine line between blackmail and liberation.'

'It always is a fine line.' He smiled. 'But I have walked it many times before.'

'And this time?'

'Mrs Penrose has a deep desire for liberation. She is trapped in a suburban life into which she was never meant to fit. Her mind is far too good to continue on the twinset and pearls luncheon circuit, on charity work and giving up one half day a week to run the Oxfam shop.

'But she needed an excuse, a reason she could give to herself for taking another step towards rediscovering sex and her own identity.'

COMPULSION

'And the next step was masturbating you in the back of a car?'

He grinned and stroked a bulge that had appeared in his trousers.

'Yes, and she was very good. A fraction of her mind believed that she was being compelled to perform the act, but the rest of her knew damn well that she wanted to.' He spread his arms at a *fait accompli*. 'All that needs to be done now, is to peel away one or two of those layers of social conditioning.'

'And you believe you can do that?'

'Mrs Penrose had reverted to a chrysalis: with help, she will emerge a butterfly instead of a moth.'

Amy said: 'You are very poetic. What is the next stage in this awakening?'

'The next stage will occur, I hope, this morning. I have sent a car for Mrs Penrose. If she chooses not to come, that is the end of the matter. But I believe she will come. She enjoyed the seduction too much; she enjoyed the back of the car too much. She will be here.'

'And when she arrives?'

'I shall introduce you. You see, I have offered her a job as well.'

'What sort of a job?'

'Entertaining business clients.'

'Sexually?'

'But of course.'

'And will she?'

'She will feel compelled to, but by now the compulsion is changing. It is not me who is the driving force;

I have simply provided the excuse. Mrs Penrose will proceed towards liberation because she wants to.

'She may use me, and my machinations, as the continuing reason for her submission.' He leaned forward slightly to emphasise his next words. 'But there will come a time, sooner rather than later, when she will admit she is succumbing to her own compulsions rather than mine.'

'And when she does?'

'Ah! Then it is time for her to make her confession.'

Amy glanced at the confessional box. She was wet and itchy between her legs at what her father-in-law had said and at what might unfold.

'Do all your women, your subjects, have to make a confession?'

'Yes.'

'To whom?'

'To me, of course.'

'What do they confess?'

'A story of compulsion from their past.'

'What if they have never experienced one?'

'Everyone has done things that, at the time, they told themselves they did not want to do.'

'Do you think I have?'

'I am sure you have.'

Amy coloured slightly under his frank gaze.

'You are the most devious man I have ever met.'

'Thank you.'

'What do you want from me?'

'Nothing that you do not wish to give.'

'Then it is nothing you shall receive.'

COMPULSION

'We shall see.' His smile was confident. 'Compulsion takes many forms.'

Amy licked her lips. Was it really so hot in this room?

'Would you like to fuck me, Sir Alec?'

She uncrossed her legs and stretched in the chair, her thighs slightly apart, so that the skirt stretched open. He would be able to see the wet white triangle of cotton that covered her pubis.

But her position or her question failed to shock him.

He stared openly up her skirt before looking her in the face.

'I would like you to ask me to fuck you, Amy. But, more than that, I would like to hear your confession.'

A shudder touched the nerve centre of her body and she felt as if she was being carried on a wave of sensuality that she had never experienced before.

Sir Alec got to his feet.

'Time to meet Mrs Penrose. Shall we?' He indicated the door. 'Will you lock it after you leave, my dear? I'll see you in the hall in ten minutes.'

He left the room and Amy got unsteadily to her feet. Her juices were running again and she moved her hips to find relief. The confessional beckoned, exerting a strange force upon her, and she walked to it, pushed open a door and stepped into the cool, silent, privacy of the box.

Amy leaned back against the wall and looked down at the grill through which petitioners for understanding told all. She could smell the wood and the dust.

She pulled the cotton dress up around her waist and twisted the narrow panel of her panties together at the front, until it matched in width the strip that ran down between her buttocks. Two fingers of her right hand opened the lips of her vagina and she lay the material along the groove of her sex.

The tight band now touched three pleasure points: between her buttocks, through the aching chasm of her vagina, and across her clitoris.

Amy gripped her panties near the waist and pulled the band of material backwards and forwards in short, exquisitely slow motions.

'My name is Amy,' she said to the grill. 'And my confession is that I want to be fucked.'

Her head twisted sideways as the pleasure became uncontrollable and a tweak of the cotton caught her clitoris in just the right spot. She climaxed, her right leg twitching so much that it banged a tattoo on the wooden side of the confessional.

Now the box smelled of sex and her perfume, as well as wood and dust. She could have stayed there and repeated the motions of pleasure but she knew her father-in-law would be waiting.

Amy left the strip of cotton taut between the lips of her vagina and pushed the dress down. She took a deep breath and left the confessional box and the private library, locking the door behind her with the key that promised entry to great and unending excitements.

Chapter 10

Caroline Penrose did not know why she was even considering going to Sir Alec's house. If what had occurred in the back of his Rolls Royce constituted a job interview, then she could hazard a guess as to the type of employment he was offering.

The man was a monster. He had to be, to have filmed her making love with a man. No, she should be honest, they had not made love, they had fucked.

It was a word she had rarely used and which her background had declared to be socially offensive. But it was very apt and emotive. It was basic and to the point. D. H. Lawrence had shocked Victorians with it and it was still possible to shock suburbia with it. She would read Lady Chatterley again with new insight.

Fuck was a beautiful word.

Caroline moved about her home as if she had a mission to make it neat and tidy, except of course, it already was. Her home was always neat and bloody tidy. Tom insisted upon it, as he insisted that she should not work because, financially, she did not need to work.

All right, so if she was supposed to stay at home, what was her purpose? To be an accessory? Certainly not for making love, or even sex. Even sex? She meant fucking. It had been wonderful two nights before.

Tom had arrived home after eleven o'clock the previous night and had slept as close to his side of the bed as was possible, as if touching her might give him a disease.

Or perhaps the wine and her hangover had made her more sceptical than usual?

His morning departure had been as impersonal as his bedroom habits. He had eaten breakfast with hardly a word, preferring to study the *Telegraph* rather than exchange more than the briefest glance.

Whatever the reason, she knew she was dissatisfied with her marriage and her life. Being shown the video had shocked her into confronting the ongoing situation of her existence, and it certainly was not life. There had to be more to it than this? There had to be more to it than being just an ongoing situation.

As the time approached for the arrival of the car that Sir Alec had said he would send, she found herself in her bedroom looking through her wardrobe. The responsible part of her mind tried to question what she was doing, but she put it on hold until she was so far committed that she could not turn back.

She chose a dark blue dress with a full skirt and a bodice that buttoned down the front. It could be worn for both casual and formal occasions. How did you class the rendezvous she was about to keep?

Caroline did not wear the scarlet basque beneath

COMPULSION

it, after all. Without half a bottle of red wine, it no longer seemed appropriate. But her recent experiences, and the fact that she was dressing for an unknown encounter with a man, had filled her with a mixture of arousal and fear – two emotions, she discovered, that were extremely close to each other and, in combination, extremely potent.

Black underwear would be safe, she decided, with tan stockings and black high-heeled shoes.

She had a shower, touched up her make-up and hair, and dressed. The sensation of putting on stockings in the middle of the morning was an added thrill. Tom used to like her to wear stockings but that, like many intimacies, was long in the past.

Her appearance pleased her but left her worried in case it did not please Sir Alec. Suddenly, the part of her mind that had been on hold escaped and asked once more, what on earth she thought she was doing?

The most honest answer was that she did not know.

Perhaps this was defiance: to Tom, marriage, respectability and boredom. She looked good and she was embarking on some kind of adventure. She also felt more nervous than she had for years, much more nervous than when she had been with Jean-Paul, for then she had been able to blame the wine.

Now she could blame no one but herself and a tycoon with a tape.

The doorbell rang and made her jump.

Unsteadily, she walked down the hall and opened the door.

Charles, the chauffeur, removed his peaked cap.

'Mrs Penrose,' he said.

Behind him, the Rolls Royce waited.

Wherever she was going, she was going there in style.

Sir Alec and a beautiful, blonde girl met her in the hall of the house.

'This is Amy,' he said. 'My private and personal secretary.'

Caroline and Amy shook hands. There was a tingle, like static electricity, when they touched. Caroline could see the girl felt it, too.

'I feel you have brought me here under false pretences, Sir Alec.'

'Certainly not, Mrs Penrose. I have asked you here for our mutual benefit and pleasure.'

He smiled that avuncular smile that seemed to hide so much, and led the way along the corridor that she remembered, and into the bedroom that she remembered. Except that it was no longer a bedroom.

It was furnished as a drawing room, with drinks and glasses standing on a sideboard, armchairs and a large sofa.

Sir Alec went to the sideboard and poured himself a scotch, to which he added a small measure of water.

'Mrs Penrose?' he asked.

'I think perhaps I should. A vodka and tonic, please.'

'A sensible choice. Amy?'

'No, thank you. Not for me.'

He added ice to the vodka and handed it to Caroline. She tasted it.

'It's strong. Is that necessary?'
Sir Alec laughed.
'Please, sit down.'
They turned towards the chairs and Caroline noticed the line of the thong through the dress that Amy was wearing. The girl was slimly curvaceous and young and the sight of her body aroused feelings in her that she had never known existed. Or perhaps they had never been released before?

When they were sitting, Sir Alec explained.

'Public relations is an important section of business and it is my experience that beautiful women, such as yourself, can achieve far more goodwill on an individual basis than any mere male.'

'Sir Alec, I am here under a certain duress. I suspect the public relations you would wish me to provide would be better described as personal services. Please get to the point.'

'Well said. And to further get to the point, I will tell you that Amy is fully aware of the duress to which you refer. She knows that you were filmed, in this very room, having sex with a man other than your husband. She also knows the small kindness which you performed for me, yesterday morning.'

Caroline looked at the blonde girl and neither flinched at the eye contact. Caroline felt the hint of a blush in her cheeks, but then the blonde girl licked her lips with the tip of her tongue. The action was so exciting that it robbed Caroline of words and made her stomach unstable with that enticing combination of fear and arousal.

Sir Alec said: 'You believe, Mrs Penrose, that I have

blackmailed you into coming here. I may assure you that I will not send the video to your husband, but you do not know if you can believe me. That is why you held my prick yesterday, and why you handled it until my sperm ran over your fingers.'

The use of such direct language after a guarded conversation shocked both Caroline and Amy, who again exchanged glances to gauge each other's reaction.

Sir Alec continued: 'So, when I say that there is an immediate opportunity for you to help me with a very important business deal, you will no doubt believe that if you do not comply with my wishes, I will, indeed, send the video.'

Caroline was overcome with a heavy feeling of inevitability sinking to meet the turmoil in her stomach. Defiance had been in her mind earlier, but now it was on the line she could not retreat.

Her voice was suddenly hoarse.

'You want me to ... entertain someone else?'

She had steeled herself into entertaining Sir Alec.

'Yes.'

'You want me to have sex with someone else?'

'Only if you want to. I will be your guide, but you will make the decisions about where you wish to draw the line.'

'Do I have a choice?'

'You always have a choice.'

Caroline looked at the mirrors on the walls.

'And you will film what happens?'

'Of course.'

She gulped. There was no other way. She did not wish there to be any other way.

'All right,' she said. 'I agree.'

Sir Alec smiled widely.

'I knew you would. And you will not regret it, I assure you.'

Caroline looked at the blonde girl.

'Where will you be?' she asked.

Sir Alex answered on her behalf.

'She will be behind the mirror, watching,' he said.

Caroline's stomach lurched and the girl licked her lips again, the lust naked on her beautiful features.

The tycoon said: 'There are also conditions that you may find bizarre, but which will be most effective.'

'What sort of conditions?'

'You will not speak unless spoken to. If you are addressed directly and you have to speak, you will call the person sir. You will keep your eyes lowered. You will follow all instructions to the letter.'

'Without knowing what they are in advance?'

'If you knew what they were, it would spoil the surprise.'

'I don't know if I can do that.'

'Then do you best, Mrs Penrose. Look upon it as an initiative test.'

'Why may I not speak?'

'I am making you a sex object. I am removing your personality. You will find the isolation will enable you to do things you would not normally consider doing.'

'What if I can't do them?'

He waved towards the door. 'You may leave at any

point and no one will attempt to stop you. Charles is outside with the car and will take you home whenever you wish.'

Caroline was confused at the way he was changing the emphasis. He had a video that he could send to her husband if he so wished, yet he had not said that he would. She no longer knew whether she cared or not if her husband saw the video or whether her marriage survived. She no longer knew whether she was embarking on this experience because she was being forced to, or because she wanted to.

'You are a very clever man, Sir Alec.'

'And you are a beautiful woman, Mrs Penrose, who deserves to be fucked.' He held up a finger. 'I use the word deliberately and not to offend. You are a beautiful and sexual woman at the peak of her desires. You deserve to have those desires fulfilled.'

Sir Alec got up and stretched.

'Are you ready?'

'Yes.'

'And still of like mind?'

'I am.'

'Good. Then it is time to begin.'

He walked to the door.

Amy and Caroline got to their feet and the blonde stepped closer, as if to say something, but did not. Instead, they stared deep into each other's eyes.

Caroline's lips had become dry and she moistened them with her tongue.

She said: 'I hope you enjoy it.'

The beautiful blonde girl lifted her hand and gently

stroked Caroline's cheek with the back of a finger.

'I will,' she said.

Sir Alec and the girl left the room and Caroline gulped down her drink, then went to the sideboard and poured another. She had only taken a sip when the door opened and Sir Alec returned.

He looked at her and said, almost formally: 'Let me introduce Jack Benson... and his son, Denzel. Gentlemen, this is Mrs Penrose.'

My God, she thought, they were black and there were two of them.

Chapter 11

'Alec, you sure know how to combine business with pleasure,' said Jack Benson, his accent unmistakably West Indian.

Both Bensons were at least six feet in height and well built. The senior was clean shaven, had grizzled grey hair and looked about fifty years of age, while the younger man was in his late twenties and had a shiny bald head and a goatee beard that gave him an air of danger.

They were both elegantly dressed in dark suits, white shirts and ties, as if ready for a board meeting.

Sir Alec said: 'Gentlemen, will you have a drink?'

Benson senior said: 'A white rum and Coca-Cola would hit the spot.'

His son said: 'Bourbon, on the rocks.'

Caroline was still standing by the sideboard and Sir Alec indicated, with a look, that she should get the drinks.

Her hands, she noticed, were shaking as she reached for glasses and bottles but she controlled them and, when the drinks had been poured, she carried them across the room.

Benson senior was talking to Sir Alec and accepted his glass with a slight bow. Even with her eyes lowered, she was aware that his gaze was admiring the curves of her body. His son was by the window, staring out at the grounds.

He took the glass with his right hand and held her wrist with his left. Slowly, he moved her hand down to the front of his trousers and placed it, palm open, upon the bulge that they contained.

'You want it?' he said in a low voice.

Caroline, her eyes fixed on the strong black hand gripping her wrist, did not know how to respond.

'Yes, sir,' she said.

He chuckled lazily and moved her hand backwards and forwards over the bulge until it stiffened. It felt huge.

'I'm going to enjoy making you yell,' he said.

'Denzel!' his father shouted. And, in an aside to Sir Alec: 'He could never wait. Always impatient. Always wants to charge in like a bull.' He laughed. 'Built like one, too.'

Benson junior released her wrist and she walked back across the room. Sir Alec lifted an arm, indicating that she should join him and Benson senior. She did so, her arms by her sides, her thighs trembling slightly.

Sir Alec said: 'I have noticed you looking at her body, Jack, but what do you think?'

'I think you've gone one better than last year. She is one hell of a lady.'

'Yes, I think so.'

Benson senior said conversationally: 'Have you fucked her yet?'

'Not yet. But I have watched her perform. She needs drawing out of herself, you know. There is a great deal of passion inside her, of which she is unaware. It needs bringing out.'

'Denzel can drive rivets into steel with his prick.' He laughed. 'He'll bring out her passion.'

'And what about you?'

'I don't rush things any more. My ladies appreciate me taking time. I like to watch a good man and his tool at work, it gets the juices jiving. Then I dip in and take my pleasure.'

'Do you think she will be suitable?'

'I'm sure of it.' Benson senior reached out and stroked her hip, running his palm down over the skirt of the dress, over her buttocks. He gripped her flesh, as if testing its softness. 'Feels good,' he said.

'She looks good, too,' said Sir Alec. 'Remove your dress, Mrs Penrose.'

Caroline was still numb from listening to the conversation and had steeled herself to be mauled by father and son, but to be formally told to remove her dress was again unexpected. Almost everything the tycoon said or did was unexpected.

Automatically, her hands went to the buttons of the bodice and began unfastening them. If she simply obeyed instructions, as she had been told to, it seemed easier. Things would just happen without her making them happen. In a way, she would be innocent of anything that occurred.

Even so, she hesitated at the final button, realising that the bulge of her breasts in the black brassiere could be seen. It was now or never, she realised; now was her last chance to walk out of the door and tell the chauffeur to take her home.

Caroline slipped the dress from her shoulders and let it pool around her feet. She stepped out of it, throwing it to one side over a chair.

The room was warm but even so she felt goose pimples on her flesh and was glad she had been told to keep her eyes lowered. Her cheeks were flushed, she knew, and the three men were now staring blatantly at her body.

Amy, the beautiful blonde girl, would also be staring and Caroline straightened her shoulders, adjusting her position so that her breasts thrust out more proudly and the curves of her buttocks quivered beneath the black silk of the french knickers she wore.

She played sport and looked after her body and knew that she looked good. Her breasts and buttocks might be full, but her legs were long and her waist trim.

Sir Alec touched her thigh, his fingers gently feeling their way from stocking top to flesh. His palm spread and moved smoothly upwards, beneath the loose panties, to hold a buttock. His touch was almost reverent, almost unsure.

He sighed.

'Truly beautiful,' he said. 'I am almost tempted to join you, Jack.'

'Why not?' The humour had gone from the voice of Benson senior and he also seemed a little overawed.

COMPULSION

'There looks like plenty for all of us.'

Benson senior now reached out and pushed the black strap of the bra from her shoulder. Caroline watched his large black hand gently following the strap and slipping into the cup of the bra to take a breast. It filled his hand. He squeezed and she closed her eyes for a moment, unsure what emotion she was feeling inside, knowing only that it felt like she might explode.

Sir Alec moved away and Denzel joined his father and stood behind her. He touched her buttocks through the panties, until his fingers began to grip and pull at the silk as if he were impatient to remove them.

'You're moving too quick, boy,' warned his father.

Both of the Bensons had put down their drinks so they could use both hands upon her, the older man concentrating on her breasts. He pulled down both bra cups to release the globes of flesh and was caressing them with his palms, tweaking the nipples with his fingers.

'Beautiful,' he said to himself. 'Beautiful.'

Behind her, Denzel continued to maul her buttocks and pushed a hand between her legs, forcing her thighs apart, his fingers going beneath the material and digging into her softness as they searched for her opening.

Caroline gasped at his roughness, but he found the destination that he sought and, with practiced dexterity, he parted her labia with two fingers and pushed a third inside. She gasped again, her eyes closing once more.

Maria Caprio

Benson senior said: 'Is she ready, Denzel?'

Denzel's breath was quickening and he opened her wider with two fingers. This time, she groaned.

'She's ready.'

Benson senior unclipped her bra and took it delicately from her arms. His son relinquished his grip upon her, as if at a command.

'Kneel, girl,' said the elder man.

Flustered and breathless, she knelt on the carpet before him.

'Get it out,' he said.

Caroline reached for the zip of his trousers and pulled it down. She felt inside, moving the shirt to find he wore boxer shorts. His erection was still incomplete and she guided it through the garments and pulled it free from his trousers. It was black and shiny, its head purple and pink, and it grew in her hands. The colour and texture shocked her: she found it almost beautiful.

'Suck,' said Benson senior.

She placed it between her lips and sucked, feeling it surge with sudden strength so that it filled her mouth. It tasted salty and it pulsed with life. She gripped it in both hands at the base and moved her head up and down upon it, lubricating it, making it slick with her saliva.

Her body quivered like the penis in her mouth, her breasts shook as she dipped and sucked, her vagina was becoming as wet as the male member in her grasp.

A hand on the back of her head stopped her.

'Enough,' Benson senior said.

COMPULSION

He removed his penis and took her hands, helping her to her feet, before stroking her breasts again.

'Are you ready, son?'

'I'm ready.'

'Then take her. Get her juiced.'

Denzel guided her by her shoulders from behind, propelling her to the large sofa and throwing her face down upon it. The sofa was soft but, even so, the abruptness of his action made her cry out.

She looked round in a daze and saw Sir Alec sitting in an armchair, sipping whisky and watching. Benson senior was pouring himself another drink but watching at the same time. He had made no attempt to cover himself and his erection remained stiff, projecting from his immaculate suit. A pile of clothes on the floor made her realise that Denzel had stripped completely for the assault which he now launched.

He gripped the silk panties and made no attempt to take them down, simply ripping them until they shredded at the seams and lay useless around one thigh. The material dug into her flesh and the violence of the act made her cry out again, but even she could not tell whether they were noises of fear or anticipation.

His fingers went between her legs, spreading her thighs and digging into her area of most sensitivity. Two fingers went in easily and squelched in the wetness.

Then he was upon her back, his knees spreading her thighs wider, his hands guiding in the weapon she had not yet seen. Its head found the mouth of her cavern and began to enter. For once, he controlled his impetuosity and pushed it in slowly, pausing to allow her vaginal passage to adjust, before pushing inwards again.

My God, she thought. Will it never stop?

Caroline was trying to lift her buttocks to persuade her body to accommodate it but, whether her body wanted to or not, Denzel was not going to be denied.

When she felt there was no more room within her, he pushed again and, through the haze of swollenness, she finally felt his testicles lying against her buttocks. He was fully inside and she realised she was wailing.

Denzel lay upon her without moving for a few moments, his breathing as ragged as hers, his hands groping her thighs and breasts greedily, gripping the flesh as if he might rip chunks from her body.

Caroline turned her face from the cushions for fresh air and felt as if she had been spitted. It was a feeling of complete possession and he had yet to start his strokes.

He flexed his penis without moving it and the sensation sent thrills through her being. She yelled at each twitch and tried to respond but was simply too full. His movements began so slightly that, at first, she mistook them for a continuation of the flexing.

The strokes became more discernible, growing in strength and, amazingly, her vagina adjusted and accepted them; more than that, it began to move in concert with the man upon her back, demanding that he give her more, and yet more.

Denzel was now heaving upon her, his hard abdo-

COMPULSION

men flattening her lush buttocks with each stroke, his hands grabbing at her breasts. His power was immense and she did not attempt to stifle her cries. Through it all, she heard him crying out too as he pounded in and out upon her.

Caroline was now only dimly aware of her surroundings and was close to being completely taken by the experience, when a vision of Amy appeared in her mind from somewhere; the beautiful blonde girl who, even now, was watching from concealment.

The thought was enough to tip Caroline into her first orgasm and she screamed at its power and bucked beneath Denzel who rode her as if she were a steed that had to be broken.

Denzel did not discharge but maintained his rhythm, pushing her body about on the sofa with his power. Within a minute of her first coming, she came again, taken this time by the friction of the cushions upon her clitoris.

Now he withdrew and turned her over onto her back. She gazed immediately at his penis and wondered how anything that size could have entered her.

He straddled her breasts, pushing the monster between the globes of flesh, squashing them around it so that she could feel its beat against the beat of her heart.

'In your mouth,' he hissed, and moved his body higher.

Caroline did her best but could only take a small portion of it between her lips, which she sucked and licked whilst her fingers gripped it around its base, working rhythmically to bring about his satisfaction. She could tell he was close but he refused to come, preferring to watch her mouth at work while he held her head in one hand, his body curled above her.

His father was now by the sofa and she could see him masturbating while he watched.

'Is she ready, son?'

'She's ready.'

Benson senior opened his trousers and pushed them midway down his thighs before kneeling between her legs upon the sofa. His hands slid beneath her buttocks and he raised her hips and pushed his now very firm erection into her vagina. It slid into her heat with ease.

'You're well juiced, girl. Well juiced.' He began to move his penis in and out. 'Let's do it, boy.'

The elder man held her hips as he fucked her whilst his son now concentrated on reaching his climax. Caroline lay beneath them, helpless and not in her right mind but lost in a world of sexual smells, sounds and tastes that was making her delirious.

Denzel's movements were getting more frantic and her strokes around the shaft of his weapon became more determined and demanding, her sucking and licking degenerated so that her whole face was wet from where she had rubbed the head of his penis.

Between her legs, the thrusts of his father were shortening, his grip upon her hips becoming more possessive.

'Do it, boy. Do it!'

COMPULSION

Denzel came, lifting himself backwards and slightly away from her, so that his father could see him ejaculate into Caroline's open-mouthed face. His disgorgement was immense – great bursts of white sperm shooting onto her cheeks, into her hair and eyes, and across her mouth. Her tongue licked at what it could reach.

His father gasped at the vision of such beauty abused and he orgasmed inside her. His pelvis locked against hers and he rocked backwards and forwards as he discharged.

They left her, but Caroline remained sprawled upon the cushions of the sofa. She no longer belonged to a world of neat houses and luncheon dates with safe suburban friends but, for the moment, was lost in a never-never land whose existence she had not imagined in her wildest dreams.

'Mrs Penrose? Are you all right?'

It was Sir Alec, standing alongside the sofa with his glass of whisky in one hand, looking down upon her benevolently.

'I am not sure,' she said.

She was aware that her body was more open and exposed than it had ever been and that the smearing trails of lust still covered her features, but she felt no inclination to cover or clean herself.

'They have gone,' he said. 'You were a great success. I do hope you enjoyed yourself?'

'Enjoy?' she said.

The term had no relevance to what she had been through.

'I shall send Amy to help you clean up. There is a bathroom down the corridor.'

He left the room and, moments later, the blonde girl entered. She crossed the room to the sofa and looked down at her. Amy's face was flushed, her eyes wild.

'You were marvellous,' she said.

Caroline smiled and felt the sperm going cold upon her cheek.

'You liked watching?' she said.

'Yes. I liked watching.'

'Sir Alec will be watching now. Hoping.'

They were talking in whispers, to avoid the microphone picking up their words.

Amy said: 'I know.' She knelt by the side of the sofa. 'Let's give him just a little. To whet his appetite.'

The blonde girl leaned over and licked some of the sperm from Caroline's face. Caroline groaned and closed her eyes.

'Taste me,' Amy said, and offered her fingers to the older woman.

Caroline's nostrils twitched at the unmistakable smell. Amy had not just been watching; she had been masturbating. She opened her mouth and accepted the fingers; she sucked and tasted the girl.

Amy said: 'You are so beautiful. One day, I would like to make love with you.'

'I would like that very much.'

The blonde girl smiled, the flush now fading as she got herself under control.

'But not now. Sir Alec has had too much for now.'

Caroline smiled back.

'So have I.'

Amy picked up the discarded dress, bra and handbag, as well as the ripped silk panties, before helping Caroline along the corridor to the bathroom. Helping her necessitated touching her and they both enjoyed the experience without letting anything develop.

It seemed inevitable that they would make love together, but they both sensed that the time was not yet right – even when Amy knelt before her and rolled the stockings from her legs, her face close to Caroline's still gaping vagina, her nose twitching at the smell.

Caroline climbed into a hot bath and Amy stood by the door.

'Do you need anything?'

'Just a rest.'

'What about these?'

Amy held up the ripped silk panties.

'Beyond repair,' Caroline said.

'May I have them?'

Caroline smiled, inordinately pleased at the request.

'Of course.'

'Thank you.'

The blonde girl raised them to her face and kissed them before she left the bathroom.

Chapter 12

The three of them had lunch together; Amy looking fresh and innocent once more in her white cotton dress, white socks and tennis shoes; Caroline aware that she sat at the dining table without any knickers on.

They ate salad and fresh salmon and drank white wine.

Sir Alec said: 'Do you feel a certain fulfillment, Mrs Penrose?'

'I am still not sure what I feel.'

'But the encounter, it was not unpleasant?'

'It was strange. I still cannot believe it happened.'

'Oh, it happened. You can have a copy of the tape if you wish.'

'No, thank you.'

'It might actually be useful if you did watch it. I do not think you appreciate how liberated was your behaviour.'

'Liberated?'

'You may have begun with a certain reserve, nervousness perhaps. But you eventually embraced lust as completely as that young gentleman filled you. The soundtrack alone is highly arousing.'

Caroline blushed briefly and was amazed that she still could. She remembered that she had made a lot of noise.

They drank and ate in silence for a while.

'Is this the end of my engagement?' Caroline asked.

'Certainly not. I believe you are very close to attaining your personal and sexual freedom, but there are still crucial moments yet to face.'

She smiled at him across the table.

'And I attain this personal and sexual freedom by allowing men to fuck me at your discretion?'

He smiled back.

'In part.'

'It seems a little one-sided.'

'It does, doesn't it, and I do not deny I gain great satisfaction from being in control and watching beautiful women do my bidding. And while my motives are not altruistic, neither are they totally selfish.'

'You said, in part. What other schemes do you have, apart from using me as a prostitute?'

He raised a finger.

'An odd choice of word. Would you like to be a prostitute, Mrs Penrose?'

She hesitated before answering.

'I do not think so.'

'I appreciate the qualification. Sometimes, our hidden fantasies are so well hidden that they need to be driven out into the open.' He smiled across the

COMPULSION

table at Amy. 'And everybody has fantasies.'

Caroline said: 'I do not think I would enjoy being a prostitute.'

Sir Alec nodded.

'Perhaps not, even though you alluded to your role today as being just that. But let me assure you, I have no intention of using you as a prostitute. I agree, I have gained a great deal from what transpired with the Bensons but it was, I believe, to our mutual benefit, Mrs Penrose.'

'So you keep saying. You also said that fucking men at your discretion was only part of what you had planned.'

Every time she used the word fucking, Caroline got a thrill.

'Yes. I use that as a release, to ease the valve of your inner tensions into a state where you can finally open it fully yourself.'

'You are talking in riddles, Sir Alec.'

'Then I will speak plainly. When you feel you are ready, I would like you to make a confession. To unburden yourself of some sexual secret or desire. One of those secrets which you have tried to forget, to deny its existence. I want you to make your confession formally. Doing so will show you have become strong enough to face it, strong enough, even, to enjoy the memory. It will demonstrate your new belief in yourself. It will demonstrate your new freedom.'

'It sounds like another game.'

He smiled disarmingly.

'Oh, it is, but a game with marvellous side effects.

It works, my dear Mrs Penrose. It really does.'

Caroline pushed her plate to one side.

'You are serious about wanting me to make a confession?'

'Totally.'

She looked at Amy.

The blonde girl smiled and nodded.

'He is serious. He even has a confessional box for the purpose. And,' she glanced at him before looking back to Caroline. 'I believe, that in certain cases, it does work.'

'You mean, as a kind of therapy?'

Amy nodded.

'Something like that.'

The conversation had released memories from her past. She tried to avoid them.

Sir Alec said: 'Go home and think about it, Mrs Penrose. I'll send the car for you in the morning, at the same time. I hope that tomorrow, you may be ready to confess.'

After Caroline Penrose had departed in the Rolls Royce, Sir Alec also left the house, driving himself in an open BMW convertible.

Amy was inevitably drawn to the private library, which she opened with her own key, locking the door again once she was inside.

The shelves and boxes awaited her pleasure and she wondered whether she should actually start work, cataloguing the tycoon's erotic collection.

She thought she had been sated with sex after

watching Caroline that morning through the two-way mirror. As soon her father-in-law had taken the two men into the drawing room, the sexual anticipation within her had become a need for fulfillment. At first, she had stroked herself gently through her dress, aware that the mirror on the wall behind her could also have a camera hidden behind it, for Sir Alec's machinations were machiavellian.

But as soon as the men began to touch Caroline Penrose, she gave up any pretence and had hoisted the tight cotton dress around her waist, standing in her tennis shoes and white socks, with her fingers between her legs.

Amy had masturbated throughout the ensuing action, sometimes pushing her fingers deep inside herself, sometimes using the material of the panties to rub that most sensitive part of her body. What a sight she must have looked, if the other mirror did have a camera behind it, with the cheeks of her bottom quivering and shaking as she came, perhaps seven or eight times.

Being a voyeur, she had discovered, was, in the right circumstances, extremely exciting. Being watched during sexual activity was also arousing, for she now suspected that many of the rooms in the house were under the scrutiny of hidden cameras.

There was no doubt in her mind that the mirror in her bedroom had a camera behind it. Tarquin had probably suspected as much, and the thought of being watched by his father had aroused him in some way.

Perhaps it had provoked him to display that, despite

his gentleness, he had power over such a beautiful creature as Amy; perhaps he enjoyed displaying her body to his father and declaring that she was untouchable.

And was she untouchable?

The realisation that she was probably being watched in her bedroom had dawned slowly. At first, she had been shocked that Sir Alec had been able to see her most intimate moments. As the shock wore off, she realised it was something else for her to use in goading her father-in-law – flaunting that which he wished to possess and which she would not give him: her body.

And now, thinking of what she had done that morning, of what she had watched, filled her once more with desire. But the choice was so great.

The confessional again attracted her; perhaps the morning had provided enough visual stimulation and something more restful would be suitable.

Amy took down the box of audio cassettes from the shelf and picked up one of the clear plastic cases at random. She read the handwritten label. It said: Confession – Sarah.

She could play it on the cassette deck, but she wanted more than the privacy of this room; she wanted the privacy of the confessional box itself.

Surely, there must be a portable machine amongst all this paraphernalia?

The girl moved boxes and magazines and, behind the television set, she found exactly what she was looking for: a Walkman cassette player.

Amy slotted the tape in, switched on and the cassette tape turned: the batteries were fine. She switched off, put the headphones on and walked to the confessional box. Inside, that now familiar smell of wood and dust greeted her and she imagined the thousand secrets it had heard.

She closed the door and sat in the dim light, wondering what might be in store. Even without the stimulation of the tape, she was aroused by her location and anticipation. She eased her bottom from the seat and slid the tight cotton skirt up around her waist.

Her hips moved experimentally and the panties twitched against her. Time for them to go as well, she thought. She slid them down her golden thighs and kicked them over her tennis shoes and onto the floor.

Amy sat back, her legs open, her fingers already touching herself. She rested her head against the wall and switched on the tape. It was as if she was taking the confession – or making it – herself.

It started – a young woman's voice identifying herself – and almost the first words sent a shock of eagerness through Amy's body.

Chapter 13

Sarah's Confession

My name is Sarah and this is my confession.

Bondage always fascinated my husband, Robert. He gained his greatest sexual enjoyment on those occasions when I was tied to a bed and unable to resist any of his demands. He would further fantasize about other men using my body.

The night he put all his fantasies into practice, I was twenty-one years old and we had been married for two years.

Robert was fifteen years older than me. He was a wealthy impresario and I met him when I was eighteen and working for a promotions company. I was attracted by his success and his charm, although physically he was not particularly handsome. He was of medium height and overweight. His hair was prematurely grey.

Needless to say, I was an obedient wife for I had had a sheltered upbringing until them: my father was a country parson, and my husband was the only man with whom I had ever slept or had sex.

Maria Caprio

At the start of our relationship he had been extremely romantic and passionate. So passionate, that it had been a struggle to keep my virginity. I believe it was because I would not surrender it that he proposed. After our marriage, his passion was at first intense but, as the weeks passed, it eased.

He explained that this was because I was not fulfilling my duties of arousal properly and, eager to learn – for I had enjoyed the early passion as much as he – I did all that he suggested. I wore sexually provocative underwear for him, undressed for him, and allowed him to tie my hands and feet with ropes in the different positions that fitted his particular inclinations.

But each aid to arousal seemed to last for a short time and then his passion waned once more.

On the particular occasion about which I am making this confession, we were attending a gala evening at a large hotel in London and had booked a room in which to spend the night.

It was a grand and jolly affair; the men wore dinner jackets and I wore a low-cut red dress. I'd even had a little too much to drink. My husband had struck up a friendship with two American businessmen, who also had rooms at the hotel, and we all left the proceedings sometime after midnight and took the lift to our floor.

We had exchanged personal details with our new friends and Jay had said he was sixty. He was taller than my husband, of lean build, and almost totally bald. Bruno was forty-five and about the same height as Robert but fatter. His hands were large, his fingers like sausages.

COMPULSION

The motion of the lift – and the wine – made me stagger just a little and I fell against Jay. One of his hands brushed my breasts and the other held my hip as he steadied me, and I noticed the sudden sharpness in the expression of my husband.

Perhaps it was then that he decided to allow a situation to develop.

We all walked down the corridor together and, at our door, Robert invited the men in for a nightcap. The room had a double bed, a bar, two easy chairs and an upright chair at a desk. He dispensed the drinks, insisting that I, too, have another glass of wine, and we sat about the room and he led the conversation.

He commented on how pleasant the evening had been and said he knew some couples whose interests were so limited that they had to play games to make entertainment.

'Trivial Pursuit, Monopoly, things like that.' He scoffed at the very idea. 'I mean, it would not be so bad if they indulged in adult games.'

'Such as what?' Bruno said.

'Blindman's Buff,' said my husband with a smile.

'That does not sound very adult,' Bruno replied.

'It depends how it is played.'

Jay laughed.

'You must tell us.'

'Well, the way I played it,' and he glanced across at me, 'and it was before I met Sarah, a man was blindfolded and he had to guess which girl kissed or touched him.'

Bruno said: 'And if his guess was incorrect?'

'He paid a forfeit.'

Bruno chuckled.

'Not enough of us to play that,' he said, 'with only your delightful wife to give us a peck on the cheek.'

'No,' said my husband, thoughtfully, 'but there is an alternative.'

Jay said: 'What is that?'

'We could always blindfold Sarah.'

I was sitting on the edge of the bed and I laughed at this silly suggestion before sensing that the mood had suddenly changed.

'You cannot be serious?' I said.

My husband stood up and went to the dressing table.

'Why not?' he said. 'A little harmless fun.'

He picked up a silk scarf and approached me.

I was still unsure.

'You mean it?' I said.

'Of course. Stand up and I will blindfold you.'

I felt I had no alternative – who was I to spoil some harmless fun – so I stood and he tied the scarf around my eyes. It was a very strange experience being in a room with three men and not being able to see what they were doing, or how they were behaving.

'Now,' said my husband, 'one more thing, to make sure you do not cheat.'

I heard him walk away and return a moment later.

A stocking,' he said, for the benefit of our two friends. 'My wife always wears stockings.'

Jay said: 'How extremely arousing.'

My husband said: 'Yes, it is.'

COMPULSION

He took my arms, positioned my hands behind me and tied my wrists together. Being tied and blindfolded made me feel vulnerable. My insides trembled with trepidation and not a little excitment.

'Is this really necessary?' I asked.

My husband was still behind me and he placed my hands against the front of his trousers. I could feel the hardness of his erection.

'But of course,' he said, 'if we are to play the game correctly.' He moved away. 'Now, my darling, you must guess the identity of the person who kisses you.'

Bruno, from somewhere on my right, said: 'And if she doesn't?' His voice had become throaty.

My husband said: 'Then she pays a forfeit.'

Jay, the elderly American, said: 'Are you sure about this, Robert?'

My husband coughed. 'Of course. We enjoy games, don't we, darling?'

These were two important men and I had been flattered by their attention. Besides, I had never disobeyed my husband; if he said this was all right, then it must be.

'Yes,' I said. 'We enjoy games.'

Jay's voice was also edged with desire, although he controlled it better.

He said: 'Are you sure, Sarah?'

'I am sure.'

'Okay. Then let's play.'

My husband chuckled and he led me into the centre of the room, turning me round until I lost track of my bearings. Then his hands were gone.

The men moved about me and one came close and kissed my neck, his lips apart. The contect made me shudder.

'Who was that?' said my husband.

'Jay,' I said. 'That was Jay.'

'Well done,' said Jay.

Someone else came close and took my hair in his hands to tip my head backwards. His mouth covered mine and his tongue forced a way between my lips. His body was against mine and I could feel his erection against my groin.

When he broke away, I gasped. Surely, this could only be my husband?

'Robert,' I said.

'Wrong,' said my husband, suddenly moving close behind me so that the word was hissed into my ear. He placed my captive hands around the bulge in his trousers. 'You will have to pay a forfeit, my darling.'

His hands took the straps of my dress and slid them from my shoulders so that the bodice hung down from the waist and left my breasts exposed in a half-cup brassiere made of red lace.

'Robert?' I whispered, but my mouth was covered once more.

Lips mashed against mine, pushing them apart, and a tongue slid inside my mouth. The man held me with one hand around my waist, pulling me against an unmistakable bulge, whilst the other hand caressed my bottom.

When he released me, it took a moment before I

realised they were waiting for me to name my assailant.

'Was that you, Robert?'

'Wrong,' he said.

Of course, I do not know if I was right or wrong, for this was a game of his creation that he was playing to his own rules.

'What do you think, gentlemen?' he said. 'Should we have the breasts?'

Bruno said: 'Yes. The breasts.' His voice came from deep in his throat.

Hands slid the straps of the brassiere from my shoulders and palms eased the cups of the garment from my breasts so that they were totally naked.

I was breathing heavily and I sensed that my breasts rose and fell accordingly.

'The nipples,' Bruno said. 'They're erect.'

'Darling,' my husband said. 'Are you aroused?'

I did not know what to say, so I said nothing. Hands gripped my breasts and mauled them.

'Are you?' he repeated.

'Yes,' I said. 'I am aroused.'

At that moment, I do not know if I was saying these words because I knew they were what my husband wanted to hear, or because I was aroused.

The whole experience was so new and totally strange to me. I was helpless and half naked before three men and felt that I did not have any choice in what was happening. Having no choice had given my senses a kind of freedom.

My husband was behind me again, wrapping my

hands around his bulge, before his hands felt my breasts. He kissed my neck and licked my ear.

'You naughty girl,' he said.

He stepped away and someone took his place, positioning my hands around a new bulge. The newcomer also licked my neck and his hands caressed my buttocks through my dress. Other hands took my breasts and another mouth sought mine and kissed me, another erection pushed against me.

They were in no hurry and moved their bulges against my hands and my body, while their hands explored my contours. I realised that with my senses dazed, I had forgotten what any of them looked like, including my husband.

I had no choice about what was happening; I was the object of the game, the object with which they were playing.

When they broke away, I staggered a little and hands held my shoulders.

My husband said: 'Identify the two who embraced you.'

'I cannot,' I said.

'Then you must pay another forfeit. I think, this time, gentlemen, her arse. Come.'

I was led across the room and pushed onto the bed, falling across it on my stomach. Hands went beneath my skirt, across the top of the stockings and onto the flesh of my thighs. The hands went higher, beneath my panties to grip my buttocks.

A mist was descending upon my senses and through it a voice said: 'Whose hands?'

COMPULSION

'I do not know,' I said.

'Then you lose your panties,' said Robert.

My panties were pulled down and I was rolled around on the bed to loosen them when they became trapped against a suspender. They were removed and I was positioned upon my back, my skirt around my waist and my legs spread.

I had never felt so naked or so exposed, nor had I felt so frightened or aroused. Without warning, a head went between my thighs and a mouth nuzzled at my vagina.

My hips bucked and I let out a cry.

Robert said: 'Whose mouth, darling?'

The mouth opened the lips of my vagina and a tongue slid inside. Suddenly I was wet and I moaned with embarrassment. My face flushed beneath the blindfold and I could not stop my hips moving against the intrusion of the tongue.

'Whose mouth?' Robert said.

I shook my head and my hips continued to move. 'I do not know.'

'Then another forfeit,' my husband said.

The mouth left me and I was aware of the heat of the room and the sound of heavy breathing from the three men. I was lying on my back, my hands tied behind me, my breasts exposed and heaving uncontrollably. My dress was around my waist and my thighs spread to reveal my pink and open sex, framed by black pubic hair and the red arrows of suspender straps that held taut black stockings.

The mattress shifted with the weight of the men

moving around me. A mouth descended to suck at my breasts; a hand slid up my inner thigh, across the stocking, across the flesh, one finger pointing at its target. The finger reached its goal and pushed inside, a fat finger, and it released more wetness as it moved in and out.

Noises were coming from my throat that I was at first unaware of, until a mouth came down upon mine and I heard the echoes of my cries. Someone kissed me, a tongue pushing between my lips to lick my teeth.

This was beyond all experiences, beyond all belief. Surely my husband could not be allowing this to happen?

They changed positions again, the finger and mouths were removed and someone was now kneeling between my legs. A penis pushed at the entrance of my vagina.

Surely not? My husband would stop it now. But he did not stop it and the penis forced an entry, taking my breath away and causing me to arch to meet it with my pelvis and hips.

It was a large penis, full of strength and heat.

From somewhere above me, Robert said: 'Whose prick?'

He repeated it but I did not think I was capable of speech.

'Whose prick, Sarah? Tell me, whose prick?'

'I do not know. I do not care.'

My mind wanted to be left alone. I did not want to answer any questions or confront what was happening. It was happening and it was by my husband's

COMPULSION

design, was that not enough?

The man lying upon me was heavy and, through the mist of oblivion I had attempted to draw about myself, I guessed it was Bruno, the fat American. His hands held my hips and he thrust inside me with increasingly vicious strokes.

'I'm going to come,' he said.

My legs were spread and raised and his stomach slapped against me. His penis was a giant and filled me and made me cry out.

He gave a strangled groan and pushed deeper still and came, pulsing like a burst water main inside me until I was flooded with his juices.

Bruno moved off me and for a moment I lay dazed.

My husband said: 'More forfeits, Sarah. More forfeits.'

I was rolled onto my stomach, for which I was grateful as my arms had begun to ache because I had been lying on them whilst Bruno had used my vagina.

My shoulders were raised and I was positioned between the naked legs of one of the men. As my head was raised higher, I knew it was being led towards a familiar smell.

'Suck, Sarah. Suck, my darling.'

My husband pushed his penis into my mouth and I began to suck while he held my head in both his hands. Behind me, I felt Jay kneeling between my legs. He lifted my hips and slid a slim penis into the hole that Bruno had only recently abused. His naked abdomen lay against my buttocks and he moved slowly for maximum enjoyment.

'Bruno, you are too goddamn big,' he said. 'You have stretched this little lady too much.' His penis slid out and lay in the groove between my buttocks. 'With your permission, sir, I will take another route?'

Another route?

What was this bizarre conversation all about? There should be no conversation. Conversation made it real.

My husband was breathing heavily, his erection the biggest I had ever known and threatening to choke me with the intensity of his movements.

'Go ahead,' he said, his breath ragged, his voice high with excitement.

No, I thought. They do not mean that?

But they did. Jay scooped the mixed juices from my vagina, and rubbed them into the crease between my buttocks, a finger easing itself into my smallest orifice.

I could not cry out, either in opposition or pain, for my mouth was fully occupied. I could not struggle because my hands were tied behind me. Jay proceeded to push his penis where his finger had been.

He gained full entry and slid inside. Although slim, his penis found a snug fit in my anal sleeve and his gasp of satisfaction strangely eased the immediate pain of the sensation.

My husband had become even more excited and had rolled onto his side, presumably to see what was happening more clearly and also to gain a greater depth of thrust into my throat.

I was helpless, a victim of male oppression in my mouth and my anus, and totally bereft of responsibility for what was happening. It was a glorious way to be sodomised.

My husband was close to his orgasm but Jay came first, swiftly and unexpectedly, jarring me with a sharp piercing as he discharged his sperm, his thin fingers gripping my hanging breasts so fiercely that they hurt.

The pain in my breasts and the sudden thrust from behind, caused me to twist and move my mouth, dislodging Robert's penis.

Seeing me squirm so violently took him to the final frontier and he pushed it back between my lips as he came, holding my head steady with hands that were tight in my hair as he shuddered and twitched. I swallowed all that he gave me.

None of the men said a great deal afterwards and I heard the sounds of clothes being put on or rearranged, a mumble of parting exchanges, then the door slammed.

Robert returned and said: 'You naughty, naughty girl. You liked that, didn't you?'

I answered as I knew he wanted me to answer, which again removed from me any need to question whether I had or not.

'Yes,' I said. 'I enjoyed it.'

He turned out the light, unfastened my wrists and stripped me down to my stockings and suspender belt. He pulled back the covers of the bed and lay me upon the sheet, tying my wrists above me to the head of the bed. Only then did he remove the blindfold, in the dark, and climbed onto the bed with me, naked and erect once more.

My husband used me through the night, falling asleep after each orgasm. I would drift into slumber only to awake with him upon my body again. And right from the start to the finish – until dawn withdrew the blindfold of night – I never climaxed.

Although my body had screamed for release, neither my husband nor the two Americans had been interested in providing it; they had only been interested in their own pleasures. And even at those times when my sensations had risen to boiling point, a vestige of guilt had stopped my senses from letting go and slipping into orgasm.

From Robert I gained an insight into male desires and how jealousy can be used to fire impotence, but I gained no emotional satisfaction and little sexual satisfaction. It was a learning experience from a man who was, basically, sexually incompetent.

Afterwards, he wanted to repeat the experience but I had had enough and I left him.

This is the end of my confession. Thank you for allowing me to make it.

Chapter 14

Amy gave herself satisfaction three times while she listened to the tape in the confessional box. Using so much energy made her lethargic and she decided against starting the task of logging the contents of the private library.

Perhaps, when she had overindulged in masturbation, she would be able to concentrate better. She smiled sweetly to herself. It could be a long wait.

But right now she felt like doing nothing more arduous than sunbathing.

Amy locked the door of the private library and walked through the main library into the hall, carrying the key in one hand and her panties in the other. She hesitated.

There was the terrace or she could open the folding glass doors that surrounded the swimming pool. Neither suited her mood. What about the conservatory? That could be a suntrap with a difference.

The conservatory was extensive and she found that sections of the glass roof and windows slid open to allow the sun's rays to shine through. One central section was perfect. It even had a camera concealed in a tree, so perhaps her father-in-law would still be able to watch.

Amy found a house phone near the entrance to the conservatory and called Rupert the butler. He arrived within a minute.

'Is it possible, Rupert, to open some of these windows?'

'In this house, madam, anything is possible.'

She smiled. Indeed, what he said seemed to be totally true. She pointed out what she wanted.

'I would also like a hammock positioned here. I believe there is one on the patio?'

'There is, madam. I shall attend to it.'

'Thank you. I shall return shortly.'

Amy went to her bedroom and contemplated changing, but saw no reason to. She collected a bottle of suntan oil and a pair of dark glasses and returned to the conservatory. Everything had swiftly been arranged to her directions.

A section of the roof was now open to the sky and the sun beat down upon the flagstones and foliage. The hammock, which was suspended on a tubular steel frame and hung two feet above the ground, was positioned in the middle of the area. Alongside it was a large rug, upon which were scattered several cushions. Also on the rug was a portable house phone, in case she wished to summon service.

Rupert was very efficient, she thought. She must tell him so.

Amy pulled the white cotton dress over her head

and revelled in her nakedness. She now wore only the white ankle socks and tennis shoes. The hammock looked comfortable and she lay back upon it experimentally. It swung gently and she let one leg dangle over the side to steady it.

Perfect, she thought.

When she sunbathed, Amy needed no distractions. The heat was enough of a pleasure. She sat up and stroked suntan oil upon her legs and thighs, across her stomach – which bore no bikini line – over her breasts and shoulders and down her arms. It was part of a delicious ritual that she enjoyed.

At last her body glistened and she could already feel the growing heat of the suntrap. She lay back in the hammock, a cushion beneath her head, eyes shaded by the dark glasses, and rocked herself gently to sleep.

Some time later, she was aware of a presence nearby.

A girl's voice said softly: 'Madam?'

Amy half opened her eyes, which were hidden behind the glasses, but gave no other sign that she was awake. Greta, the maid, was standing by her feet.

'Madam?' she said again.

Still Amy did not respond and watched as the girl's gaze slide from her face and down her body. The look made Amy realise that she had opened her legs in sleep. Her golden left limb was still in the hammock but the right one had slipped over the side and her foot rested on the floor.

More than that, her right hand had strayed once

more to delve among the golden curls at her pubis and had been subconsciously stroking the gateway of her sex which, she could tell, was open.

Greta stared in fascination at the finger which lazily stroked the pink dampness between the lips.

'Mmm...'

Amy stirred and stretched, but did not remove her finger, and the girl diverted her gaze to look at her face.

'I am sorry, madam. I did not mean to wake you.'

'That is all right, Greta.'

She removed the glasses and smiled at the girl.

'Rupert asked me to see if there was anything you desired. It is so hot in here. Perhaps a drink?'

'That would be lovely.' She continued to stroke herself between her legs, unself-consciously. 'Iced lemonade, perhaps?'

'Certainly, madam.'

The girl left and Amy saw that the sun had moved and that the hammock was now in the speckled shade of a tree, although her skin tingled from the exposure it had already received. Her hand covered her sex. She must be careful. She did not want to get suntanned inside as well as out.

Greta had looked charming. She had also looked interested in what Amy had been doing. Just how much did the staff know of what was going on?

Perhaps it would be diverting to find out?

The girl returned carrying a silver tray that contained a glass of fresh lemonade, in which ice cubes clinked, and a large jug containing more. Amy took the glass and had a long drink.

'Delicious,' she said. She smiled at the girl. 'It is very hot in here. Do you not think so?'

'It is indeed hot, madam. But you tan so beautifully.'

'Thank you. Do you ever sunbathe?'

'Sometimes, madam.'

'I love it. It is so relaxing.' She smiled. 'It makes me feel sexy.'

The girl remained standing alongside the hammock in the continental uniform of blue cotton dress with pleated skirt, blue knee socks and flat shoes. The fact that Greta was fully dressed made Amy feel more naked.

'Do you like living in England, Greta?'

'It is a fine experience. It helps me to learn the language, madam.'

'Is that all you have learned here?'

'I have learned many things, madam.'

'Including discretion?'

'Yes, madam.'

Amy smiled at her and her fingers idly stroked amidst the golden curls at the junction of her thighs.

'One danger about sunbathing nude, is that you can get burnt in the most sensitive of places.'

The girl's eyes flickered down her body and back again.

'Yes, madam.'

'I think I need something to soothe the heat. Do you have such a thing as whipped cream?'

'We have a cannister of whipped cream, madam.'

'Good. Would you bring it for me? And some

bananas. Do you have bananas, Greta?'

'I am sure we do, madam.'

'Good.'

The girl left and Amy lay back and wondered what might happen. She had no formal plan, just a recipe of ingredients and a renewed itch for sexual experimentation.

Greta returned a few minutes later. Upon the tray was a dish, a spoon, a knife, a bunch of bananas and an aerosol canister of whipped cream.

'Perfect,' Amy said. 'Put them down here.'

The girl placed the tray alongside the hammock within reach of Amy, who picked up the canister and read the label.

'Greta, bring a cushion and kneel beside me,' she said.

The maid did so.

Amy shook the canister. She opened her legs, reaching down to open the lips of her sex with her left hand. Her right hand pointed the canister at the opening and pressed the nozzle.

White cream squirted out, into and around her vagina.

Amy gasped.

'Oh, that is so cool, so soothing.'

She handed the canister to Greta and pushed the cream into herself with her fingers.

'More, Greta. I need more.'

The maid hesitated, then leaned sideways so that she had an unrestricted view of Amy's sexual area, and sprayed more cream inside.

'Delicious,' Amy said, and this time left the mound of cream in place. 'But it needs to go further inside. Pass me a banana. Not too ripe.'

Greta looked startled, smiled and flushed, all at the same time. She composed herself and picked a large banana from the bunch, which she gave to Amy.

The blonde girl peeled the fruit and discarded the skin. Its flesh was large, curving and firm.

As if holding a holy relic, she raised it in both hands and kissed the tip gently, before lowering it between her legs and pushing the end into the cream.

Amy did it carefully so as not to cause the banana to break, but her passage was so ready and so well lubricated, that the first three inches slid smoothly inside. She moved her hips sensuously and sucked in another two inches. Now she held it there with her left hand and let her right hand hang over the edge of the hammock.

'Greta,' she said. 'I believe my nipples are burnt as well. Please put some cream upon them.'

There was sweat on the girl's face now, and it was not simply due to the fact that they were in a suntrap. But she picked up the canister and sprayed two small spirals of cream upon the tips of Amy's breasts.

Amy moved her body in pleasure.

'Too much,' she whispered. 'Lick it off, Greta. There's a good girl.'

Greta did not hesitate. She leaned over the hammock, dipped her head, and licked as gentle as a kitten at the left breast.

Amy groaned.

'That is so nice, Greta. So nice.'

As she spoke, her right hand went beneath the maid's skirt and touched her naked thigh. Greta hesitated for a second, then continued lapping. Amy's hand went higher between the girl's legs, to the crotch of the cotton panties that she wore. They were damp.

Amy rubbed gently with one finger against the patch of wetness and felt it spread. The girl continued to lick, her tongue trailing across the flesh between the breasts of her mistress to the other cream topped nipple. Amy's forefinger delicately slipped beneath Greta's panties and burrowed into her pubic hair.

The girl opened her mouth to cover the other breast and sucked off the cream as her tongue circled the rosebud nipple. Amy's finger suddenly found direction and headed downwards through the curls and dipped into the small trough of wetness between Greta's legs. It slid over her raised clitoris and the maid shuddered.

Amy said: 'I think my breasts are clean now, Greta. Thank you.'

The maid knelt back, her lips parted, cream in the corners of her mouth that she now licked away, and waited for further instructions. Amy held her gaze with her own as her finger continued its journey, pushing gently but deeply into the depths of Greta's sex.

Greta's eyelids flickered and the membranes of her vagina contracted around the solitary finger.

Amy said: 'You are very patient, Greta. Very understanding.'

The mistress removed the forefinger and used her

thumb to lift the edge of her panties, allowing her whole hand to slip inside. Her fingers cupped Greta between the legs while her thumb slid up the trough to rub the clitoris.

Greta moaned, for the first time, and Amy slid two fingers inside her. The maid moaned again, her eyes misted and her jaw sagged.

Amy began a slow movement of her hand, pushing the fingers deeply into the girl's wet softness and, as they withdrew nudging her clitoris with her thumb.

The maid continued to contract and release the fingers and her hips began to move imperceptibly. Amy added a third finger to crowd the mouth of Greta's vagina and was rewarded with a louder gasp.

Her thumb now rolled her clitoris with more determination, for Amy could tell that the girl's senses were about to fuse in pleasure. Her coming was heralded by a series of small gasps, followed by a slow intake of breath.

The maid shook gently upon the hand of her mistress, her eyes wide. She stared, still slightly surprised, into the smiling angel face of Amy.

When she had finished, Amy removed her hand and the girl sank back upon her haunches. Amy raised the three fingers she had used to her nose and her nostrils twitched delicately. She lowered them into her mouth and, with the tip of her pink tongue, slowly licked them clean.

Amy smiled again, her eyes sensuous, and said: 'The banana. Take it out.'

Greta leaned over the hammock, took hold of the

fruit and eased it out from between Amy's legs. Cream and sexual lubrication clung to its sides, making a squelching noise as the slot of passion relinquished its grip.

The maid held it up in triumph. It was intact and very sticky.

Amy licked her lips.

'Do you like banana, Greta?'

'Yes, madam.'

'Taste it.'

Greta put the end of the fruit that had been inside her mistress to her mouth and bit off a piece with small white teeth. She chewed and swallowed it. Her tongue licked her lips clean.

Amy said: 'Is it to your liking?'

'It is delicious, madam.'

'Then we must share the rest.'

Amy took the banana from the maid and broke the fruit where the stickiness stopped. She discarded the clean section and was left with a piece that was perhaps four inches in length that was covered in cream and her inner juices.

'We shall share this,' she said.

She put it between her teeth, so that the stump remained protruding from her mouth, put her right hand behind Greta's neck and pulled her head down towards her face.

The maid parted her lips and accepted the piece of banana being offered. Amy pulled gently on the back of her head and the fruit mashed between their mouths.

They ate slowly, their tongues pushing the goo backwards and forwards between each other's mouths, licking pieces from each other's teeth and lips, adding saliva as they masticated the mixture with gasps and moans. As they ate, Greta shyly held Amy's right breast in her palm.

Finally, it was gone but Greta was assiduous in making sure the face of her mistress was clean and Amy lay supine, her lips parted, allowing the girl to lick and suction every small part of her mouth and cheeks and chin.

Amy stroked her hair.

'You are very efficient,' she said. 'But there is still one part of me that needs to be cleansed.'

Greta, mouth open, tongue ready, gazed into Amy's face with eyes that still showed her heat.

'Down there, Greta. Lick me down there.'

The maid changed her position and crouched near the bottom of the hammock. Amy spread her thighs and Greta leaned over and licked.

At the first wet touch of her tongue, Amy's slim and golden body arched in pleasure. The reaction encouraged the maid, who used the whole of her wet and open mouth to suck cream and small pieces of fruit from her inner thighs and the soft tangled curls of her pubic hair.

Amy groaned and twisted gently in sensuous turmoil.

When most of the cream had gone, Greta began to use her tongue to explore every crevice and fold of skin in that sensitive place, putting her hands beneath

Amy's buttocks so as to better control her delving.

Amy's eyes closed and she tipped her head backwards. Her breathing became a series of sighs.

Greta licked ever lower between those slim and golden thighs, and Amy raised her hips. The maid parted her buttocks slightly with her hands and the delicious tongue dug between their curves to explore that other tight-closed rosebud.

Pleasure waves were carrying Amy away, when Greta made her final sortie between the open lips of her mistress's labia, covering them with her mouth and digging inside with her marvellously proficient tongue for the last traces of cream.

Amy gasped, crying out softly, and her body went rigid. The centre of her universe was between her legs and the shockwaves spread from there, where the maid's mouth was wetly clamped, and shook her slim body upon the hammock.

The golden girl, who wore only white ankle socks and tennis shoes, lay beautifully exhausted and smiled up at Greta who was now standing alongside her, a semblance of composure back in her face and her attire undisturbed by what had transpired.

'Will there be anything else, madam?' the maid said.

'No, thank you, Greta. I think all I need now is to sleep.'

Chapter 15

Her own home seemed restrictive to Caroline Penrose, and not just because it was a great deal smaller than the mansion of Sir Alec Ramsden.

There were signs of her husband throughout the place, from the choice of prints in the dining room to the water colours bought in Portobello Road in the drawing room; from the golf clubs in the garage to the way he had commandeered a spare bedroom as his study.

Was she really simply an accessory in his life? Someone he took for granted would be there when he got home?

She undressed in her bedroom and looked at her body in the mirror. There were no cameras watching her this time, but she preened at the memory of how the three men had reacted to her that morning. Her vagina twitched even more positively when she recalled Amy and the casual touches they had exchanged as the blonde girl helped her to the bathroom.

Amy had watched and had been so excited that she had masturbated.

My God, how long was it since she had done the same? It was back in adolescence. She did not think she could remember how. Even after her recent sexual awakenings, she did not think she could bring herself to do it now.

But the taste and smell of Amy's fingers aroused her and the touch of her tongue as it licked kitten-soft at the masculine milk upon her cheek, made her go wet.

Did she smell like that, too, Caroline thought?

Her fingers slid across her stomach towards the black curls of her pubic area, but she could not watch herself in the mirror and she closed her eyes. One finger slid between the lips of her vagina, hesitated and then dipped deep inside. The hot liquidity contracted around the intrusion and she groaned.

No, she couldn't.

She removed her hand and raised it to her face to tentatively test the aroma. It was not unlike the smell of Amy. She moved the finger across her lip, and licked the wetness. The taste, too, was similar.

Now, if Amy was here, she might be tempted to do other things that remained untried but which lurked questioningly at the back of her mind. Would she like them? She would not know until she tried.

The sexual intoxication of the morning refused to leave her and she wandered the house naked. The tycoon had invited her to make a confession and the concept had opened the door of a memory long sealed away because of the guilt attached to it.

And yet, was it her guilt or that of her husband?

COMPULSION

Would her husband come home this evening? Would he notice her tonight?

Perhaps she could make sure that he did notice. She had a new confidence in her body that had shaken off the fears of already being too old at thirty-seven. The discovery that she could arouse amazing passion in men of all ages had been a marvellous boost to her ego. More than that, she had also discovered that she could reciprocate the passion without effort.

There was a well of desire within her that was still waiting to be released, that was almost frightening in its intensity.

Tom was due home at seven and she would test it upon him. She put on the scarlet silk basque that she had worn the night before, with the silken thong that enhanced the lush curve of her buttocks rather than hid them.

As she fastened the black stockings, she looked up and caught sight of herself in the mirror and smiled. Her large breasts appeared to be falling from the half cups of the basque. She slipped on the high-heeled black shoes and admired herself.

Sir Alec had asked if she wanted to be a prostitute.

Perhaps once. In memory.

She pirouetted and her shape, the underwear and the colours took her breath away. What would it do for Tom? Her fingers went between her legs and touched herself briefly. Caroline could identify the smell of sex coming from her body. It made her hips twitch.

Nice suburban ladies did not smell of sex in the

early evening, nor did they don outrageous underwear for the return of their husbands. Or did they?

The sound of the front door opening downstairs surprised her.

'Caroline?' Tom shouted. 'It's me. I'm home.'

'You're early,' she said.

But he had already left the hall and entered one of the rooms.

Caroline mooed her lips at her image in the mirror and left the bedroom. She went down the stairs and into the hall. The sound of Tom's voice came from the drawing room. He had brought someone home with him.

Her first reaction was annoyance that he had spoiled her surprise. Then she reconsidered and realised the surprise could be even more effective. She went to the partly open door of the drawing room and listened.

Through the slight opening between the door and the jamb, she could see a young man sitting in an easy chair across the room. He had a sheaf of papers upon his lap and was listening to Tom.

Caroline composed herself, licked her lips and pushed open the door and entered the room.

'Tom, darling, you're early.' She stopped and stared in pretended surprise at the young man. 'Oh, I didn't realise you had company.'

'Good God,' Tom said, behind her.

The young man stared open-mouthed, not knowing quite where to look.

Caroline smiled and continued to walk across the

carpet, her body swaying in the high-heeled shoes. The young man attempted to gain his feet and the papers spilled upon the floor.

'No, don't get up.' She held out her hand and he took it, hesitantly. 'I'm Caroline. Tom's wife.'

'I'm . . .' He gulped. 'I'm David Bagley. From the office.'

She squeezed his hand.

'You've dropped your paperwork,' she said. 'Let me.'

Before he could protest, Caroline knelt on the carpet in front of him and picked up the scattered papers. She did it leisurely and without looking up, so that he could gaze without embarrassment at her breasts that were spilling from the basque.

'There we are.'

Caroline handed him the documents and stood up.

'Thank you,' he said.

She walked back to her husband who was sitting in a chair opposite. His flushed face continued to register shock, and possibly anger. Or was it desire?

Caroline bent forward to kiss him on the cheek and, in so doing, gave David Bagley a full and complete view of her buttocks, giftwrapped in the red strips of the thong and suspender straps.

'What the hell do you think you are doing?' he hissed.

'Just saying hello.' She turned abruptly and caught the young man's eyes fixed on her bottom. 'Can I get you anything. David? My husband is a terrible host. Tea, coffee, scotch?'

'No, thank you. Nothing at all.'

Tom put his documents to one side. 'In fact, we've finished our business. David has to go.'

'What? Oh yes, of course.'

Caroline smiled sweetly at the young man.

'So nice to have met you. I hope we see you again.'

'Yes, thank you. So do I.'

She left the room and returned upstairs to the bedroom, only now her face flushing from the outrageousness of her behaviour. But the sense of arousal within her had intensified. She wondered how Tom would react.

The front door slammed and she heard his footsteps on the stairs. He burst into the bedroom to confront her.

'Have you lost your mind?'

'No. I think I've found it.'

'Walking around in front of a complete stranger dressed like that?'

'Should it have been someone we know?'

'For God's sake, you know what I mean. What on earth will he think?'

'That you have a very desirable wife.'

'Desirable?' His face was red, his eyes staring. 'You look like a slut.'

'Really?'

Caroline confronted him. She was standing with her legs apart, her breasts jutting forward. She welcomed his outburst for it allowed her to release her own anger.

'A slut,' he repeated.

'You were always good with words, Tom. Shame about your prick.'

'What?'

'I've wondered recently what you must use it for. Stirring your coffee at the office? Or something else at the office?'

'What the hell are you implying?'

'I don't care if you are screwing somebody on the side, Tom. But I refuse to be ignored any longer.'

'Ignored? How can anyone ignore you, dressed like that?'

'Yes. How can you?' She pulled a breast free from the basque and held it in her hand. 'Do you remember sex, Tom? Aren't you tempted? Even with a slut? Particularly with a slut?'

He shook his head, as if to clear it. He was extremely agitated and she could feel his sexual tension. He desired her, but his ego was in the way of his erection.

'Feel it, Tom.' She stepped forward and put his hand upon her breast, holding it over the mound of flesh. 'Do you like it? Do you want to suck it? Do you want to fuck me?'

'You've gone mad,' he said.

'Perhaps. But it beats your kind of sanity. Do you want to fuck me, Tom?'

'No.'

He pulled his hand free, yet she could almost taste his desire.

'Perhaps we should have asked young David to stay. He would have fucked me. I could see it in his eyes. You could have watched, Tom. You could have watched him stick his prick inside me, watched me suck it, watched him come. Then you could have fucked me.'

He shook his head again and backed towards the door. His hands trembled and she could see the erection pushing against the material of his trousers.

'You would have liked that, Tom, wouldn't you? Or wasn't he rough enough? Maybe if he had dirtied his hands in the garden, or had a tattoo, that would have made it better for you. But you would have liked it, wouldn't you?'

Tom turned and ran out of the bedroom and down the stairs. The front door slammed. She heard his car engine start and listened as it left the drive.

Caroline turned and looked at herself in the mirror again. Her left breast still hung free and she was almost as flushed as her husband had been, but she was flushed with triumph and excitement. She touched herself between her legs and moved her hips against her hand.

No, she decided. She would wait for Tom to return, for she was sure he would.

Caroline remained dressed in the basque and stockings. Wearing them whilst walking around the house gave her an exquisite sense of disgraceful freedom.

She opened a bottle of wine, watched television and wished she had a copy of the videos in which she had starred. Tom, she guessed, might be gone as long as two hours. He would be drinking in a local public house, trying to come to terms with this new woman that his wife had become.

But, while he would not be able to understand the motives, she knew he would be driven mad by her displaying her body to his young colleague – and he would be driven home by the knowledge that she was available for him right now.

He returned after nine o'clock. In anticipation of his arrival, Caroline had turned off the television, drawn the curtains and switched on a table lamp. A Smokey Robinson tape played on the cassette deck.

The front door opened and slammed.

'In here,' Tom said.

Once again, he was not alone.

Caroline stood in the middle of the room, her hands on her hips.

A slut, he had said. Did she want to be a prostitute, Sir Alec had asked?

He came in and stopped in his tracks inside the door.

Behind him was a large man who needed a wash and shave. He was possibly in his late thirties, although his dishevelled appearance made it difficult to judge his age. He wore boots, old trousers tied with a belt, a check shirt with frayed cuffs and collar and a torn jacket with a ripped pocket.

'Hello, Tom?' she said quietly. 'Who is your friend?'

'Gerry.' His bloodshot eyes stared at her. 'This is Gerry. He's from Ireland.' His words were slurred from drink.

'Hello, Gerry. I'm Caroline.'

She smiled and walked forward and held out her hand. The Irishman was confused by her appearance and her formality, but he took her hand. His own was dirty and hard.

'Hello.' His gaze slipped from her face and went over her body, lingering on her breasts. 'Tom said . . .'

He ran out of words.

'Yes. What did Tom say?'

Tom walked to the cabinet and got a bottle of whisky.

'I said we could have a drink.'

He poured two neat whiskies into tumblers, came back across the room and gave one to Gerry. The Irishman downed it in two gulps.

Caroline turned around and walked back towards the stacked music centre, allowing him a look at her buttocks. She turned to make sure he had been enjoying the view and saw that he had.

'Do you like Smokey Robinson, Gerry?'

'Oh yes. Fine music.'

'Then we should dance to it.'

She opened her arms, walked back towards him and waited in the middle of the room. Gerry glanced at Tom briefly, before putting down the glass and joining her.

She said: 'Don't you think you would be more comfortable without your jacket?'

'Oh yes, sure thing.'

He allowed her to push it from his shoulders before he threw it behind him without looking where it landed. Tom, still nursing the glass of whisky, slumped into an armchair.

Caroline put her arms around the Irishman's neck and drew him close. She felt totally in command.

'Don't be frightened to touch,' she whispered in his ear. 'I won't break.'

At first he placed one hand on her back and the other on her hip. She pressed against him as they swayed to the music. He smelled of dirt, alcohol and body odour, as if he had been digging trenches all day, before going to the pub to wash the dust from his throat.

His stubble was rough against her cheek and she took great delight in gently rubbing herself against it. The itch in her vagina was becoming intolerable and she moved her hips against him and grunted in satisfaction as she felt him grow against her.

The Irishman's hands became bolder and one strayed down over her buttocks, feeling the flesh gently.

'Do you like what you feel?' she said in his ear.

'I do.'

'I like you feeling it.' She pushed her hips against him. 'Do it some more.'

Both hands now descended upon her buttocks, big strong hands that took one cheek in each palm and felt and groped and pulled her against his hardness.

'What did my husband say?' she asked, licking his ear.

He shuddered.

'He said all sorts of things.'

'Did he say he wanted you to fuck me?'

At the use of the word, the Irishman gripped her

buttocks more tightly and she feared he might become overexcited.

'He didn't say that.'

'Would you like to?'

The man gulped and tipped his head back so they could look at each other's faces.

'What about him?'

'He likes to watch.'

Caroline opened her mouth and kissed him, pushing her tongue into his mouth. He responded, kissing her in return, and his hands began to grip the flesh of her buttocks with more force and passion.

She broke away and took his hand.

'Come on.'

'Where?'

'Upstairs.' She ran her tongue across her lips and glanced at Tom, still in the armchair, hunched over as if protecting his private parts. 'Where we can fuck in comfort.'

She led him upstairs, his hands touching her bottom and thighs as they went. In the bedroom, she stripped the covers back from the double bed and climbed upon the white sheet. She pulled off the red silk thong, opened her legs and stroked her vagina. The lips parted immediately.

'Come on, Gerry,' she said. 'Fuck me. I need it.'

The Irishman pulled off the shirt and dropped the trousers, which he kicked off. He wore no underpants and his erect penis jutted from the mass of black curls at his pelvis. He had a tattoo of a dagger on his right arm. His body was muscled from manual toil, his torso tanned and streaked with dirt, as if he had been working stripped to the waist.

It was a sculpted body, a hard body. He was not handsome but he was all man. A man who would work and drink and fight and rut in exactly the same way: without quarter.

He reached down to unfasten the boots.

Caroline said: 'Leave them on.'

He smiled for the first time, as if his role had been defined. He climbed upon the bed and knelt above her.

'You're ripe, my darling,' he said. 'And your husband's a fool. Which way do you want it?'

'Any way you like.'

He knelt between her legs without further ado and guided the head of his penis into her vagina. He thrust, swift and sure, and buried it inside her.

Caroline yelled out and arched her back to meet him. Over his arm, she saw Tom standing in the doorway, watching, his face strained, one hand clutching the bulge in his trousers.

The Irishman fucked her furiously and without mercy, holding himself above her, the beer and whisky on his breath enveloping her. She raised her legs and clasped them around his back so he could dig deeper still, and each stroke brought yells and groans from them both.

At last he withdrew and, kneeling back, he pulled down the half cups of the basque to reveal her breasts. His hands devoured them.

He leant forward and clasped his lips around each

in turn, sucking large amounts into his mouth, flicking the erect nipples with his tongue.

His mouth trailed up her body to her neck and, as he licked her ear, he whispered: 'You've got me on the boil, darling. I'll not last long. If you want to come for your husband, you'll have to fake it or be quick.'

She sucked at his neck and whispered in return.

'I'm ready to come now. I'm on fire.'

'Then how do you want it, darling? How do you want it for your husband?'

Caroline, glorying in the sordidness of the situation, with the dirt from the man's body and his boots smearing the sheets and her own body, arched herself against him.

'From behind,' she said. 'Fuck me from behind.'

'Aye,' he said. 'It's a shame to waste such an arse.'

The Irishman knelt back, picked her up and flipped her onto her stomach with ease. She opened her legs and he knelt behind her, groping her buttocks and laying down upon her back for a moment, so that his penis lay along the groove between them.

'With such a fine cushion it won't take long,' he whispered.

'Good,' she said, pushing backwards to raise herself against him.

He lifted her hips and guided his penis into the hot tunnel of her vagina once more. This time he yelled out loud as he sank deeply within her and his rock hard stomach and abdomen smacked against the yielding flesh of her bottom.

Caroline bucked beneath him and she pushed her

right hand between the sheet and her stomach until her finger touched her engorged clitoris.

The Irishman pounded with great fervour against her buttocks, his yells trailing into one long cry. Caroline yelled back and spasmed into orgasm, her legs and body twitching.

Her labourer lover lasted longer than he said and kept on pounding. Her first orgasm became a second and then a third, before the Irishman gulped for air and exploded within her.

His climax continued through his own spasms as he rocked upon her body. Her finger touched her clitoris one more time and she slipped into the fourth successive coming with a sigh like death.

For a moment she felt she lost consciousness, but a light kiss on her neck from Gerry brought her round.

'I'll not be stopping,' he whispered. 'But you're a great fuck, darling. Any time you and your hubby fall out, come and get me at the Jug and Bottle.'

He climbed off the bed and she heard him pull on his clothes.

'I'll be seeing meself out,' he said to her husband, but Tom made no reply.

Caroline remained lying on her stomach and listened to the Irishman's footsteps go down the stairs. There was a slight delay, while he collected his jacket from the other room, and then the door opened and slammed and he was gone, as if a dream had ended.

Was Tom still there?

She rolled onto her side, aware of the curve of her hip, and of the dirt upon the bed – much more than she had envisaged – and looked towards the doorway.

Her husband was half in and half out of the room, a leg tight against the door frame, as if he were holding on to it for strength.

'Isn't that what you wanted, Tom?' she said. 'He even had a tattoo.'

'Bitch,' he said.

She smiled and licked her lips.

'Satisfied bitch,' she corrected. 'I came four times. When was the last time you made me come four times?'

His face was red enough to cause a haemorrhage.

She said: 'How about you? Do you want to fuck me?'

Caroline opened her legs and dipped a finger between them. She pushed two inside herself, raising her hips and giving a little moan as she did so. When she removed them, they were wet and sticky and she held them up for him to see.

'Come on, Tom. You want to. Push your prick into another man's sperm.'

With a strangled cry, her husband staggered into the room and began to pull at his clothes. He shed the jacket of his suit, but the tie became stuck halfway down and he left it like that. The shirt button at his collar burst open of its own accord. He pulled open his belt and pushed down his trousers as he reached the bed, so that they were still around his thighs.

His penis was gorged with blood and as red as his face. He pushed between her spread legs and she reached down and took hold of it. At her touch, he

COMPULSION

cried out and she felt it begin to throb and knew he would not be able to hold it for long.

Swiftly, she guided it into her gaping hole and pulled him in by the hips. He uttered a series of three moans, each a breathless octave higher than the last and, as his hands grabbed at her breasts, he came. His body shook so violently that he was in danger of falling from her but she trapped him inside her with her heels digging into his twitching buttocks.

As the convulsions subsided, he began to cry.

Caroline allowed him a moment before she spoke.

'Gerry was better,' she said. 'You didn't make me come. Do you make the girl in the office come? Or do you think maybe she fakes it.'

'Oh my God,' he said.

He pulled himself from her and staggered away from the bed, his trousers entangling his legs. He did not look back but with his trousers almost pulled up to his waist, he picked up his jacket and escaped from the room.

'Tom,' she called, and she heard him hesitate on the landing. 'Don't come back without an invitation.'

His footsteps went down the stairs and he stumbled towards the bottom. She heard him fall. He was still sobbing to himself as he opened the door and slammed it behind him. The car started and she listened to its engine fade as he drove away.

Downstairs, Smokey Robinson had stopped singing about love.

Upstairs, Caroline reached out, switched off the light and pulled a cover over her. She was content to slip into a satisfied sleep while the mingled lust juices of two men seeped from her vagina to stain her marital bed.

She could think of no finer statement of freedom than that and the confession she would make tomorrow.

Chapter 16

Amy awoke feeling sexually aroused. It was impossible not to in this house, she told herself. She also had the urge to continue to play her father-in-law at his own game.

Rupert, the butler, had now become the focus of her attention. He was aged about forty and of a definite male gender, for she had noticed the way he looked at her when he did not think he was being observed.

He was also, she hoped, very obedient.

The morning was dull and rain sporadically splashed the window panes. It was a morning for staying in bed and amusing and abusing oneself. She had abused herself the night before, several times, and could smell her own sexuality.

Amy touched the sensitive area between her legs and was instantly wet. Perhaps her dreams had been erotic, too. She reached beneath the pillow for the torn black silk panties that belonged to Caroline. She had used those during the night as well.

With a sigh, she got out of bed, stretched and went

into the bathroom. She brushed her teeth and washed her face, applying understated make-up, before putting on a short white silk slip that just covered her buttocks. However, she omitted to wear the matching panties.

The slip was, she believed, exactly suitable for the occasion. She felt, and looked, incredibly young. She hoped Rupert was attracted to young girls.

She walked down to the breakfast room where Sir Alec was reading his newspaper and drinking tea.

'Good morning, my dear.' He appraised her attire. 'You look very fetching this morning.'

Her smile was almost challenging.

'Good morning, father-in-law. Except that it isn't. I dislike the rain. It makes me wish to indulge myself. I shall have breakfast in bed and watch an educational film.'

She held up her key to the private library.

His smile was tolerant.

Amy went through the main library, unlocked the small door at the end of the room and entered the inner sanctum. Even now, with other plans on her mind, she was drawn to the confessional box but she resisted its lure and took a video from the top of a pile on the shelves.

Locking the door behind her, she re-crossed the main library into the hall and looked in on Sir Alec who was still at the breakfast table.

'Would you ask Rupert to bring a bowl of strawberries to my room?' she said innocently.

'Of course. Is that all?'

COMPULSION

'Just the strawberries. And Rupert.'

Amy turned away before her smile broadened and saw the butler coming from the kitchen into the hall. She raised a hand and waved her fingers at him before taking the stairs quickly, so that he could appreciate her nakedness beneath the slip as he passed below.

It was a temptation to look down at his reaction, but she held herself in check, taking the steps leisurely now and bending forward at one point to pick up an imaginary item from the carpet.

Had he seen? Would he be interested?

How could she doubt herself? She was certain of her beauty, certain of her ability to attract any man and most women.

In her room, she put the video in the machine and stretched upon the bed, pushing up the pillows to make herself more comfortable.

The video film started and she saw an office setting. The room and furnishings were modern and did not look as if they belonged to this house. The man in it appeared vaguely familiar, although she did not know why.

He was maybe forty, with a paunch, and fading looks, although the girl was much younger. She wore large spectacles and her dark hair was plaited and pinned upon her head. Both the man and woman wore business suits.

The office belonged to the man, for he was sitting in the chair behind the desk when the girl entered. They stared at each other without speaking for a moment.

He leaned forward and pressed a button on his telephone and said: 'No calls.'

Amy almost laughed with delight. The situation was a cliché.

Now he said to the girl: 'Lock the door.'

She turned back and did so before facing the man again to wait for more instructions.

'Show me,' he said.

The girl smiled, put the file in a tray on his desk, placed both hands on her hips and slowly raised her tight skirt.

As it crept higher, he leaned forward in his chair for a better view. The rising hemline revealed shapely legs, dark stocking tops and black suspender straps. She hesitated deliberately.

'Higher!' he said, his voice almost croaking.

The girl took the skirt all the way to her waist, with a giggle, for she wore no knickers.

Behind the desk the man had unfastened his trousers and released his erection. As if in a practised move, she walked around the desk, then bent over it, presenting her rear to him. He rolled his chair forward, his knees slipping between her legs, used both hands to open her vagina and guide his penis, and she sank backwards upon his lap.

They both gasped.

So far, Amy noticed, the girl had not said a word.

A knock at the door brought her back to the present. She had been, without noticing it, touching herself between her legs, making it more wet and pungent, and making her insides squidgy with lust.

Squidgy. She liked that word. It was precisely how her insides felt.

Amy used the remote control to switch off the video.

'Enter,' she said.

The door opened and Rupert came in. He wore his normal black suit, with a white shirt and tie, and carried a silver tray upon which was a silver bowl of strawberries and a spoon.

'Your strawberries, madam.'

Amy sat up on the bed, causing her legs to part slightly.

'Delicious,' she said.

She wondered whether her father-in-law was watching her live from behind the mirror or filming it for a later viewing.

The butler offered the tray and she took the dish. He could not fail to see that by sitting up, a strap had slipped from Amy's shoulder leaving one of her delightful breasts almost exposed.

'Thank you,' she said.

He straightened.

'Would there be anything more, madam?'

His voice was remarkably controlled.

'Yes,' she said. She looked up at him and smiled, half innocently, half seductively, the tip of her tongue peeping between her lips. 'I would rather like some cream.'

Rupert's expression remained unchanged, although he licked his own lips before he replied.

'I will bring you some, madam.'

'There's no need,' she said.

Amy put out a hand to stop his departure. As if by accident, the back of her fingers came to rest against the front of his trousers.

'It would be no trouble, madam. I have been instructed that anything that madam wants I should endeavour to provide.'

'Good.' The word came out as a purr. She tipped her head coquettishly to one side. 'Because I want a special kind of cream.'

Her shoulder strap had slipped further and she felt that the slip was remaining in place only because it had lodged upon her nipple.

Rupert coughed.

'What kind of cream is that, madam?'

'I hope you will not find me too demanding, Rupert, but I am an innocent in this house. I feel I have so much to learn.'

'I will do my best to advise you, madam.'

His eyes were gazing down the front of her slip.

'I have heard that it is possible to milk a man. To obtain from a man, a kind of cream. Is that true?'

'It is true, madam. But it is a cream that may not be to your liking.'

'Oh, but how will I know if I do not taste it? You see, I have led such a sheltered life, even though married. My husband, Tarquin . . .' she shrugged her shoulders without finishing the sentence.

'I understand, madam.'

'So I would be grateful if you would show me how to milk a man, so that I may taste his cream. Would you help me, Rupert?'

'I will do my best, madam.'
'And may I taste your cream?'
'If you wish, madam.'

The back of her fingers stroked the front of his trousers and detected a rising bulge.

'Am I right in assuming that this is the limb which I should milk?'

'That is correct, madam.'

Rupert's voice was no longer so steady and, while his expression remained constant, his eyes were staring.

'May I release it?'
'Please do, madam.'

Amy placed the bowl of strawberries on the bed alongside her and swivelled her hips so that her legs dangled over the side of the bed, facing the full-length mirror.

The movement caused her slip to ride about her thighs and the parted and swollen lips of her vagina could be seen in the reflection. At the same time, the slip had lost its hold upon her nipple and one side of the silken garment had dropped to her waist, exposing her breast.

In her concentration, she did not appear to notice this deshabille. She used both hands to unzip the black trousers and delve inside. The butler's erection was already full and difficult to manoeuvre but she eased it through the tangle of undergarments and shirt flaps until it plopped through the open fly.

He remained unmoving, his hands by his side, his palms pointing behind him, his shiny black shoes at ten to two, his jacket still fastened.

'Rupert,' Amy said, in a small voice. 'This is very large.'

'Thank you, madam.'

She took hold of it with one hand and began to slowly move the loose sheath of skin, backwards and forwards.

'Is this how it is done?'

He caught his breath.

'That is one way, madam.'

She put both her hands to the task, using two fingers delicately towards the base of the shaft to move backwards and forwards, while rubbing the circumcised head of the penis delicately in the palm of her other hand.

He gasped.

Through her lowered eyelids, she caught a glance of herself in the mirror opposite. Her legs parted, her vagina exposed, looking like an innocent angel in white, her blonde hair tumbling about her shoulders, the rosebud nipple rising and falling upon the naked breast.

And alongside her were the straight, darkly clothed legs of the butler, his shiny shoes steadfast on the floor, his penis stiff and flushed, inches from her face. Her nostrils flared to get its smell and her squidginess caused her to press her thighs together for momentary relief.

'Am I doing it correctly, Rupert?'

'You are doing it very well, madam.'

His voice was strained and she knew he must be watching what was happening in the mirror, just as she was watching.

COMPULSION

As her hands continued their work, she leant forward until she was close enough to lick it but, instead of doing so, she blew upon the head with her soft warm breath.

He shuddered slightly and her fingers moved more quickly.

'Am I milking fast enough?'

'Quite fast enough, madam.'

'The shaft seems to be getting damp, Rupert. As if you are leaking your cream.'

'Only a little, madam. There is a lot more to come.'

'Perhaps, if I were to kiss it, Rupert?'

Her voice was small and innocent.

He groaned and his penis quivered in her hand.

Leaning forward, she positioned her face directly in front of the butler's erection, puckered her lips and gently brushed them against the tip of the weapon.

He gasped and it bucked again in her hand.

'I don't think it likes that very much, Rupert,' she said, resuming her position sideways on and continuing to masturbate him.

'It liked it very much, madam, but it is about to discharge its cream.'

'Now, Rupert?'

'Very soon, madam.' He moaned and the dark trousers began to quiver as his legs shook. 'Very soon.'

Amy maintained her strokes with one hand while she picked up the bowl of strawberries in the other and held it below the head of the penis.

She felt the tensions in her hand.

'Now, Rupert?'

199

The blonde girl looked up into his face, her features still innocent despite the slight flush about her cheeks. His eyes met hers, his mouth opened, and he looked lost.

'Now, madam.'

The butler began to ejaculate and Amy directed the spurts of white fluid into the bowl. When he was finished, she delicately replaced the now flaccid penis back inside his trousers and underpants, taking care to straighten the garments beneath the grey flannel. She zipped him up and patted the material on either side of his genitals with both palms.

'Thank you, Rupert. You have been most kind.'

He coughed.

'Thank you, madam.'

His voice was strained.

Amy slid back onto the bed, careless of how the slip or her legs lay. She sat up against the cushions and picked up the bowl of strawberries.

The butler watched and waited.

'Is there anything else, madam?'

With her fingers, she picked up a strawberry that was sticky with his sperm and inspected it closely.

'Yes,' she said.

Staring at him, she placed the strawberry in her mouth and ate it.

'Your cream is delicious.'

'Thank you, madam.'

'That is all, Rupert. You may go.'

'Happy to be of service, madam.'

He bowed, picked up the silver tray and left.

COMPULSION

Amy stretched out on the bed as the door closed, causing the slip to ride higher still. Her hands went between her legs and touched an area that was screaming for relief.

One, two, three strokes and she was almost there. She pushed the fingers of her left hand inside herself and rolled her clitoris with the fingers of her right hand.

The orgasm engulfed her, a high tide of emotion that caused her hips to rise from the bed. Her body became rigid as it shook with sensation. She was gone, over the top of the breakwater, floating out to sea.

When her senses slowly returned, like driftwood on a beach, she rolled onto her side to face the mirror and the camera and, with great relish, slowly ate the strawberries, one by one.

Chapter 17

When Caroline arrived at the house, she was shown to the indoor swimming pool by the butler.

Amy waved from where she lay submerged near the waterfall.

'Come on in.'

'I don't have a suit.'

'Neither do I.'

The blonde girl swam across the pool towards her and pulled herself out onto the tiled side. Droplets of water fell from her naked body and she looked as golden and perfect as a nymph.

Caroline realised she was staring. 'I'm sorry.'

Amy smiled. 'I like it. I want to see you naked.'

Caroline flushed and felt silly.

'Perhaps it is a little early in the morning.'

'I started early.'

'Doing what?'

Amy licked her lips wickedly.

'I masturbated the butler.'

'You did what?' Caroline stared back to the door through which she had entered, but the butler had gone. 'That butler?'

'Yes. I enjoyed it.'

'I'll bet he did, too.'

'He did.'

Caroline shook her head.

'I am still getting used to all this.'

'But still enjoying it?'

'Oh, yes.'

'Then take your clothes off and join me. Sir Alec will not be back until after lunch.'

Caroline looked around the swimming pool, with its mirrors and foliage and windows.

'Are you sure he is away?'

'Who cares?' said Amy.

She turned and dived back into the water.

There was a changing room and, rather than disrobe at the side of the pool, Caroline entered. It was not that she was shy, but she felt it inappropriate to remove her clothes by the side of the pool.

Out there nakedness was acceptable, not erotic underwear. Besides, she had noted the inevitable mirror fixed to a wall of the changing room, which made its privacy dubious.

Caroline removed the beige summer dress and admired herself in the delicate white underwear she wore beneath it. Off it came, along with the high-heeled shoes and tan stockings, and she looked at herself again. With or without clothes, she looked good.

Different from Amy, but certainly good.

A few days ago, she might not have thought so but her confidence was now restored and she felt better

COMPULSION

about herself than she had for years.

Caroline went outside and Amy applauded from the far side of the pool. She dived in and swam across to her.

Amy said: 'You are a good swimmer.'

'My breasts help.'

'They are magnificent.'

They trod water together and Amy reached out and held one of Caroline's breasts. As if carried by the current, they came together, their limbs entwining.

Caroline laughed and put out a hand to hold onto the side of the pool. Amy remained in her arms, an arm around her neck, her legs straddling the older woman's thigh. The slim blonde rubbed her pubis against her.

The laughter died. Their eyes locked and they knew they both felt the same desires. Amy moved closer and they kissed. It started gentle and became passionate. Their mouths locked, their tongues snaked together.

Suddenly, Amy broke away and swam a few feet on her back to put distance between them. The blonde curls of her pubis, now dark with the water, were revealed by the swimming position and Caroline could not take her eyes from the temptation.

'I want you so much,' Amy said.

'I want you,' said Caroline.

'But not yet.'

'When?'

'When we are ready to explode, When the time is right.'

'When will that be?'

'Soon. It has to be soon.'

Amy turned in the water and swam below the surface, emerging again fifteen yards away.

'I am full of sex,' she shouted. 'But I am a miser. I am saving it, holding it, keeping it under control.'

Caroline said: 'And when the time is right?'

'Then I will be Vesuvius.'

'And I will be Pompeii.'

Amy laughed, her voice still brittle with the pent-up desire, and Caroline laughed too. They swam and splashed and allowed their ardour to cool – but it remained smouldering, a glance away.

'Did you enjoy yesterday?' Amy said.

'I loved it.'

'What did you do when you went back home, back to normality?'

Caroline giggled.

'I fucked a labourer while my husband watched.'

Amy stopped swimming to stare at her.

'Really?'

'Yes, really. His body was hard and dirty and he made me come four times.'

'Oh, Caroline.'

The blonde girl dived beneath the surface again, as agile as an eel, and swam between Caroline's legs to fleetingly touch her vagina.

Caroline shuddered and then swam after her as she made for the side of the pool, but the blonde girl was too quick. Amy clambered out and pointed to the jacuzzi.

COMPULSION

'Come on,' she said. 'I have been playing with myself all day. Tell me a story and make me come again.'

Amy stepped into the bubbling water of the jacuzzi and Caroline climbed from the pool and followed her, sitting opposite. Her large breasts floated just below the turmoil of the surface.

'Do you masturbate often?' Caroline asked.

'All the time,' Amy said. 'Do you?'

'Never. I think I lost the knack at school.'

'Are you sure it's not embarrassment? Being ashamed afterwards?'

'Perhaps.'

'It was with me. But once I let go, wow. It is one of the greatest pleasures in life, a desert island to which you can go and indulge your fantasies.' Her fingers went between her legs beneath the water and she closed her eyes and tipped her head back. 'Oh, yes.'

She suddenly opened her eyes and stared at Caroline.

'How can you be ashamed of such pleasure? It hurts no one and it feels so good. Do not worry that it is a substitute for sex, it is simply a variation of sex.' She licked her lips and her eyes tilted backwards as her fingers went to work again. 'Try it, Caroline. Tell me about last night, and we'll do it together, beneath the water where no one can see.'

The sight of the blonde girl making herself excited aroused Caroline, but she was still reluctant.

Amy said: 'Touch yourself, now. Like I'm touching

myself. Do it, Caroline. Do it.'

Beneath the water, among the bubbles that had already made her open vagina tingle, the woman's fingers went to the source of sexual pleasure.

'I have two fingers inside myself, Caroline.' The blonde girl moaned. 'You do it. Put two fingers inside yourself.'

Caroline moaned in reply. 'I have. They're inside. I'm moving them Amy. I'm moving them.'

'And your other hand. Use your other hand, as well. There is so much to touch. Use your other hand.'

The fingers of Caroline's other hand made the same journey and began exploring and touching and stroking her clitoris. She gasped.

Amy said: 'Do it for me, Caroline. For me.'

The girl was staring at her, her eyes wide, her mouth slack, as she concentrated on the work of her own fingers.

Caroline followed her example and felt the orgasm building beneath her touch. Their eyes locked, their tongues lolled, and they masturbated in unison.

Amy's breath began to shorten first, her eyes to widen further and, as she gasped her arrival, Caroline convulsed upon her own hand and they came together. Their cries were strangled and their legs thrashed the already frothing water.

They regained their breath slowly, relaxing in the foam, allowing the turbulence to hold them upright as they lounged in the jacuzzi.

The blonde girl, still breathing through her mouth, smiled.

'Worth it?' she asked.

'Oh yes. It was worth it.'
'Now, tell me about last night.'
'I will tell you, but I do not think I can manage another.'
'You do not know what you can manage until you try.'
'That is true. Even so, I have a confession to make this afternoon.'
'You mean, *the* confession?'
'Yes.'
'You have decided?'
Caroline nodded. 'I have decided.'
Amy's expression was one of yearning.
'I would love to hear it.'
'I thought you wanted to hear about last night?'
'I do. First.'
'Then I will tell you.'
Caroline told her what had happened the previous evening, about her reasons for forcing a confrontation with her husband and its unexpected outcome when he had come home with the labourer.

All the time she talked, Amy's fingers worked at herself beneath the water, eliciting small moans which she sometimes tried to stifle.

Watching the beautiful girl play with herself this way made Caroline enjoy her role more, and she told her story with a wealth of detail and description.

When she had finished, Amy had still not come but was holding herself on the edge once more.

'Go back to the bedroom. When he turned you over. Tell me again. Tell me.'

Amy's eyes closed and Caroline retold the final part

of the labourer's passionate attack upon her body.

'He pushed it inside me from behind. His cock was huge, as hard as steel. But it was throbbing and I knew he could not last much longer. He fucked me and fucked me. His weight squashed my bottom; he was fucking me so hard it sounded as if he was spanking me.'

Caroline noticed with eagerness that each time she used the word fucking, Amy twitched in response.

'He told me he was going to come but I came first. I stuck my fingers inside me, Amy. I finger-fucked myself. It felt so good. I finger-fucked myself as he fucked me from behind, with my husband watching from the doorway. I came and he came and I kept on coming.'

She timed it perfectly to the gasps of the girl sitting opposite, so that Amy came at the moment of mutual orgasm.

They relaxed again among the bubbles.

The blonde wiped trailing wet hair from her face.

'You tell it well. I hope I am able to hear your confession.'

Caroline bit her lip and wondered when Vesuvius would erupt. Perhaps her confession might be the catalyst.

'So do I,' she said.

Amy stood up and stepped out of the jacuzzi.

'Time for a swim to cool down,' she said. 'And then lunch. My father-in-law will be back soon.'

'Your father-in-law?'

'Yes. Sir Alec is the father of my husband.'

Caroline shook her head. 'We know so little about each other. It has been only sex, so far.'

Amy smiled. 'The sex has been good. It is less complicated without history.'

'Even so, I would like to know about you. You already know something of me.'

'All right. Come and swim. Then we will talk by the waterfall, where it is cool.'

Chapter 18

The girls ate lunch together, talking and exchanging information about their backgrounds.

Caroline had put on her underwear and summer dress and she enjoyed the feeling of her body being dressed for sexual pleasure rather than for practicality.

Outwardly she might appear to be respectable and yet, beneath the dress, she was attired for erotic indulgence.

Amy had slipped into one of her favourite casual outfits – white ankle socks and tennis shoes, worn with a simple blue dress in brushed cotton. She had again omitted to wear panties.

Caroline said: 'I am sure my husband is having an affair with someone at the office.'

'Does it bother you?' asked Amy.

She did not confirm Caroline's suspicions, even though Sir Alec had already given her the details of Tom Penrose's infidelity. Her friend may wish to save her marriage and if she did, a suspicion might be easier to live with than hard evidence that he had strayed.

'It did. It still does, I suppose. My pride is hurt that he can find someone else more desirable than me.'

Amy strongly suspected that the unfaithful husband was the featured player in the video she had watched that morning. If he was, then perhaps she could find a way to use the knowledge to her friend's advantage.

'Perhaps he does not find them more desirable,' Amy said. 'Perhaps it is a different kind of desire. Why should we be restricted to one sexual partner when there are so many desirable people? It is society that dictates monogamy, not sexual response.'

'That is true. A relationship can have advantages, but no matter how good, you lose that first spontaneity of desire.'

Amy smiled.

'Spontaneity of desire. It is good, is it not, when you are able to react to it?'

'It is marvellous.'

'So what about your relationship with your husband? Is your marriage over?'

'I do not know. I am not sure that it was ever much of a marriage.'

'Why do you say that? You have been together for many years.'

Caroline shrugged.

'We never talked, not properly. There were secrets we both kept that were never divulged, questions that were never asked, never answered. Eventually, we both devised our own ways of coping with life together, or pretending that everything was fine. But it annoyed me that he took me for granted and refused to acknowledge my own potential as an individual.'

'Did you have a sex life?'

'We used to. Tom would indulge in sex at regular intervals. He was always the instigator. But it was sex on a plateau, if you see what I mean, with few mountains to climb – at least for me. An orgasm was falling off the edge of the plateau rather than reaching the heights.'

Amy laughed.

'You are saying that now because you have new comparisons.'

Caroline grinned.

'Very likely. Anyway, eventually even the sex finished. That was when I suspected him of having an affair. He banned me from calling at the office or even telephoning him there. He said it was bad for his corporate image.'

Amy chuckled to herself, remembering the corporate image he had presented on the video with his trousers down.

They were having coffee when Sir Alec arrived home. He had with him a young man in his mid-twenties, wearing the cassock and the collar of a priest.

'This is Father Michael,' he said, making the introductions. 'This is Caroline and Amy.'

The young man had dark, wavy hair and fine features. He blushed as he shook their hands and said hello in a soft, shy voice.

Perhaps, Amy thought, he blushed because of the

way they looked at him. It was without reverence and, although they were a little surprised, both of them assessed him speculatively.

Was this a real priest, the blonde girl wondered, or another of her father-in-law's games?

Amy said: 'How fortunate that Father Michael is with you. Caroline tells me she is ready to make her confession.'

Caroline shot her a glance.

Sir Alec said: 'Is that correct, my dear?'

'That is what I told Amy.'

'But you are having second thoughts?'

Caroline smiled at Father Michael.

'I did not realise you would be bringing a priest.'

'Does that bother you?'

'I am not sure.'

Sir Alec said: 'Michael is well equipped to deal with anything you might divulge.'

'I am sure that he is.'

'But you would rather confess to me?'

'It was probably my fault for making an assumption. I should have realised that this is no place to assume anything.'

'But you would prefer to confess to me?'

Caroline looked at the young man, who was still blushing, and thought it might, after all, be rewarding to make her confession to him.

'No, Father Michael will be fine.'

'Good. I have explained the nature of the confessions that are made in this house.' He smiled at the young man. 'He realises that they are told without euphemism. Is that not so, Michael?'

The young man coughed.

'That is so.'

Amy licked her bottom lip.

She said: 'So if one of us was to talk about being fucked, you would not be offended?'

He gulped and his blush deepened.

'I would not be offended, my child.'

She grinned and added: 'But would you enjoy it, Father?'

'It is not for me to enjoy your confession. It is for me to be a recipient, so that you can unburden yourself.'

'Yes, Father,' said Amy, 'but if I tell you all the details of how a man fucked me, and all the details of how I fucked a woman, would your cock go stiff?'

The young man's face was red all the way to the roots of his hair, although he tried to maintain his composure before the sweet smile of the girl with the angel face.

'As I said, my child, I am simply a recipient.'

Sir Alec said: 'I think you are being naughty, Amy. Michael may wear a cassock, but beneath it he has the body of a healthy young man. It may be his calling to deny himself the pleasures of the flesh, to deny natural desire, but he cannot stop the natural human reactions of his body.'

'But surely,' Amy said, 'that in itself is unnatural.'

Sir Alec said: 'There are several schools of thought on the subject, and every religion and sect and schism has its own interpretation on lust, love and libido.'

Amy said: 'And to which religion, sect or schism does Father Michael belong?'

'Suffice it to say that he has agreed to hear confession.'

'And denial?' Amy said.

Sir Alec said: 'Sometimes, denial can be the greatest aphrodisiac. As you well know, Amy.'

Which she accepted was perfectly true.

The longer she played out her own games, the more intense her desires grew. How much longer could she hold out? She smiled again at the priest.

Sir Alec said: 'Anyway, it is time we prepared. I think, Amy, it might be a good idea if you were to play a tape of a previous confession to Caroline, so that she is under no illusion as to what is required.'

Amy nodded and her father-in-law smiled at Caroline.

He said: 'The only other requirement is that at the end of your confession, you must agree to accept whatever treatment or undertaking is meted out to you.'

'I agree.'

'Good. Then Father Michael and I will leave you for now. We will all meet again in the private library in an hour.'

Amy played Caroline a confession on the cassette deck in her bedroom. They sprawled upon the bed together and listened. They were both aroused but kept their distance from each other.

Afterwards, the blonde girl touched herself

between her legs again, gently but without serious intent to raise an orgasm.

'I just cannot stop any more,' she said. 'The whole ambience of this house is to remove repressions.' She smiled lazily. 'I suppose I am making up for lost time.'

Caroline said: 'You mean you have not had an active sex life until now?'

'I still haven't. It is mainly a sex life dominated by myself. A singular sex life, if you like. I feel secure when it is my own fingers that are in control rather than someone else's.'

'When will that change?'

'When I make my confession.'

'When will that be?'

The blonde girl's smile grew wide and she bit her bottom lip.

'I think it will be very soon.'

'Is that why you agreed to stay here when your husband went back to Spain?'

'Probably, although that motive had not formulated itself quite so clearly at that time. When the chance arose and I realised the potential of the house, a certain fatalism came over me – as if I knew that I was meant to experience all that my father-in-law could provide or offer.'

Caroline held her hand.

'And yet, you still pick and choose. You have still not given yourself up to passion.'

'In a way, that is part of the process I have chosen for the release of my own repressions. As my father-in-law said, denial can be a great aphrodisiac.'

Caroline got off the bed and picked up the video cassette on top of the television. It was the one that featured her husband.

'How many of these tapes does he have?'

'Hundreds. Possibly thousands.'

'It seems a degenerate occupation.' She glanced at Amy with a smile. 'And also a wonderfully thrilling and fulfilling mission in life.'

'Try explaining that in polite society.'

They both laughed.

'And yet it is,' Caroline said. 'Sex is an important part of the human condition and yet it is so often misunderstood or swept into the cupboard beneath the stairs. There is a need to shed repression, to fight suppression.'

Amy said: 'You are beginning to talk with the fervour of a convert.'

Her friend raised an eyebrow.'

'Which brings us to Father Michael. Do you think he is a real cleric?'

The blonde girl slowly sucked the finger with which she had gently penetrated herself, as if it were a lollipop of exotic flavour.

'Does it matter?' she said.

Caroline smiled and looked back at the video.

'Do we have time to play this?'

'No,' Amy said, slipping her legs over the side of the bed, so that the skirt of her dress rose high enough to display the golden curls of her pubic hair. 'It is time to go.'

Sir Alec and Father Michael were already in the private library and Caroline gazed around the room with curiosity.

The tycoon said: 'Are you ready?'

'Yes. I am ready.'

'Then let us begin. Father Michael?'

Sir Alec indicated the confessional box and the young man in the cassock entered his side and closed the door.

Caroline felt nervous as she faced Sir Alec and his daughter-in-law.

He said: 'Amy and I will leave you now, Mrs Penrose. We will wait in the annexe until you have finished. I do feel it is important that you make your confession in private and without an audience. I feel it can be a much more cathartic experience that way, when you are ready to enter, please do so.'

Sir Alec led Amy to a door at the back of the room. He opened it, allowing her to go through first before he followed.

Caroline looked around at the shelves of books, magazines and tapes and wondered what other secrets they contained. She also wondered whether she would gain access to them with her own confession.

Her own confession.

She had rehearsed it in her mind and it had revived delicious and depraved memories. And now it was time to deliver it.

Caroline entered the confessional box and knelt down.

The annexe was a room in which Amy had not been before. It was small and without windows. Illumination was supplied by two diffused spotlamps in a corner, which provided warm shadows and atmosphere. It contained two armchairs, a capacious sofa and Father Michael.

Sir Alec smiled.

'Please, make yourselves comfortable. All that Mrs Penrose says will be relayed into this room. Relax, enjoy.'

He opened a section of the wood panelling, which provided access to the confessional box, entered and took his seat behind the grill.

Amy should have guessed the confession would not be as straightforward as her father-in-law had said. She also guessed that she had been closeted here, with the priest, as an act of two-way temptation.

She smiled at Father Michael and sat on the sofa. The young man, still blushing, sat in an armchair facing her. The blonde girl stretched out full length on her side, raising one leg so that the skirt of her dress fell back.

Caroline's voice suddenly came from a concealed speaker. It was as intimate as if she were telling her story in this very room, to the priest and the girl with an angel's face.

Father Michael crossed his legs and tried to make himself comfortable beneath his cassock, and Amy parted her thighs and raised her hips for the touch of her hand.

Chapter 19

Caroline's Confession
My name is Caroline and this is my confession.

I married my husband Tom soon after I left university. My childhood had been normal and I had grown up as part of a middle-class family in Sussex. There had been boyfriends but nobody serious, although I had purposely had an affair when I was eighteen because I wanted to lose my virginity. I felt it might be in the way in case I met someone wildly exciting. Unfortunately, I did not. I met Tom.

He was intelligent and witty, although never really handsome, and he always liked to dabble with life on the wild side. At least, he thought he did. He had been to university in Liverpool where he had gone drinking with student friends in seedy public houses, where he had mixed with working-class people and the unemployed.

After we were married, we lived in an apartment near the East End of London – one of those areas that had been converted for wealthier young couples at the expense of the families who had grown up there for generations and who now had to move out.

He began to frequent a public house, once or twice a week, that was beyond the limits of the new money and in the real East End. It seemed to give him a thrill to mix with real people and the small-time crooks and confidence tricksters who used it regularly. A few serious criminals also called in but there was never any real trouble. Tom was tolerated rather than liked.

I went to the place with him from time to time but on this particular occasion, he insisted I go along. He said a party was being held for a man called Ratchett who had been in prison for three years.

It did not appeal to me but he insisted and, as I was something of an immature twenty-two year old and we had been married for barely a year, I agreed, although I did not know what to wear.

Afterwards, we were supposed to be going on for supper and I supposed Tom was looking forward to being able to use gossip from the party to entertain the friends from his own class.

Anyway, I had to choose something that would also be appropriate for our second engagement and I wore a simple pink crepe-de-Chine dress, with a scoop neck that buttoned down the front. With it I wore white stockings and flat, white shoes.

We arrived when the party was almost over and I noticed that the few regulars I knew by sight had kept well away from the hardcore who were still celebrating.

Ratchett was a tall, angular man with short spiky grey hair, aged about forty-five to fifty. He wore a crumpled suit and a white shirt that was open at the neck. Upon his feet he wore hard-toed boots.

I noticed his footwear because Tom had been at pains to explain such things on a previous visit. Men who were used to fighting always wore hard-toed shoes and boots, he said, with which to kick their opponents.

Tom and I were accepted into this motley and drunken crowd as minor celebrities, which pleased Tom enormously. My usual drink was gin and tonic, but then only sparingly. In this company, however, no one drank sparingly and it seemed impolite to refuse what was offered.

At one point, I could not help myself from staring at the tattoo around the man Ratchett's neck. He saw me looking and laughed, putting his arm around me and pulling me tight against his body. It felt like it had been carved from granite.

'Can you see better, now gel?' he said, and tilted his head back.

The tattoo was of a dotted line with the words 'cut here' beneath them.

He had pulled me to him because he had been amused at my fascination but as he continued to hold me I felt an extra hardness begin to grow from his body. His grin changed slowly into a leer and he made no secret that he knew I could feel it.

'I've been banged up for three years,' he said in a low voice. 'No female company for three years. It can send a man mad just thinking about it.'

Someone shouted him and during this distraction,

I broke free and went to stand closer to my husband. Tom had been drinking whisky at a much faster rate than I had been drinking gin, in an effort to impress his new friends, and was already drunk.

I said to him: 'I think we should go,' but he just laughed and said he was enjoying himself.

Ratchett had seen my move and, in retrospect, I believe that it prompted him to speak quietly to one or two of the company, for the party began to break up soon afterwards. At last, there was only Tom and myself, and Ratchett and his friend, Mo, a man who was perhaps ten years younger than Ratchett.

Mo was a little shorter in height but extremely broad in the chest. He wore jeans, Doc Marten boots and a white T-shirt from which the muscles of his arms bulged. He had tattoos on each forearm and the words hate and love tattooed across the knuckles of his hands.

Tom said: 'Great party,' to Ratchett, who put his arm around his shoulder.

'Things to do,' Ratchett said, and tapped the side of his nose as if imparting knowledge about the underworld. Tom tried to look impressed. 'Bugger,' said Ratchett, 'Harry's taken the car. Can you give us a lift, Tom?'

He squeezed his shoulders and Tom said: 'Of course. Where to?'

'Mo will direct you,' Ratchett said.

Outside, I felt whoozy in the fresh air and Tom looked unsteady but he got into the driving seat of the BMW and Mo got into the passenger seat. Ratchett and I sat in the back.

COMPULSION

'Do you know what I was inside for?' he asked Tom.

'No, actually,' said my husband, as if to ask would have been impolite.

'GBH. Grievous bodily harm.' Ratchett placed his palm over my thigh. 'I've always gone down for violence. This time, I nearly killed the bastard.'

He laughed, and Mo joined in, and then so did Tom, but rather nervously. As they laughed, Ratchett's fingers traced the suspender strap that ran along the top of my thigh through the thin material of the dress.

The man never looked at me but continued to stroke my thigh during the short journey that ended outside a house in a street of terraced houses, many of which looked derelict.

Mo said: 'They'll soon be knocking these down. Building more flats for your yuppie mates.'

He grinned at Tom and Tom smiled back.

Mo jumped out and opened the door on my side of the car.

'Come on you two,' said Ratchett, pushing me out. 'You've got to have one for the road before you go.'

Tom's nerves were now showing and he said: 'Well, actually, we're late for another engagement.'

I was already half out of the car and Ratchett leaned over into the front and put a hand on my husband's shoulder.

'Just the one, Tom. I owe you one for the lift.'

'No really,' Tom began to say, but Ratchett cut him short.

'And it's the least you can do, isn't it, my old mate.' He squeezed his shoulder. 'Three years has been a long time without civilised company. Just one for the road to show we're mates. All right?'

'Well, all right then. Just the one.'

Tom reluctantly got out of the car and Mo unlocked the house door.

Mo said: 'Don't worry about your motor, Tom. No one would dare touch it if it's outside my gaff.'

Tom normally loved the colour of such local words but now he looked queasy, as if the whisky did not mix with his nervous condition.

Inside, the house smelled damp, even in summer. The wallpaper was peeling and the carpet threadbare. Mo led the way upstairs and Tom followed. I went next and Ratchett came behind.

Halfway up the stairs, I felt his hand on my leg beneath my dress but I dared not say anything. He moved his palm up the stocking until it reached the flesh above it. Then we were at the top of the stairs and he removed his hand and behaved as if nothing had happened.

Mo unlocked a door and we went into a bedsitting room which contained everything from a kitchen sink to a double bed. The sight of the bed made me shudder.

'It might not be much, but it's home,' said Mo.

He picked up a bottle of whisky from the sideboard and poured two strong measures into two glasses, which he handed to Tom and Ratchett.

'Sorry,' he said to me. 'No gin.'

'That's all right,' I said. 'I have already had enough.'

He poured himself a measure into a mug that he

took from the draining board, before switching on a cassette player. Loud rock and roll music filled the room.

Ratchett leaned back against the door and said: 'Cheers,' and held up his glass. Tom did the same and then drank it down in two or three quick gulps. He drank it so quickly that it made him cough because it had been at least three or four normal measures.

'Now there's a man who can drink,' said Ratchett. 'Give him another.'

'No, really,' Tom began to say, but Mo had already picked up the bottle and poured the same again into his glass.

Mo slumped into the one easy chair and said: 'Sit down. Use the bed.'

Tom sat on the edge of the bed and I hesitated before I went and sat alongside him. Mo stared at my knees.

'So what do you do, Tom?' Mo asked. 'Something in the city?'

'Er, yes, I suppose I am.'

'Must be nice. Flash car, lovely wife, lots of cash.'

'Well, it's quite hard work, actually.'

He took another gulp of whisky in an attempt to finish the drink so that we could leave. He still hadn't seen that we would not be able to leave until they said we could go. He still had not seen the inevitability of the situation.

'Tell me about it,' Mo said and, incredibly, Tom began to, warming to his subject as the interest and the sudden fresh intake of scotch began to relax him.

I had recognised the inevitability of what was to happen. I could feel it in the room and the way Ratchett and Mo stared at me whilst they asked Tom questions and got him to talk inanely about his career in exports.

The atmosphere was electric and my insides had turned to jelly. I was frightened, of course, but there was also a sort of animalistic curiosity. No man had ever looked at me the way these two now looked at me.

It was pure, basic lust without any of the pretence of dinner and a show and being escorted home in the hope that the outlay on the evening would be repaid with tired copulation. These two hard and vicious men were not looking in hope but in certainty.

As Tom stopped speaking to take another drink of whisky, I stood up.

'May I use the bathroom?' I said, blushing at having to ask the question.

Mo waved towards the door which Ratchett opened.

'I'll show you the way,' Ratchett said.

He opened the door and I walked through. He followed and as the door closed I saw Tom, still sitting on the bed, staring forlornly after me. I heard Mo say: 'Go on then. You were telling me about Hong Kong.'

Then they were shut off and there was just Ratchett and me on the dim landing of this old house. We stared at each other for a moment and he said: 'You don't want a bathroom, do you, gel?'

I shook my head.

'The room was too warm.'

'Of course it was.'

He moved towards me and I backed away until I was level with another door. He reached out and I flinched, but he was not attempting to grab me, only to open the door.

'My room,' he said.

His eyes never left my face and I backed into a room that smelled of dirt and cooking. He followed me in and closed the door.

The curtains were only half drawn and the interior was dim. It consisted of a small area that held a sink, a chair, a table and an alcove in which hung an overcoat, a shirt and a pair of trousers on wire clothes hangers.

A partition had been built to give the room two sections, and a curtain, made of strips of coloured plastic, hung across the space where the plasterboard wall ended. The curtain gave the cell-like area beyond a flimsy kind of privacy. Upon the floor in this cell was a mattress covered with a tangle of blankets.

Ratchett watched my reaction and said: 'Do you like it? A bit different from what you're used to, I expect.' His grin froze and his eyes went down over my body. 'But then, you're a bit different from what I'm used to.'

He put his whisky glass onto the table behind him and touched my neck. I backed away, slowly, until the plastic curtain was behind me.

His hand went down over my breast and he palmed it and squeezed gently. His mouth had opened and his breathing had become peculiar.

'Three years,' he said. 'Three fucking years without a woman.' He sniggered. 'Ain't you the lucky one.'

At that point, I don't know what I was thinking. I was beyond recriminations about never having come here in the first place.

The feeling of inevitability had descended upon me as soon as Ratchett had put his arm around me in the public house. I could have insisted then that we leave but I hadn't. The danger had been too exciting.

I had gone to stand next to my husband at the bar but I kept looking at Ratchett and, unbidden, I had imagined his frenzy after three years without a woman.

There had been several opportunities to escape the situation that I hadn't taken. Instead, I had allowed it to develop until no choices were left. I did not want to admit it, but I had wanted this to happen.

The only men I had known, socially or sexually, had been extremely middle class. There had not been many lovers but most had been polite, one had been fervent and another incompetent. How would a man like this behave?

Simply being close to him and sensing his bestial qualities of violence had been exciting, and yet all the time there had been those opportunities to end the degenerate daydream and return to my own world, taking the taste of what almost happened with me.

But I hadn't. In consequence, I was here, now, alone with him in a hovel while my husband sat a few feet away in another room.

Ratchett's hand dropped again, onto my hip. He stepped closer and moved it against my buttock, feeling the flesh through the crepe de Chine of the dress.

'You want it, don't you?'

'Don't hurt me,' I said.

He pulled me to him, his arms wrapping around me like bands of steel, and his mouth clamped over mine, his tongue forcing a passage inside. It was not an attempt at a kiss but a forced entry, as if to demonstrate his power.

His hands pulled at my skirt, lifting it to my waist, and then they were beneath it, wallowing in my flesh, tearing at my panties.

He pushed me suddenly and I tumbled backwards, through the plastic curtain, onto the mattress, the skirt of the dress high around my waist. He hesitated then, to stare at the sight of my long legs encased in white stockings, the naked flesh above, and the remnants of the white panties that he had torn and which were now partway down my thighs.

His hands went to his belt. He unfastened it, pulled open his trousers and pushed them and his underpants down his legs until they reached his knees. He still wore his jacket and shirt and you might think he looked foolish except for the wild stare of his eyes, the set of his face and the iron rod that pulsated from his groin.

Ratchett dropped upon me, tearing again at my panties until they hung loose around one thigh. His fingers dug between my legs and made me yelp at his impatience and clumsiness.

'No, no,' I said, reaching down between us and pushing his hands away, so that I could help. My fingers parted the lips of my vagina, releasing the wetness waiting there, and I grasped at his prick and pushed it into the passage.

'Bitch!' he said. 'Bitch!' and he came as he thrust, almost splitting me with the force of his drive. He gripped my hips and held me in the air upon him as he knelt there. My body shook upon its impalement.

When he released me, I fell backwards onto the mattress, already shattered by the fierceness of the assault, but he was still inside me and he was still hard.

He lay upon me, his breath ragged, and his hands now explored every inch of me, digging below to grip into my buttocks with fingers like talons, opening the front of my dress to reach my breasts which he pulled from the brassiere.

Ratchett mauled my breasts and sucked them and began to move within me, each stroke lifting me from the mattress, each stroke eliciting a moan.

'You like it rough, gel? I'll give it you rough.'

He reached behind him, pulled his belt free from his trousers and pushed my hands above my head. With the belt he strapped my wrists together and then held himself above me on stretched arms as he continued to pump in and out with a powerful and inexorable rhythm.

His eyes held mine as he moved towards another climax and I twisted beneath him, in my delicate white underwear and my new pink dress, with the smells of poverty and the feel of dirt all around me, and I loved it.

COMPULSION

My mouth was open and my gasps were regular and I squirmed my groin against the rock hardness of his body to bring myself to orgasm. I was almost there when the door opened and I cried out in fear in case it was Tom; it was not fear of being discovered but fear that Ratchett would beat Tom for disturbing us.

But it wasn't Tom, it was Mo. He stepped inside the room, closed the door and watched.

'Is she good?' he said.

Without breaking his rhythm, Ratchett said: 'She's a raver.'

Mo said: 'I'll be back. Just give the pillock another drink.'

He left and Ratchett changed his pace. His expression tightened and the grip of his fingers could have broken the bones in my hips. I squirmed again but I could not quite reach the peak. He came for a second time, and for a second time his orgasm shook me as if I had been impaled.

This time he got off me and stood up, pulling up his trousers and fastening them, although he left my wrists tied with his belt.

He grinned and said: 'Mo's turn. I'll baby-sit your husband.'

Picking up the whisky glass, he left the room and I lay there, wondering at the new sensations that seemed to have captured my being. Moments later, the door opened again and Mo entered. Without preliminaries, he pulled off his T-shirt, unfastened his jeans and pulled them and his underpants off. He must have already removed his boots in the other room.

Naked, he looked bigger than with his clothes on.

His chest was hairless and his muscles shone with sweat. When he flexed his arms, the tattoos moved. His legs were like tree trunks but his penis was, surprisingly, of normal size. It was erect and he stroked it as he looked down at me.

He shook his head as if he could not believe that all this was for him, and then knelt on the mattress and began to touch me, exploring my body with his hands as Ratchett had done, groping my breasts and delving beneath me to cup my buttocks, pushing fingers into the wetness between my legs.

'Oh, yes,' he said, and moved between my thighs.

I arched my hips forward and he grinned because I was helping. Then he pushed his prick inside me. He held it still for a moment until he got used to the heat and, like Ratchett, he held himself above me as he fucked me, so that he could watch my face.

It was not long ago that I had been close to orgasm, so now it did not take long to arouse my feelings to the brink once more. As he watched, my head dipped back and my eyes rolled upwards and I tensed and came, wrapping my legs around him to hold him inside me, the heels of my shoes digging into his buttocks.

A cry escaped from my throat but I tried to stifle it so that my husband would not hear. But I could not, nor did I wish to, disguise the fact that I was shaking against this muscle-bound man in ecstasy.

The orgasm went on and on until I thought I had lost my mind. When I slipped back into a dazed reality, Mo was still pounding into my body and giggling with delight at making me come. For a moment,

I felt the tensions in his penis begin to change and thought he, too, might be about to do the same, but he stopped his action immediately and his face concentrated as he kept it at bay.

'Not too soon,' he said. 'Too much to do.'

He withdrew, turned me over, and reinserted his prick into my vagina from behind, pulling me up onto my knees. He was still doing this when the door opened again behind me. My heart lurched as before in case it was Tom. It was Ratchett.

Mo's stroke did not falter.

'How's her husband?' he said.

'Passed out,' said Ratchett.

I heard him begin to undress.

How much longer would this go on? I asked myself. How much longer did I want it to? was another question that crept into my mind. For my senses were no longer contained within me, but had seeped out with my juices to mingle with the essence of violence and lust and dirt that these men represented.

This small cell of a partitioned room was a complete world in itself, where nothing existed but sex.

Mo withdrew again and the two men moved about me, their hard, uncompromising bodies matched by their hard, uncompromising demands. Ratchett's chest was covered with thick hair and where that stopped, the wings of a large red and black tattooed eagle came down over his shoulders.

I longed to touch it, but my hands were tied; I longed to lick it, but they wanted my mouth for other things.

My body was stretched along the bed and Mo pulled my head into his lap and pushed his penis between my lips. I sucked willingly. Behind me, Ratchett lay against my back and entered me from behind, sighing as he sank upon my buttocks.

They used me this way for a long time and I wondered, and worried, whether they would eventually sodomise me, for I had heard that that was the practice in prison.

The thought of Ratchett sodomising someone in a cell not much bigger than this made my insides churn wickedly, and I groaned, even with the prick in my mouth. They both sensed my excitement and, behind me, Ratchett fucked harder and I pushed back against him.

His tempo quickened and my inner heat climbed to boiling point. I exploded into my second orgasm, shaking furiously and dislodging Mo's penis from my mouth.

When I had finished they changed positions. Mo stretched me on my back, my hands again above my head, lifted my legs onto his shoulders, and drove home.

This time, I could not contain my cry and my voice echoed through the house. He had lasted a long time and was now on his final run; I recognised it in his sweating face and my staring eyes urged him to reach his goal as I gasped with every thrust.

Standing alongside, watching my face intently, was Ratchett.

When Mo came, a noise almost of strangulation

came from his throat, as if someone had suddenly cut off his air supply. He shuddered and his penis pulsated and his discharge emptied into me.

He rolled away gasping and my legs flopped uselessly upon the mattress. Ratchett knelt by my side and unfastened the belt and freed my wrists. He took my hands and placed them upon his weapon and I caressed it.

'Suck it,' he said, and I willingly rolled onto my side and dipped my head and suctioned the head of his prick into my mouth. He gripped my hair in both hands and fucked my face as if, once more, to prove his control and power. But that was all right: I adored the control and power of this awful man.

It was not Ratchett that I adored, of course, but the alien idea of entering an underworld where strange life forms existed; an underworld where I could sample the basest of experiences.

He pulled my head up and lay me back on the mattress. His hands leisurely touched me, breasts, vagina, buttocks. A finger pressed into my anus and my eyes widened. He grinned.

'Don't worry,' he said. 'I don't do that.'

In one sense, I was delighted to have him reassure me – it was almost like an acceptance into his world. On the other hand, at that moment I could think of nothing better than to have been sodomised.

Ratchett stretched out upon me again and pushed his still swollen member between my legs and into my hot stickiness. At last I was able to stroke his shoulders and touch the wings of the eagle.

He began to fuck me, his strokes regular. I raised my head and licked his neck. He laughed and fucked harder, raising himself above me on his arms.

I ran my fingernails through the thick hair on his chest and felt a tremor of reaction. The next time, I dug my nails into the skin below the hair and he groaned and fucked harder still.

Our bodies squelched and slapped together. Moans and groans escaped our throats. I wrapped my legs around his and gouged his back with long raking strokes from my fingernails. He howled and pounded me and I howled back and he drove me into orgasm. I continued howling as he rose above me like an eagle, gulping for air, and pulsed out his seed.

Ratchett collapsed upon me and, slowly, I once more became dimly aware of the rest of my surroundings. Mo had gone. I wondered what time it was, where my husband was, and if we would now be allowed to leave.

Now I wanted to leave. The excitement had gone, been replaced by tiredness and a deep sexual satisfaction that I knew would not last in my own world.

The man climbed from my body and pulled on his trousers, not bothering with any other garment. He stared at me quizzically, before he opened the door and left the room.

I got to my feet and staggered. My dress fell back into place but I felt totally worn and exhausted. The flesh of my breasts were red from where hands had mauled them and I knew my thighs and bottom must bear similar marks. I eased my breasts back into the

COMPULSION

brassiere, wincing because they were so sensitive, and fastened the buttons of the dress.

At the sink I dabbed my face with water. Slowly I raised my head to stare at myself in the mirror and saw a stranger. Had I done all those things? Had all those things been done to me?

My mind returned from the recent events and I blocked them out. I got my handbag and tried to restore at least a semblance of normality to my features with make-up and a hair brush. At last I was ready for that awful final confrontation.

I left the room and walked along the hall to where I had left my husband. The door was open and I could see Tom, half sitting, half sprawled upon the bed. Mo, back in T-shirt and jeans, was drinking from a mug again.

He said to Tom: 'Come on, me cock sparra'. Time you were off.'

Mo put down the mug and shook Tom by the arm. My husband raised his head and opened his bloodshot eyes.

'What?' he mumbled.

'Time to go home.'

Mo took hold of an arm and pulled him to his feet. Tom staggered and saw me in the doorway.

'Caroline?' he said, in surprise. 'Where've you been?'

Ratchett said: 'She wasn't feeling well. Had to have a lie down.'

'A lie down?'

Tom stared around as if trying to remember why

he should be worried but Mo was half carrying, half dragging him to the door. Ratchett made no attempt to help but, just before Tom and Mo reached the doorway, he turned his back on them. Tom's eyes blinked as he tried to focus on the fresh weals down Ratchett's back.

'What...?' he said, before Mo got him through the door.

I waited until they had gone past me and begun their descent of the stairs, then stared in through the open door at Ratchett. I think I was waiting for some sort of acknowledgement: that I was an accomplished lover, that I was acceptable as a person, something. Even goodbye would have been enough.

But he said nothing. He glanced up and saw me, then looked away with a smile on his face and walked out of my sight.

When I got downstairs, Mo had taken Tom's keys from his pocket and opened the car.

'Hope you can drive, gel,' he said, and pushed my husband into the back where he slumped across the seats.

I took the keys and drove away. Mo remained on the pavement outside the row of houses awaiting demolition, his hands on his hips, his muscles rippling with the laughter that shook his body.

We did not go to our second engagement. We went home. I managed to get Tom into our apartment where he collapsed on the living room floor.

I ran a bath and began to undress, realising for the first time since leaving the house that I wore no panties beneath my dress. Normally I would have been scandalised at the thought of being outside without such a vital garment, but now nothing seemed to matter.

Marks were still upon my body where the men had touched me and the lips of my vagina were still swollen. I touched myself there, almost as a gentle healing gesture but, to my shock, the touch immediately aroused me once more and the memory of the fierceness of the passion flooded back.

With an effort, I reburied it, had the bath, put on pyjamas and went to bed, even though it was still early. I chose pyjamas as a reaction against the erotic underwear I had been wearing earlier, and because I did not want to provide an excuse for provoking my husband's passions when he awoke.

I could not sleep and I could not rid myself of the sights and sounds and smells of that awful room, so I resorted to gin and television, and lay in bed drinking and watching until, at last, I fell asleep.

Of course, I could not escape my dreams and when I awoke, I imagined myself to still be upon the mattress beneath the hard physiques of the two men, for someone was attempting to gain entry into my body.

When I opened my eyes, I saw it was my husband, half undressed, his eyes red and angry. The bedclothes were pulled back and he had already removed my pyjama bottoms.

It was obvious we both had hangovers and I was disinclined to fight him, although his attentions were distasteful. He was between my legs, attempting to insert a flaccid penis into me. I lay there and let him, until he rolled off me, having failed.

I pulled the cover back over myself and went to sleep once more.

The next day, Tom went to the office before I got out of bed. I heard him moving around the apartment but feigned sleep when he looked into the bedroom.

That night, his secretary called to say he had to work late. By the time he came home, I was again in bed and feigning sleep. I felt him alongside me, touching me, but not daring to disturb me. Eventually, he lay alongside me and masturbated until he came.

We avoided personal interaction and direct conversation for the next few days until enough time had passed for us to pretend nothing had ever happened.

Two weeks later, he took me away for the weekend and we had sex for the first time since Ratchett's party. Tom could not leave me alone the whole time we were away and yet he never asked me what, if anything, had happened.

He has never asked me, not out loud, but the question has been there ever since.

That is the end of my confession.

Chapter 20

They all gathered once more in the private library and Amy was surprised that Caroline looked different, as if a burden had genuinely been lifted from her.

Sir Alec opened a bottle of champagne and they toasted her.

She laughed in embarrassment at the attention.

'Feel better?' the tycoon asked.

'Oddly enough, I do.'

'And aroused?'

'That, too.'

'I think we all are.'

'All?' Caroline said.

Sir Alec smiled urbanely.

'I have a small confession of my own to make. Father Michael was not behind the grill, I was.'

'I should have known.'

The young man was even redder in the face than before and had developed a slight twitch in his right eye.

'But our young friend really did hear your confession.' The smile broadened. 'Along with Amy.

It was relayed into the annexe.'

Caroline looked at Amy, who grinned.

'How convenient,' she said.

Amy held up three fingers that looked distinctly sticky.

'I came three times,' she said proudly.

Father Michael coughed.

Sir Alec said: 'I suspected you might. Which is why I had a camera recording the fact.'

The young man said: 'Oh dear.'

Amy laughed.

'I begin to feel more like Alice ever day.'

'Perhaps you would like to watch it now?'

Caroline said: 'I would.'

'Oh dear,' said Father Michael. 'I wonder if I could be excused, Sir Alec? I believe you said you had a swimming pool? I feel in need of exercise and cold water.'

'Of course, my boy. Off you go.'

After his departure the girls both laughed.

'Did you?' Caroline asked.

'If you mean, did I seduce him, then the answer is no. But I gave him food for thought. His cassock was jumping like he had a rabbit beneath it.'

'You wicked girl,' said Caroline.

'I try to be.'

Sir Alec was attending to the television set and operating buttons on a remote control.

'Ladies, if you will take your seats, we can watch this small entertainment and hear again the rather inflammatory story of Mrs Penrose.'

Caroline and Amy sat side by side on the sofa,

while Sir Alec relaxed in an armchair.

Amy said: 'The two men who had you, was it good?'

'Good? It was fantastic.'

The film started at the same time as Caroline's soundtrack confession.

They watched Father Michael squirm as Amy became more and more abandoned as the story unfolded. In the final moments of the story that Caroline had related, Amy's skirt was around her waist and she was using both hands between her legs. Her groans mingled delightfully with Caroline's voice as she came for a third time.

Father Michael's knuckles showed white as they gripped the sides of the chair, his legs rigid before him, his body half bent as if in abdominal pain, his eyes fixed upon the sight of this blonde angel masturbating openly before him.

Sir Alec pressured the remote control and switched off the tape and the television.

Amy said: 'When I make my confession, can it be to Father Michael?'

The tycoon smiled.

'We have moved from if to when, my dear. Congratulations. Yes, of course you can have Father Michael.' He smiled at the double meaning. 'I am sure he would be delighted.'

Caroline, whose insides were liquid with desire from talking about sex and watching Amy so blatantly tempting the young man, addressed Sir Alec.

'You said I would be required to accept certain treatment or an undertaking.'

The more bizarre the better, she thought. She had begun to enjoy being told what to do.

Sir Alec said: 'I do have a task I wish you to perform. It involves a junior executive at my London office called Stephanie Lawler. Ms Lawler is an attractive woman who has no scruples when it comes to using her considerable charms in the furtherance of her career. She sometimes works with your husband. Perhaps you know her?'

His look was one of polite enquiry but Caroline sensed there was more behind it.

'No. I do not know her.'

'I have arranged for her to be brought here. She believes the purpose of her visit is to be interviewed by my new head of personnel.' He smiled. '*You* are my new head of personnel, Mrs Penrose, although she will not be given your real name or identity. She will be told you have the power to hire, fire and groom for stardom. I would like you to discover how far this young woman is prepared to go on behalf of the company and her own self-interest.'

The terms of his challenge were still nebulous in Caroline's mind.

'What exactly do you want me to do?'

'That is the point. How you play the role is in your hands. To make the situation believable, I have made arrangements for an office to be prepared for you. I even propose to make a cameo appearance myself, in support of your authority, but the rest is up to you.'

'More games, Sir Alec?'

'People play games all the time. They adopt roles

for each situation in which they find themselves. Life is a series of games, Mrs Penrose, the secret is in knowing that you are a player and not a pawn.'

'How nicely put.'

'I do my best. Now, if you will allow me to show you to your office?'

He led them out of the private library. Amy locked the door behind them and they followed him down the corridor to the room that Caroline knew so well. It had been a bedroom the night she had entered it with Jean-Paul and a drawing room on the occasion when she had entertained the two gentlemen from the Caribbean. Now it was an office.

A large and impressive leather-topped desk had pride of place. Behind it was a swivel chair of proportionate size. The sofa remained and two hard-backed chairs faced the desk. The sideboard also remained, with its drinks display intact.

Caroline looked at the large mirror.

'I take it you will be watching as usual from the other room?'

'Actually, no,' he said. 'But someone will.' He caught her glance. 'No, not Amy.'

'So who will be watching?'

'Your husband.'

'My husband?'

'Yes. I have also requested that he attend here this afternoon. But neither he nor Ms Lawler are aware of the other's presence. It is, I think you must agree, a situation filled with possibilities.'

Caroline nodded. The tycoon's planning made a

great deal of sense if she used only a modicum of hypothesis. It seemed as if he was delivering to her, for her use and amusement, both her husband and her husband's mistress.

'It is certainly that,' she said. 'What reason has been given to my husband for his attendance here?'

'The same as that given to Ms Lawler. He will also be told that you are the new head of personnel, with direct access to me.' He smiled. 'That may confuse him as much as being asked to wait in a room with a view. But people are a trifle more easy to manipulate when they are off balance, don't you think?'

'I am a trifle off balance myself, Sir Alec.'

'I have every confidence in you, Mrs Penrose. You have blossomed over the last few days. Just allow yourself to take control. You have always had the ability and now you have the power. Use it.' He smiled again and, as ever, he added: 'Enjoy.'

He began to leave the room and Amy gave her an affectionate kiss on the cheek for luck and followed him.

At the door he turned back and said: 'You have ten minutes to acclimatise to your new position. When you are ready to begin, press the button on the desk.'

They left and Caroline went behind the desk and sat in the swivel chair. The expanse of leather on the desk stretched in front of her like a protective castle wall.

The woman she was to meet was, she was sure, her husband's mistress. That alone might have made her feel at a disadvantage only a week ago. She was also a junior executive with a highly successful and competitive company in the City, which meant that Ms Lawler was similarly successful and competitive.

Again, a week ago such a confrontation would have left her shaking with nerves. But she had a new self-confidence, she was forearmed with knowledge of infidelity, and she was in a position of power.

Caroline smiled and began to enjoy.

There was a leather-bound folder on the desk and a fountain pen lying on top of it. Nearby was a cardboard file with the name of Stephanie Lawler printed upon it. She opened the file and looked at the photograph that stared out at her.

Stephanie was an attractive girl with dark hair, large, wide eyes that looked bigger still behind large spectacles, and a generous mouth.

A brief outline, that appeared to have been specially prepared for Caroline, said the girl was aged twenty-five, had attended a public school before university, was fluent in French and German and had a desire for travel as well as promotion.

Caroline closed the file, but pushed it across the desk so that it lay in a prominent position, picked up the fountain pen and opened the leather-bound folder which contained a foolscap pad. She pressed the bell that was on the edge of the desk and began to write.

Chapter 21

The door opened and Caroline was aware that someone had entered, closing the door behind them. She continued writing and did not look up.

'My name is Stephanie...'

Caroline continued to write with one hand but raised the other, palm outstretched as if she were a policeman stopping traffic. She still did not speak or look up but pointed with one finger towards the chairs. The young woman coughed and took a seat.

The fountain pen was beautiful and she enjoyed writing with it on the hard, shiny paper – and she enjoyed the discomfort of Stephanie Lawler.

At last, Caroline screwed the top back onto the fountain pen, put it down on the desk and closed the folder. She looked up and could see the nervousness in Stephanie's face.

'You are?' she said.

'Stephanie Lawler. I was told...'

This time she stopped her with one raised finger, before she reached across the table to pull towards her the file that the young woman had undoubtedly already noticed. She opened it and pretended to read its contents.

A knock at the door made her look up and Stephanie Lawler look round. The door opened and Sir Alec Ramsden put his head round.

'Sorry to disturb you, Caroline. I wonder if I could snatch a word of advice?'

'Of course, Alec.'

The tycoon crossed the room and Stephanie got to her feet in his presence. Caroline remained seated. Sir Alec smiled absentmindedly at the girl and went round to the far side of the desk. He placed a document upon it and leaned over Caroline's shoulder confidentially.

'The Tokyo appointment,' he said. 'Is it to be Walters or Mathieson?'

The finger of the hand holding the document pointed to a name.

'Mathieson,' Caroline said without hesitation.

'Yes, you are probably right. I will have him notified this afternoon.' He looked up at Stephanie, as if remembering there was someone else there, and smiled again. 'Sorry for interrupting. I'll leave you to it.'

He left the room and the girl resumed her seat. Caroline could see she was impressed by the neat subterfuge.

'How long have you been with the company, Stephanie?'

'Three years. Three very enjoyable years.'

'Yes. Of course.' She gave her a tired smile. 'Are you ambitious?'

'Naturally. That is why this company was my first choice. It is the leader of its field and, with the dynamism of Sir Alec at its head, it is no secret that it will stay there. In such a company, there will always be opportunities for talent to be given its chance.'

Caroline closed the cardboard file.

'You have been told I am head of personnel.'

'Yes.'

'You are aware that Sir Alec has been known to use unorthodox methods in the past?'

'Of course.'

She smiled at the girl.

'He continues to use them in choosing the right people for the right job.'

The girl nodded.

'I believe that a company needs the right corporate image. It needs attractive people in the right positions of power.' She picked up the fountain pen, tapped it on the folder and stared coldly at the girl. 'Anybody who attains a high-profile position in this company, should have personal dynamism and sexual magnetism. Their qualities should reflect the dynamism of the company. Don't you agree, Stephanie?'

'Er, yes, of course.'

'I am a great believer that the sex drive is linked to ambition. Do you have a high sex drive, Stephanie?'

The question took the girl unawares.

'I . . . suppose so.'

'I am not looking for false modesty of any kind, Stephanie. I want the top five per cent of achievers in my team, and the top five per cent are invariably highly sexed. I shall ask you again. Think carefully about whether you wish to answer the question at all and, if you do, whether you intend telling me the truth. Do you understand the question, Stephanie?'

'Yes, I do.'

'And are you highly sexed?'

'Yes.' Her eyes took on a hard glint although she blushed. 'I am.'

'You enjoy sex?'

'Yes.'

'Of all kinds?'

'Yes. I do.'

'In all circumstances?'

'Yes.'

The girl's answers were becoming breathless.

Caroline paused and held her gaze.

'You really enjoy fucking, do you Stephanie?'

'Yes.' She licked her lips. 'I enjoy fucking.'

Caroline sat back and smiled, as if they had completed a test, and girl relaxed perceptibly.

'Why don't you call me Caroline?'

'Thank you.'

'And why not fix us both a drink? I'll have a vodka and tonic on the rocks.'

Caroline nodded in the direction of the bottles and glasses on the sideboard and Stephanie immediately got up and went to mix the drinks.

The girl was petite, probably no more than five foot three in high heels, but she had a good shape. She wore a charcoal grey business suit of tight skirt and double-breasted jacket without a blouse beneath it.

'You are very attractive,' Caroline said.

'Thank you.'

'Do you get much harassment from men at the office?'

'Nothing I can't handle.'

'Do you fuck at the office?'

For a moment, the girl's new-found composure wobbled and she dropped an ice cube. She glanced across the room at the head of personnel.

'Yes. I occasionally fuck at the office.'

Caroline smiled.

'It can be invigorating, can't it?'

Stephanie smiled, more sure of herself.

'Very.'

'Have you ever indulged in group sex?'

A shadow of doubt passed across her face again but she decided to tell the truth.

'No. I haven't.'

'You should try it.'

The girl nodded, as if promising that she would.

'Have you ever fucked two men at the same time?'

By now, she had prepared herself for more shock tactics. She carried the drinks across and handed the vodka and tonic to Caroline.

'Yes. At university. It happened after a party and I'd had a lot to drink.'

'Did you enjoy it.'

Stephanie held her eyes this time.

'I would have enjoyed it more if I had not been drunk.'

The girl resumed her seat and they sipped their drinks.

Caroline raised her glass.

'Perfect,' she said.

'Thank you.'

'These questions do not embarrass you?'

'No.'

'But you do not understand their relevance?'

'I'm not sure.'

She was reluctant to admit that she had not got a clue.

'Modern business is not just done in the boardroom with balance sheets. It can be effectively done in bedrooms between the sheets. It can be done even more effectively bending over an office desk. I am not suggesting that my executives should prostitute themselves, but neither would I condemn any of them for using all their God-given talents to the best interest of the company.

'The right sexual person in the right executive job can influence clients and opposition with their body language, never mind fucking the president. It's attitude and sexual drive. The centre of man and woman's universe is the genital region. Work on that and everything else will take care of itself. Of course, you have to have the other abilities as well.'

'Of course.'

'You have the looks. Your file says you have the other abilities. I have to decide where the centre of your universe lies.'

They both drank. Caroline took a sip; Stephanie took a gulp.

'Would you stand up, Stephanie?'

'Yes, of course.'
'Would you remove your spectacles?'
She took them off and placed them on the desk.
'That is a very nice suit.'
'Thank you.'
'Please take it off.'
'Pardon?'

Caroline did not repeat the request, but sat back and continued to sip the vodka and tonic.

The girl slowly unbuttoned the jacket and removed it. She looked round before deciding to put it on the chair. Her bra was black lace; her breasts curvaceous. Caroline did not react and the girl's hand went to the waistband of the skirt. She unfastened the button and the zip at the side, then pushed it down over her hips and stepped out of it. That went on top of the jacket.

Stephanie wore black panties that were cut high at the side, a matching suspender belt and dark grey stockings. Colour had returned to her cheeks but she also had a look of defiance in her eyes.

Caroline put down the drink, got out of the chair and walked round the desk.

'That took a lot of nerve, Stephanie. Well done. But you have no need to be bashful. You have a beautiful body.'

The flush changed slightly, as if she were pleased with the praise, and her shoulders straightened.

Caroline stood alongside her and touched her shoulder. The look in the girl's eyes changed again, as if in nervous anticipation.

'No need to worry, Stephanie. I am not a lesbian.'

She leaned forward and kissed the girl's shoulder. 'But I do admire beauty.' Her hand slid down into the small of her back and down again, over the curve of her buttock. 'And you really are beautiful.'

The girl's breathing changed.

'Do you like being touched, Stephanie?' Caroline's other hand crept up her body at the front to cup a breast over the brassiere. 'Have you been touched by a woman before?'

'No.'

Her voice was small.

'By a girl, perhaps, at school?'

'A long time ago.'

'Was it good?'

'At the time, I thought so.'

'Of course it was. Male, female, it doesn't matter. It's all sex.'

The hand holding the breast relinquished its grip and slid down over her stomach, over the lace of the panties and suspender belt. Its fingers followed the crease where Stephanie's thigh met her body, the crease that led down and inwards towards her vagina.

Caroline's voice had dropped to a whisper and her mouth was close to the girl's ear.

'I envy you your body, Stephanie. I envy you your youth and all the sexual enjoyment that awaits you. You are so beautiful.'

Her fingers reached their destination and still there was no resistance from the girl. Caroline licked her lips and wondered what her husband was thinking as he watched from the two-way mirror.

She bent down to kiss Stephanie's ear, her tongue licking inside and, as the girl shuddered, her fingers went beneath the panties and found her vagina was already wet.

One finger slid inside and, even though Caroline had never done this before with another woman, she felt totally in control because the girl expected her to be in control.

The finger delved deeply and the girl gasped. As it withdrew it ran its wetness up the furrow and over the bud of the clitoris. Stephanie opened her mouth and her eyes half closed. Caroline took her in her arms and kissed her.

Any thoughts of resistance had been banished and the girl responded passionately. Their mouths moulded together and their tongues entwined. Stephanie opened her legs and wrapped them around one of Caroline's thighs so that she could rub her pubis against her.

Caroline continued to speak, breathing the words into Stephanie's mouth.

'I was right,' she said. 'You are highly sexed, aren't you?'

'Fuck me,' breathed back Stephanie.

'All in good time.'

Caroline's hand slipped between them and this time was more forceful. It parted the lips of her sex and two fingers dug inside her, eliciting a moan that was part-pleasure and part-theatrical. The girl moved herself against the hand and there was nothing theatrical about her body language now, as she squirmed and thrust against the fingers.

When she seemed to be close to coming, Caroline moved her hand and kissed her deeply to calm her down. She was still in charge, after all. She put her hands on Stephanie's shoulders, pushing her down, and the girl dropped to her knees.

'Remove my panties,' she said.

The skirt of the beige dress was full and Stephanie lifted the material and eagerly went beneath it, dropping the material over her head.

Caroline faced the mirror, knowing that her husband was watching his half-naked mistress beneath the skirts of his wife. She closed her eyes in pleasure as the girl's hands delved around between her legs, as if exploring a wonderland: stroking her buttocks, opening her sex, slipping a finger inside. Her mouth left a wet trail across her thighs above the stockings.

Her fingers tugged at the white briefs and eased them over her bottom. As they came down, the girl's mouth went above them, to lick at the soft flesh of her inner thighs and probe towards her open vagina.

Stephanie's tongue was like a delicious viper, darting in and out, and it was Caroline's turn to groan. She gripped the girl's head through the material and held it whilst she pushed herself against her, mouth to sex mouth.

She stopped short of an orgasm and released the girl, stepping out the briefs as she emerged from beneath her skirt.

They kissed again and exchanged words on their breath.

'I think you are destined to go far,' whispered Caroline.

'Fuck me,' replied Stephanie. 'Do anything you want, but fuck me.'

'I think what we both need is a stiff cock.' She kissed the girl again. 'I have someone else to see. Another executive.' She smiled into her face. 'You are both up for the same posting, but he is a mere male. Why don't we put him through his paces together and see how he makes out?'

Caroline's tongue bridged the fractional gap between their mouths to lick along Stephanie's bottom lip, as if in promise that the girl's future was assured.

Her eyes, still heavy with lust, contained a hint of suspicion that her position could be undermined.

'What do you say?' Caroline whispered with a smile. 'Shall we fuck him dry?'

Stephanie regained her assurance in her own sexuality.

'Whatever you say, Caroline.' She returned her kiss. 'You are the boss.'

They broke apart.

Caroline said: 'I will get him. Why don't you take the bra and panties off and fix yourself another drink. If you are nonchalantly naked by the vodka bottle, it's bound to put him off balance. And people who are off balance are more easily manipulated.'

Stephanie laughed and reached behind her to unclip the bra as 'the boss' left the room.

Caroline was full of sex and power and control – it

was a marvellous feeling. She went into the room next door to be confronted by her husband, standing red-faced and open-mouthed by the two-way mirror.

'That is not a pose that suits you, Tom,' she said.

'What the hell do you think you are doing?'

'And that is no way to address a superior. I have been close to Sir Alec for some time, in an undercover capacity. You heard what I told the delightful Stephanie. Sex does play an important role in business and if you can't get it up, you are going to have a problem getting anywhere with this company.'

'Caroline, have you gone mad?'

'We have been through this before.' Her mantle of authority was comfortable. 'I really am head of personnel. If you cannot live with that, you may leave now and tender your resignation forthwith.'

'You cannot mean that?'

'Tom, this is not your wife speaking. This is not even your housekeeper speaking. This is your superior speaking. Now, make your mind up.'

'I can't believe . . .'

Caroline looked at the ceiling impatiently.

'And I cannot waste time on executives who are unable to make decisions. Clear your office as soon as you get back to London.'

She began to turn away.

'No, wait.' She looked back at him. 'It's just that this is all such a shock.' He looked through the mirror. 'Stephanie and everything.'

'You know Stephanie, of course, but she does not know my identity. I prefer to leave it that way. Now, are you coming? Stephanie is in need of a good fucking.'

'You mean you want me to . . .?'

'I most certainly do. And you will give a first-class performance if you value your job.'

'But . . .'

'There are no more buts.' She started through the door. 'You come with me, do as you are told and fuck Stephanie, or you leave now. Your choice.'

He followed her, still nervous in his light grey suit, pulling at a shirt collar that was suddenly too tight.

The entered the office-drawing room. Stephanie was leaning against the sideboard with a glass in her hand. The sight of her lover caused her eyes to widen a fraction, but otherwise there was no sign of their intimacy. Caroline gave her credit for composure.

'Stephanie, I think you know Tom Penrose. I have just given him a brief outline of the company placement policy.'

'Hello, Tom.'

The girl walked across the room on her high heels, her breasts bouncing, and held out a hand to shake as if they were at a board meeting.

Tom took her hand briefly.

'Stephanie,' he said.

Caroline put her arm around Stephanie's shoulders and closed her right hand over the fingers that held the glass. She lifted it to her own mouth to demonstrate their intimacy by sharing a drink.

The girl preened against her in response.

'Stephanie and I decided we need a prick,' Caroline said, aware of her choice of words. 'Perhaps you would undress and provide us with one, Tom?'

He still looked lost in his suit and shiny shoes, hair neatly laquered into place.

Caroline smiled.

'I realise we have a head start on you.' She bent down and kissed Stephanie on the mouth. 'And very good head it was, so perhaps it would be better if we started without you?' She smiled at her husband. 'Come and join us as soon as you are ready.'

She led Stephanie to the sofa that reminded her so powerfully of the two West Indians. Tom might not be able to match them, but the situation was certainly varied enough to be highly enjoyable.

Caroline lay the girl down and took the lead, kissing her mouth and neck and breasts, while her fingers went between her legs. She was extremely wet and took three fingers easily. How did she know to do all this, Caroline wondered to herself? It just came naturally.

Stephanie moaned loudly and rhythmically to the thrust of the fingers, her petite frame twitching madly on the sofa. Behind them, Tom was pulling off his clothes, excited by the scene despite discovering that his wife had become his boss.

This time, Caroline allowed the girl to reach her orgasm and she spasmed around the hand.

'Was that good?' Caroline asked.

'Marvellous,' she whispered breathlessly.

Caroline moved her from the sofa and took her

place. She raised her skirt to present her vagina to the girl who was now kneeling between her legs.

'Suck, you little sex machine,' she said. 'Do what you do so well.'

Stephanie dipped her head willingly and her mouth enveloped Caroline's sex, the delicious viper's tongue going straight to work. Behind her Tom was now naked, except for his socks and shoes, and had a respectable erection. He was preparing to join them until Caroline, with an imperious finger, pointed at the offending articles. he obediently pulled them off and waited for permission to approach.

'Come and join us, Tom.' Caroline smiled distantly as she enjoyed the girl's wicked tongue. 'Stephanie wants fucking.'

He knelt behind the girl, his erection in his hand, and she moved her hips to accommodate him. He slotted it home and his thighs slapped against her buttocks.

'Fuck her well,' Caroline said. 'She needs it.'

Perhaps her husband was responding to the challenge in her voice, perhaps he was intensely excited by the sight of his mistress performing loud and lascivious oral sex upon his wife, perhaps he enjoyed being ordered about. Caroline did not know the reason, but he summoned energy she did not know he possessed to pound away at the small girl from behind.

Caroline enjoyed lying back and watching. The combination of bodies had been her decision and Stephanie really was very good with her mouth. Perhaps she could recommend a posting to Lesbos. She felt her own climax approach and allowed it to steal up gradually and tilt her over the edge.

It was another plateau orgasm, but immensely satisfying for the way in which it had been achieved.

Stephanie raised her face from between Caroline's thighs and looked up her body. Caroline blew her a kiss.

'Delicious,' she said.

She extricated herself and left her husband still fucking the girl from behind as she leaned onto the sofa.

'Do it as you will,' she said to them both, 'but do it. I want a fuck to the finish.'

Caroline refilled her glass with vodka and tonic and went back behind the desk, upon which lay her white briefs, resumed her seat in the swivel chair and watched.

Stephanie and Tom appeared to be locked in a battle of stamina and sexuality, for whatever reasons, and they displayed animal lust as they went at each other's bodies. First Tom was on top and then the lithe Stephanie rode him; he copulated with her mouth so fiercely that Caroline worried in case he might damage her, but she had revenge by locking his head between her thighs.

They fucked and sucked and pulled and heaved until Stephanie's breath was rendered from her in yelps and screams, until his breath was a gasp this side of collapse. She came many times; he came once and revived swiftly to maintain the competition.

Even from the other side of the room, Caroline

could smell them and she was intoxicated by their adrenaline and lust. Her hand went beneath the desk and beneath her skirt and she indulged in masturbation as Amy had taught her.

Finally Tom orgasmed again, against his wishes but beneath the fingers and mouth and viper's tongue of Stephanie. He fell exhausted onto the sofa and she got to her feet, put her high heels back on, and went and poured herself a drink.

Her body was streaked with sweat, her hair was tangled and her breathing was extremely shallow.

'Is there anything I can do for you, Caroline?' she said.

'No thank you, my dear. You have done splendidly. There is a bathroom down the corridor on your left. Please, feel free to relax in a hot bath. You deserve it.'

'Thank you.'

'And you can be assured that I will be making specific recommendations to Sir Alec regarding your potential.'

'Thank you.'

'When you have finished bathing and resting, I will have a car ready to take you home.'

The girl collected her clothing and belongings and looked back at Tom Penrose, lying naked and exhausted upon the sofa.

'Goodbye, Tom.'

He raised a feeble hand in farewell.

The girl left the room and Caroline walked from behind the desk to the sofa and looked down at her husband.

'When you are once more capable of walking, I wish you to get dressed and drive home and wait for me there. Remove your clothes and lay on the bed until I arrive. I do not wish you to wash. I want you to remain in this state so that I may lick the smells and secretions of that delightful girl from your body. Is that understood?'

'Yes, Caroline.'

'Good. And I want a performance from you this evening, to equal the one you have given here today.'

Caroline turned and left the room.

Chapter 22

Sir Alec and Amy toasted Caroline with more champagne in the dining room.

The tycoon said: 'You were superb, my dear. You have created for yourself a new career. As well as looking upon me as a friend, I hope you will accept the role which you, yourself, have created.

Caroline was surprised.

'What is that?'

'A genuine position as executive personnel officer, with special responsibility for making sure that the right executive is in the right job. I liked what you said: how did you put it? That the sex drive is linked to ambition; that sexually magnetic executive officers can reflect the magnetism of the company.

'You have a flare for image and a flare for handling people. I think you could do a fine job for me as a troubleshooter of lust. Of course, it will involve quite an amount of travelling to different parts of the world. What do you say?'

Caroline's smile filled her face.

'I would be delighted, Sir Alec.'

'Marvellous.' He held out his hand and they shook on it. 'Welcome aboard, Mrs Penrose. I trust your judgement, tact and common sense. You will be directly responsible to me alone. It will give us chance, perhaps, to explore other avenues of mutual enjoyment in the future.'

'It will, indeed. I look forward to it.'

Amy said: 'What about your husband?'

Sir Alec spoke before Caroline replied.

'If I might interject. He is scheduled to go to Amsterdam tomorrow for three days. Might I suggest you go with him, Mrs Penrose? It will give you a chance to cast your expert eye over our Amsterdam operation.'

'That sounds like an excellent idea, Sir Alec.'

'Good. I will have a car collect you both in the morning, to take you to the airport. The driver will have the tickets and hotel reservations, files on our senior staff in Holland, your company gold card and a sufficient amount of ready cash to meet your needs.'

'As always, Sir Alec, you are extremely efficient.'

He smiled.

'That is why I own the company.' He put down his glass and prepared to leave the room. 'I will say goodbye for now, Mrs Penrose, and wish you all success in the future. I look forward to our next meeting.'

The tycoon bowed formally and left.

Caroline looked at Amy.

She said: 'It looks as if I am going to miss Vesuvius erupting.'

Amy shrugged.

'I will be here when you return,' she said.
'Will you?'
'I think so.'
'And Tarquin?'
'I don't know yet. But I rather like the idea of commuting to Barcelona at weekends. It provides options.'

Caroline said: 'So does Amsterdam.'

Amy grinned and added: 'And Paris, and Berlin, and Vienna, and New York, and Los Angeles, and I could go on for ever.'

'Why has he given me such a job?'

'Because he understands that the essence of life is sex. Because he can afford to and because he believes you are good with people. It is also because he enjoys playing the game of life. He is one man and there is only so much he can do, but you can play the game for him by proxy and bring home full reports, photographs, videos and perhaps, even confessions.'

Caroline finished her glass of champagne and put her glass on the table.

'But first,' she said, 'I have a husband to deal with.'

Amy said: 'Will you keep him?'

'For the moment. I think he may respond to being told what to do. It's in-bred in them, you know, at public school.'

'You think the marriage may work?'

'No marriage is perfect.' She smiled. 'But this is a definite improvement.'

Amy crossed the room and gave her a chaste kiss, for no other seemed appropriate.

The blonde girl said: 'I look forward to the next time we meet.'

'Will you have made your confession by then?'

'Yes.' Her lips puckered in a mischievous smile. 'I shall make it tomorrow, to Father Michael.'

'I wish I could be here to share it.'

'Do not worry. I will tell you all about it. Besides, the tapes will be in Sir Alec's private collection. We can play them together and Vesuvius will erupt.'

They laughed and kissed farewell. After she was gone Amy reflected upon the following day, now that she had committed herself to the confessional.

Did this mean that her father-in-law had won?'

Amy thought not. She preferred to believe that by this time tomorrow, they would both be winners.

Father Michael joined Amy and Sir Alec at dinner. He seemed refreshed after his swim.

He still wore his cassock, but Sir Alec had changed into a lightweight linen suit, and Amy had put on a pink silk shift that was knee length. She believed simplicity was best; particularly with a body like hers.

Amy said: 'I have decided I would like to make my confession tomorrow. Would that be suitable, dear father-in-law?'

Sir Alec nodded over a glass of claret.

'Perfectly suitable, my dear.'

'And may I make it to Father Michael?'

'But of course.' The tycoon looked across the table at the young man who had started blushing already. 'That is all right by you, isn't it Michael?'

He coughed.

'Certainly, Sir Alec.'

'Good. Then I would suggest we meet in the library about eleven-thirty.' He smiled over the rim of the glass at Amy. 'We can build up an appetite for lunch.'

They ate in silence for a while, as if each were mulling over their thoughts. Amy wondered at quite what she would say in the morning and kept shooting small glances at Father Michael, who seemed uncomfortable.

Her father-in-law was at ease and she wondered what role he would cast for himself in the penance that would follow her revelations. Until now, he had been content to be a voyeur rather than a participant.

At least, as he had said himself, if he did become physically involved she would be keeping it in the family.

Amy said: 'Father Michael, are you really a priest of some religion?'

The young man stared across the table at Sir Alec for guidance and the tycoon considered a moment before speaking.

'Michael is in a state of confusion. He believed he had a calling and answered it, and has spent two years in study and meditation. He is at that point where he has to make the decision whether to continue with a life of isolated contemplation, or whether to rejoin society.

'His problem is sexual, which is often the case for many men of the cloth. He is young and his libido is at its peak, particularly after such a long time of self-denial. There is no shame in discovering that he is not meant to spend the rest of his life in the sterilised safety of a cloistered world. But he must discover for himself if that is not meant to be; he must discover for himself where his true destiny lies.

'I invited him here to help him confront his desires. He will receive no greater temptations than can be found in this house. Tomorrow will be the culmination of a journey for both of you, Amy.

'If Father Michael decides his future does not lie with celibacy, that will not be a denial of his beliefs. Rather, it will be the release of a burden he has attempted to carry but for which he is no longer suited. If, on the other hand, he decides denial is the way forward, then he will have proved it in grand fashion.'

Father Michael concentrated on his pudding, embarrassed by the disclosure.

Amy smiled. It added even greater piquancy to her confession, for she was already sure of the outcome. She knew that the young man had already made his decision, but had not yet admitted it to himself. She felt it was her duty to convince him.

The meal complete, Sir Alec retired to his own apartments and Amy suggested to Father Michael that they might take a short walk on the terrace. The rain had stopped and, although cloudy, the evening was very warm.

As they walked they looked across the lawns to the lake.

'Have you ever fucked a woman, Father?'

Even in the dim light she could tell he was blushing.

'I do not think that is a proper question for a young lady to ask.'

'But I am not a proper young lady, Father. I am most improper. Have you?'

It was a long time before he answered, but she waited, using the lengthening silence as a bludgeon to force a reply.

'No. I have never had carnal knowledge of a woman.'

'Have you ever fucked a man?'

'Good grief, no!'

'I am sorry if I offended you, but I thought that if you had been cloistered with other men for any length of time, you might have fallen victim to temptation.'

'Never.'

'So it is women that you find attractive?'

'Yes.'

His answer was qualified, as if he suspected he was being led into a trap.

'Do you find me attractive, Father?'

'Of course, my child. You are very beautiful.'

It began to rain suddenly from a summer cloudburst and the young man stepped beneath the portico of the building. Amy remained standing in the rain, allowing it to soak her thin dress.

'Would you like to make love to me, Father?'

'What sort of a question is that?'

'A straightforward one that demands only the truth in reply.' The rain had quickly saturated the dress and it now clung to the contours of her body. The chill made her nipples erect against the wet silk and she shook droplets from her long hair. 'Surely you may tell the truth and admit it? Admitting a fact does not constitute a sin.'

He nodded, tongue-tied. He could not take his eyes from her body.

'Of course I would like to make love to you, my child.'

'If you did, would that be a sin?'

'To me, it would indeed be a sin.'

'Even though I wanted you to make love to me? Even though, to me, it would not be a sin?'

'Even under those conditions.'

'And is sin a human condition, Father?'

'Yes, my child. It is a human condition.'

'And should sins be forgiven?'

'Of course, my child, they should . . .'

Amy smiled at him.

'Good, I thought they were. So tomorrow, when I confess, you can fuck me with a clear mind, Father, safe in the knowledge that sin should be forgiven, and then you can repent at leisure.'

'Oh, Amy,' he said, his eyes devouring her body. 'You are such a temptress.'

'Wait until tomorrow, Father Michael. And see if you can resist.'

At eleven-thirty the next morning, Amy walked into the library all in white, as if dressed as a bridesmaid.

Her knee-length pleated skirt and simple long-sleeved white blouse that buttoned to the neck were made of jersey silk. She wore ankle socks and flat shoes and had tied her hair behind her head so that it hung in a long, blonde ponytail. Her make-up, as ever, was minimal.

Sir Alec raised his eyebrows in approval and Father Michael's eyes widened without hope, as if he were a drowning man.

'You look absolutely stunning, my dear,' said the tycoon.

'Thank you, daddy,' she said, goading him one last time.

She felt nervous and longed for the game to start, longed to be able to slip into the cool, dark, illusion of privacy of the confessional box and begin.

Sir Alec sensed her mood.

'I think we have all waited long enough,' he said. 'Let us proceed.'

He unlocked the small door into the private library and she walked through ahead of Father Michael. Sir Alec locked the door behind them. For a moment they all stood around the room and stared at each other.

'Please,' he indicated the box. 'Let us take our places.'

Father Michael cast one last glance at the vision of loveliness that Amy presented – a vision that spoke of innocence and sweetness – and entered his side of the box.

Amy took a deep breath, exchanged a look with her father-in-law, and stepped into the confessor's side that she knew so well, where she had sat and fantasised alone.

The smell of dust and wood enveloped her and the outer door shut out distractions. It was like coming home. The only difference was that this time, beyond the grill, was a young man in a cassock.

Her lips were suddenly dry and she licked them and coughed softly. She knelt on the padded stool, leaned her head towards the shadow of the grill and began.

Chapter 23

Amy's Confession.
My name is Amy, and this is my confession. I have always been beautiful. I say this not from pride or conceit but because it is true. But my beauty acted as a barrier to a normal teenage sexual upbringing. My parents travelled a great deal and I went with them. We were never in one place long enough for me to have boyfriends or enjoy even mild flirtations.

Consequently, I was eighteen when I lost my virginity to my first real boyfriend. Gary was twenty-six and worked in television as an assistant producer. I was at college and attempting to survive on my own in a small flat in London. I was impressed with his job and the names he dropped into conversation and the fact that he took me to parties which were attended by minor celebrities.

Gary was good-looking and very self-assured, while I was still in awe of the circles in which we mixed and of his dominant personality. We had been going steady for two months when he told me I should be a model and introduced me to a photographer.

Maria Caprio

The photographer was called Mike and had a studio in Shepherd's Bush. He explained I would need a portfolio of photographs to submit to agencies and said he would be happy to take the pictures.

I left the arrangements to Gary and met him in the BBC bar at Shepherd's Bush at seven o'clock in the evening, when he told me he had fixed up a photographic session for that night. He assured me that I did not need any special clothes as Mike's studio had its own wardrobe department.

After a few drinks we went to the studio, which was a series of connecting rooms above a row of shops. It was centrally heated and extremely hot. Mike, who was trendy in sports shirt, shorts and bare feet, poured wine and we talked like old friends.

When I was ready, he showed me into a small dressing room and suggested I wear a swimsuit for the preliminary shots. I undressed and chose a one-piece costume and, after repairing my make-up, I walked out before them.

At first I was nervous, but then I began to enjoy being directed beneath the hot lights, particularly when Mike was shouting words of encouragement and telling me how great I was. I responded when he said look sexy or surprised and I got used to the poses he wanted me to adopt with extreme ease.

'That's a great start,' he said. 'But we need a variety. We also need sex.'

He said it in a matter-of-fact way, as he changed the roll of film in his camera.

Gary said: 'What do you mean sex?'

'I mean lingerie shots, maybe topless. There's a selection of underwear behind the screen.'

I had expected to show my body, although not totally nude, and underwear was only like swimwear, so I was not unduly worried. Behind the screen were boxes of lingerie but there was so much I could not decide.

Gary joined me and gave me an open-mouthed kiss, touching my bottom.

'Excited?' he said.

'Yes. It's fun.'

'Mike gives value for money. This will be a hundred pounds well spent.'

For a moment I was shocked.

'A hundred pounds?' I said. 'I did not know this was costing anything.'

'Of course. Mike's a professional.' His expression changed to one of concern. 'Don't you remember, he said a hundred pounds.'

I did have some recollection of that figure being mentioned, but I thought that Mike was doing it as a favour to me and Gary and that he was waiving his normal fee.

'I'm sorry,' I said. 'There has been a mistake. I do not have a hundred pounds.'

'Ah. That's a problem. Mike's already made an outlay by booking you the studio.' He touched my arm reassuringly. 'I'll see if I can work out a deal.'

I put on a dressing gown and felt embarrassed that I had already cost the photographer his time, equipment and studio hire. When I stepped out from behind the screen, Gary and Mike were talking on the far side of the studio.

My boyfriend came across to me.

He said: 'We have a deal. Mike will do the portfolio for nothing, if you let him take some shots he can sell.'

'But of course,' I said.

'Just a minute, Amy. He wants to take glamour shots of you. You know, lingerie, topless, maybe nude. There is a lot of money to be made from that type of photography and he knows he will be able to cover his costs if you agree.'

'Well...'

I was unsure of what I was committing myself to.

'Of course, you will get the percentage of everything he does sell.' He grinned. 'It would be your first professional modelling assignment.'

'Well, if you think it's all right.'

'Of course. I'm here, after all.'

'All right, then. I'll do it.'

Gary shouted to Mike: 'All systems go.'

'Great,' said Mike. He grinned as he walked towards us. 'Don't worry, it's painless,' he said.

He went behind the screen. Gary and I followed and watched the photographer choose underwear.

'Definitely white,' he said. 'We'll make the most of the young, virginal look.'

They left me to put on the articles he had chosen. There was a white bra whose half cups held my breasts without hiding the nipples, a suspender belt, white briefs and white stockings.

My boyfriend gave me a shock when he reappeared

without warning, carrying a white dress on a hanger and a pair of delicate white high-heeled sling-back shoes.

'You put them on so you can take them off,' he said.

Reluctantly, I put on the white underwear and the white stockings and shoes and dress, and checked my appearance in the mirror. Although I was eighteen, the pure white clothes made me look much younger. I stepped out from behind the screen.

Gary said: 'You look sensational. What do you think, Mike?'

He nodded in agreement.

'Absolutely perfect,' he said.

Their praise made me feel better and gave me confidence.

Mike led me to another part of the studio where a bed with a brass frame was lit by spotlamps.

'Sit on the edge of the bed, Amy,' he said, 'and look demure. Knees together, your hands in your lap.'

I did as I was bid and he took shots of me from several angles.

'Now stretch your legs out and lean forward as if you are looking at your shoes.'

When I did so, the low-cut blouse gaped and I knew my breasts were on show.

'Hold that position and look up at me.'

I did so, finding it easier to be directed than to think about what I was displaying.

'Brilliant, terrific,' he said, moving around me, taking photographs of my breasts. 'Great tits, Amy. Great tits. Look sexy, pout at me. Look as if you want your tits sucking. That's it, great.'

Next, it was my legs that became the focus of his attentions and I was required to pull the skirt up to my waist to reveal my limbs encased in stockings. My tan looked good where the stockings ended midway up my thigh.

Mike took more photographs and I fell easily into being directed. The incessant barrage of words was exciting.

'Look sexy, Amy. The men who see these pictures will want you. Imagine them, all those men, all those stiff pricks. Pout for them, make them believe you want fucking, Amy. Make them come quicker.'

The concept was thrilling and, after all, I was only modelling for a professional photographer and my boyfriend was my chaperone. I began to love it.

We had a break for more wine. I removed the dress and lay on the bed in the underwear and responded again to the directions and the dirty things Mike said but, eventually, he turned away in frustration, shaking his head.

'What's wrong?' I said, disappointed that he had stopped.

He turned back and stared at me.

'It's a waste,' he said.

'What do you mean?'

'We could make a fortune selling to Japan and the Far East. They love blondes, the younger and more innocent the better.'

Gary said: 'So? What's the problem?'

'They like simulated sex, bondage, stuff like that.'

I was fuddled with the wine, the heat and the excitement, but I knew what simulated sex was.

'You mean, I pretend to have sex?'

'Yes.'

'Who with?'

Mike looked at my boyfriend.

'With Gary.'

Gary said: 'Oh, now wait a minute. I'm no model.'

Mike put down his camera.

'You don't have to be. Everybody will be looking at Amy. You just have to pretend to be in a sexual situation with her.'

'I don't know,' he said and looked at me. 'It's all right for you two, you are both good at it. What do you think, Amy?'

He was right, I was good at it.

'I don't see why not,' I said. 'But what's bondage?'

Mike said: 'It's something the Japanese like. They like to tie their women up before they have sex.'

'Really? How uncomfortable.'

The photographer said: 'They find it stimulating. And if we mock up a few shots for them, I know an agency in Tokyo who will pay well.'

Gary said: 'Okay, let's try it. But you two will have to show me what to do.'

Mike said: 'First, Amy should change her outfit. I'll find something else.' He waved at the wine. 'Have another drink. It could be a long night.'

Gary and I had a drink and, in the absence of the photographer, he kissed me again and touched my body. I was already excited from having my picture taken and could not help but respond.

'I think I'm going to like this,' he said. 'I've never done it with an audience before.'

'It's supposed to be simulation,' I said.

'Of course.' His hands were on my bottom. 'It's just that this is stimulation.'

We were both hot for each other although we were treating the whole situation in a light-hearted way. I hoped we could go straight back to his flat after we had finished – he had not been as eager as this for a long time, even though our relationship was still relatively new.

Taking my virginity six weeks before had excited him, but since then he more often than not seemed to have had too much to drink, or pressure of work had made him sleepy. He had taught me how to fellate him and on those occasions when he was too tired to make love properly, he allowed me to use my mouth to bring him to orgasm.

Gary had not, in fact, given me an orgasm – I had never been given one, in any way, by a man. I had come to rely upon my own fingers for satisfaction, believing that this was the normal way of sexual relations.

But now his prick was extremely hard in his trousers and he had more energy than I had ever known. Perhaps, I hoped, this was the night I would attain a proper orgasm. But first, we had to get the photographic shoot out of the way.

Mike called me to the screen by the changing room.

'Put those on, darling, and wipe off all the make-up. Oh yes, and tie your hair back.'

On the table was a blue pleated school skirt, a white blouse a red and yellow school tie, white panties and knee socks and my own flat shoes.

I did as he requested, sipping the glass of wine I had taken with me behind the screen and tying my hair in two pigtails to heighten the youthful effect. When I looked in the mirror, I could have been back at school.

By now, I had forgotten that the prime motive of the evening was to procure a portfolio of photographs for my future career, and was carried away with Mike's sophisticated style and the thought of being a professional who sold to Tokyo.

My entrance stopped them both talking.

'Perfect, darling, perfect,' said Mike.

Gary had stripped and was now wearing only a pair of boxer shorts. He held a hand in front of him to hide the bulge they contained.

I was breathless with the heat of the lights, the wine and the continuing buzz of excitement that I had never known before. I was the centre of attention and I loved it.

'Right,' Mike said. 'Over by the bed. Gary, you sit on the edge and Amy, darling, you stand in front of him and look innocent.'

We assumed our positions.

'That's it,' Mike said. 'Now Gary, put your hands up her skirt and then lift it slowly.'

The lights were hot and Gary's hands were sweating when he put them beneath the skirt. He grabbed my bottom, feeling it, and he pulled my skirt up with both hands.

'No, no, no,' said Mike, putting down the camera. 'Look, I'll show you.'

Gary moved and Mike sat in his place. His expression was totally professional and I did not object when he placed his hands behind my knees.

'Do it in stages,' he instructed, 'and keep the action smooth.' He ran his palms slowly up my naked legs and over the white panties. 'Rumple the skirt up, like this, so I can get the shot of your hands.'

He went back to his camera. Gary resumed the position on the edge of the bed and Mike got the shots to his satisfaction.

'Now,' the photographer said. 'We take off her panties. Look, like this.'

They exchanged places again and Mike put his hands beneath the skirt in such a way that Gary could see what he was doing. Mike tugged down the waistband of the panties and slipped his hands inside. His palms slid slowly down over my bottom taking the panties with them. Then he tugged them lower, until they were mid-thigh around my legs.

'When you get here, I want you to put your hands back up and look as if you're enjoying it. You know, hands and fingers everywhere.'

He demonstrated, one hand groping the flesh of my bottom and the other moving around to the front to push between my legs. With a shock, I felt his fingers slide across my vagina. I was so hot, inside and out, that the lips of my sex opened at the touch and, more than anything, I was embarrassed that he might notice. As he withdrew his hand he most certainly did, and trailed a finger along the crease.

He stood up and smiled.

'You are doing great, Amy. Get hot, turned on. Project sex. Okay, Gary. Let's do it.'

He continued taking photographs and I got wetter between my legs. Now Gary noticed too and he had no compunction about pushing a finger inside me. It caused me to open my mouth and gasp.

'Brilliant! Great! Go, Amy, go. You've just discovered sex and you're turned on. Go for it, Amy. Go for it.'

Gary pushed two fingers inside me and Mike continued taking photographs.

'Get rid of the panties,' he said at last, and I stepped out of them. 'Leave them by the side of the bed. I'll get them just in shot next time, very emotive.

'Okay, now kneel down, Amy, in front of Gary. That's it. Gary, hold one of the pigtails as if you're forcing her. Right. It's oral sex this time, so you might as well get it out Gary. I think it needs the air.'

Gary laughed and I smiled nervously. He released his erection and it bobbed in front of my face.

'Now when I doctor these pix, there will be no rude bits on show,' Mike said. 'I don't care where you put it, Gary, but I want to pretend it's in her mouth. Okay, try it.'

This was going too far, but I could hardly back out now. Gary's penis was brushing against my cheek and I placed my hand in a strategic position at the opening of the jockey shorts and pretended I was fellating him.

'No, that's bloody useless. Come on, Amy, you can do it. Make it look good, give me sex. Sex, Amy, sex! Come on Gary, do something, stick it in her mouth if you have to.'

And he did. He held my head in position with my pigtail and pushed his erection into my mouth. I sucked.

'Great! Terrific, Amy. Come on, girl. Open your eyes wide. Look frightened. That's it. Let it bulge your cheek.'

He went behind me and pulled up the skirt until it was around my waist to expose my naked bottom and continued using his camera. I suddenly realised being a glamour model for Japan was not very glamorous, but it was very sexy. I was wetter than ever between my legs.

'Right, next position,' Mike shouted, his actions becoming edgy and frantic, his excitement and abruptness transferring to me and Gary. 'Amy, lie on the bed. On your back. Gary, use the pyjama cord to tie her wrists to the bedstead.'

We obeyed his directions as quickly as we could, caught up in the drama of our own making. Even then I believed this would all remain simulation.

I was helpless, the skirt around my waist, and Mike again demonstrated what he wanted by placing one hand on my breasts, groping first one then the other, his other hand between my legs.

'Get your fingers in there, Gary. That's it, Amy, writhe about on them, pretend you don't want them there.'

But I did and I was beginning not to care whose fingers they were.

Gary replaced Mike and groped me, his fingers digging into me, and I writhed and gasped and had another sudden thought about the embarrassing possibility of actually having an orgasm while all this was going on.

'Now,' Mike said, 'rip open the blouse, make those buttons ping.' Gary ripped it, his face heavy with desire. My breasts were exposed. 'Maul them, Gary. You're a rapist, not a gentleman. That's it. That's it. Come on, Amy. React, you bitch! React! Give me innocence defiled.'

He moved around the side of the bed, his camera clicking. When the film finished, he picked up another camera.

'Okay, now get rid of those shorts, Gary. That's it. Christ, I hope you can keep the erection. We don't want you going soft on us and losing interest, do we, Amy? And take off her skirt. That's it. The tattered shirt and tie and the knee socks – perfect. Now, get on the bed and push her legs up. Lift them, that's it. I want a simulation fuck here, Gary. Christ, you're useless. Get out of the way.'

My boyfriend got off the bed and Mike pulled off his shirt and shorts and revealed his own erection.

'You've got me going as well, darling,' he said. 'First time in years. You are going to be big.' Then, to Gary. 'Like this. Lift her legs and position your cock at this beautiful doorway to heaven.' I could feel the head of his penis lying against my vagina. 'Now simulate fucking. You can let it slip along her bum if you like.'

He demonstrated by pushing his penis between the crease of my buttocks. 'Or between her legs. She's wet enough. Whoops!' he said, and his penis went inside me.

Gary stood alongside us and watched as Mike knelt up on the bed, his penis embedded to the hilt inside me, my legs lying up his body with my feet on either side of his head.

'Well,' Mike said, and moved it inside me. 'Maybe this is a better way.' He grunted. 'Amy, you are a wonderful fuck.'

I lay there, senses reeling, aware of a desire in the pit of my stomach that was heightened by the fact that I was tied and could not ease it with my fingers; aware that my boyfriend watched while another man fucked me; aware that this other man's penis was causing waves of pleasure to course through my body.

Mike withdrew and I groaned in disappointment.

'You try,' he said.

Gary took his place, raised my legs and pushed his erection inside me. The pleasure waves began again and I did not care that Mike took photographs and shouted directions.

'Fuck her, Gary. Come on, Amy, give me sex. Show me lust in those angel eyes. Make them say, fuck me, fuck me, fuck me.'

Then he abandoned the camera and joined Gary on the bed, pretence gone, simulation gone, and he pushed his penis into my mouth and I sucked it happily because the waves of pleasure were climbing ever higher.

But, before I could orgasm, Gary came in my vagina, grunting and shuddering like a bear, leaving me stranded out at sea.

'Get the camera,' Mike shouted, as my boyfriend slumped off the bed. 'Get the shot.'

Gary picked up the camera and pointed it at my face.

'It's on automatic,' Mike said. 'Press the shutter when I say and hold it steady.' He panted as he pushed his penis in and out of my mouth. 'Now!' he yelled. He withdrew and began to ejaculate into my face.

My boyfriend pressed the shutter of the camera and I heard its electric motor whirr and click as it took shot after shot of the photographer's sperm spilling onto my features.

At last he had finished and climbed off the bed.

'Absolutely fantastic,' he said. 'You are doing great, Amy. Hang on there and we'll be with you in a minute.'

They left me tied to the bed, the sperm going cold upon my face as it ran down my cheeks and my neck, and had another glass of wine and a cigarette, while they discussed what they had done.

Eventually, Gary returned to the bed and this time actually did simulate sex with his limp penis against my body which was turned this way and that. Then their erections returned and Mike set a delayed action camera on a tripod to photograph them both using me at the same time.

By then my excitement had died, killed by their lack of concern. If I had attained my orgasm, if they had treated me like an equal, I would have willingly taken part in all they wished to do. As it was, I was a bondage victim who, after the excitement had died within me, refused to respond to whatever they tried.

I realised afterwards that my boyfriend and the photographer had been in collusion and that my feelings had never been their concern. They had simply wanted to reap their own pleasure. They might have attained some satisfaction but they were the losers for, handled correctly, they could have unleashed the passion that has been waiting within ever since.

My boyfriend and I finished and I moved away from his circle of acquaintances, but the taste of modelling had made me realise my own potential. I became a professional model, one of the best of my generation, and while I flaunted my sexuality I built around myself the protection of a reputation, refusing to trust the carnal desires of most men, soon becoming known as the Ice Maiden.

And yet, and yet. I regret so much that those two men who took advantage of me did not have the sense to treat me as an equal partner in their sexual escapade.

I have always been aware of the beauty of my body, that it was so marvellously made for sex. And I wanted so much to endure and enjoy all that I could. I wanted so much to be fucked, to embrace sex, to be dragged into its depths and experience every degeneration, to wallow in it and to emerge from it triumphant. I still do. I want to be fucked.

And that is my real confession.

Chapter 24

Amy was emotionally drained and it was several moments before she opened the door and stepped out into the private library.

Father Michael, his hands held protectively across the front of his cassock at genital height, had an expression of compassion on his red face.

Her father-in-law was not smiling for once.

'You are pale, my dear. Are you all right?'

'Yes, I am fine.'

'Well enough to accept my judgement?'

Amy licked her lips. It was a judgement such as this for which she had been waiting for years.

'Yes.'

'And will you accept the judgement?'

'I will.'

'Then let us retire to the annexe.'

Father Michael led the way into the small room, which was lit only by low red lights which made it claustrophobic. In the middle of the room was a small and strange table. It was about the same dimensions as a coffee table and the two ends and the top were of

Maria Caprio

one moulded piece of clear perspex. The ends were curved and the perspex looked as if it were a flattened letter C. To the base of this table was fixed a mirror.

Sir Alec stood in front of Amy and stroked her face gently with both hands. His fingers dropped to the blouse and, without further ado, he ripped it open.

Amy gasped in shock and her breasts jiggled in their sudden freedom.

Behind her, Father Michael pulled the remnants of the garment down her arms, quickly, as if preparing her for sacrifice, until she was totally naked to the waist.

Sir Alec pushed her into position, so that the back of her knees were against the curve of the perspex table.

'Take her,' he said.

Father Michael's hands held her shoulders and pulled her backwards and she sat upon the table. He pulled her again and made her lie upon it. She shuddered as her back touched its coolness.

Her father-in-law pulled her thighs towards him, so that the table supported her back and buttocks. He unzipped the skirt and tugged it down, again without finesse, and did the same with her white briefs, which had already become damp. While Sir Alec stripped her, Father Michael tied her wrists with silken cords to hooks attached to the base of the table.

Amy was now spread like a crab on its back. Her head lolled and her feet were on the floor. She wore only the knee socks and shoes. There was no way, even if she had wanted to, that she could have maintained a chaste position. Her vagina ached between her legs and, it seemed to her, that her insides gushed with lust.

'You have talked in tongues to Father Michael,' Sir Alec said, in a voice without expression. 'Tongues of temptation which he suffered in silence but in torment. Now you must suffer from tongues.'

He knelt at her feet and spread her legs. Her vagina opened like a flower before he touched it. His hands slid beneath her thighs and cupped her buttocks and he dipped his head and began to lick.

Amy moaned and tried to push herself against his mouth, but he was totally in control. He licked all round her most sensitive of areas, before making short, slippery forays into her wetness, nudging her clitoris with his nose as his tongue delved deep. And then his lips moved away, to the periphery of sensation, making her ache with desire and the knowledge that he would soon switch his ministrations to her core once more.

For those first, few moments, she forgot that Father Michael was kneeling at her head. Then he leaned over her and she smelled the incense of his cassock. His mouth began to devour her breasts, his tongue to lick and his teeth to nibble at her nipples.

The blonde angel howled against his chest.

Sir Alec was an expert at building and easing the tension at her vagina and yet, each time he retreated, he lifted her to a higher plateau of sensation than before. He was causing her desire to levitate steadily with his tongue.

Father Michael now moved his mouth to her neck

and face and she pulled against the bonds at her wrists, for she longed to embrace him and run her fingers through his hair. His lips were parted, his eyes glazed, his mouth salivating and he devoured her features as he had her breasts.

His tongue licked every inch of her face, her neck, her ears. It lapped at her nose, slid over her cheeks and into her mouth. Amy was salivating too, as if her juices were running from every orifice. He slobbered around her mouth so that the lower part of her face was soaking wet.

The young clergyman was grunting instead of breathing and when his mouth was not covering hers, Amy cried out with the rhythm of her father-in-law's tongue between her legs.

This time there was no holding back, this time the experience was a tidal wave that threatened to sweep her to oblivion.

Sir Alec sensed it and his mouth totally consumed her vagina. His tongue dug into the soft membranes inside and his nose rubbed against her clitoris.

Amy screamed and the pent-up passion of her frustrations were finally released. Father Michael held her head in his hands, his hot breath blowing into her mouth, and Sir Alec gripped her thighs and kept his mouth clamped in place. She shook as Vesuvius erupted.

When she was next aware of her surroundings, the two men were changing her position. Her wrists had been untied and now she was bent over the table face downwards, her knees on the floor. Her wrists were refastened.

COMPULSION

Now she could appreciate the design of the table. She could see the reflection of her body in the mirror below the perspex, from her squashed breasts to the curling hair that framed the pink slit of her vagina.

Alongside the table, Sir Alec undressed. She could not see him fully, but was aware that his legs were stocky and powerful and that he had a large erect penis growing from the curling grey hairs of his pubic region.

Amy got a better view of his penis when he knelt behind her and parted her thighs. She watched the reflection in the mirror as he manoeuvred the head of his weapon to the entrance of her vagina.

He gave it two or three gentle strokes along the wet opening and she quivered. A moan that could have been a plea escaped her throat.

'Do you have anything to say, Amy?'

'Fuck me. Please fuck me.'

He drove it inside with one long and powerful thrust.

As his penis went in, the breath left her body and she lay upon the perspex, impaled at one end, her mouth open and gasping for air at the other.

'Father Michael has made his decision,' Sir Alec said, not moving, his penis still embedded to the hilt. 'And he has a coming-out present for you.'

The young man kneeling by her head pulled aside the cassock to reveal that he was naked beneath it. A monstrous and palpitating penis stared her in the face. He took hold of it timorously in one hand, as if it might explode of its own accord.

'Amy,' he breathed. 'For what you are about to

receive, I hope you are truly thankful.'

With his other hand, he turned her head and presented his weapon. She opened her mouth and he slid it inside with a gasp. The blonde angel sucked once and that was sufficient.

Father Michael pushed and came, the head of his weapon touching the back of her throat, the force of his ejaculation causing her to swallow desperately for fear of being drowned, as two years of virgin sperm burst into her mouth.

All the time he shuddered his life's juice down her throat, he rocked on his heels and his voice keened as if in lament.

When he had finished, Sir Alec began to fuck her in earnest. She watched in the mirror as his engine of lust impaled her and was withdrawn, as its shaft heaved inside and his thighs and abdomen flattened her thighs and bottom. Each time it was withdrawn it was slicker than before and white with her secretions.

The young man had slumped back on his heels, his cassock open, his limp penis in his hand as if he held the remnants of a sacrifice. But, even as she watched, it began to stiffen and twitch with life again and she knew she was the sacrifice.

He knelt up and offered it to her face and she sucked it into her mouth.

They fucked her strenuously, in vagina and mouth, for several minutes, until she felt that neither entry had contours any more but that both were undefined caverns inhabited by slurping monsters of sex.

Suddenly, both pricks were removed and Father

Michael untied her wrists. She was rolled onto the thick rugs that lay alongside the perspex table and the young man once more used the silk cord to bind her hands together and push them above her head. That completed, he pulled off his clothes until he was naked.

Sir Alec knelt by her head, his knees straddling her arms, and allowed his erection to rest upon her forehead. Between her legs, Father Michael positioned himself. He raised her thighs and lowered his hips so that the head of his weapon nudged at her opening.

'Are you ready to accept Father Michael's second virginity?' Sir Alec said.

'Oh, yes,' said Amy. 'Please.'

She raised her hips and attempted to help the inexperienced cleric whose fumblings were a glorious torment as the penis ran across the sensitive gap and stroked her clitoris.

'Put it inside me! Please, inside me!'

He attempted to guide it with his hand and then it discovered its own way and began its inexorable slide into the cauldron of her vagina.

Amy screamed in triumph and Father Michael cried out in surprise at the heat that now enveloped his prick. She contracted around it as he attempted to pull back and suctioned it with all her membranes. He cried out a second time and came.

The thrust of his orgasm lifted her hips until he held her buttocks upon his abdomen. Father Michael did not withdraw after his sperm had gushed again, but remained embedded within her. His prick did not slacken or reduce and she continued her contractions around it, milking it with sensation, encouraging its strength.

Slowly, he began again to thrust in and out and she sighed with pleasure and tilted back her head to ease into her mouth Sir Alec's testicles, which she sucked and manoeuvred with great care and gentleness.

He emitted a gasp and his penis quivered against her chin. He eased the sensitive sac free, raised himself above her, and stroked her face with the wet end of his weapon.

Amy's mouth was open and her tongue darted out to lick at the shaft whenever she could. The sight caused Father Michael to groan as he laboured between her thighs and made him thrust deeper and fiercer still.

At last, Sir Alec allowed her to take him into her mouth and she sucked wildly again, dipping the tip of her tongue into the eye of his weapon and nibbling gently at the glans with her delicate white teeth until he stopped the unbearable pleasure by pushing it long and deep to the back of her mouth and into her throat.

Amy did not know how long this lasted, or how many times the two men changed her position and their own, to approach her mouth and vagina from different angles, to sink upon her buttocks and her breasts, to make her come with finger, mouth and tool.

Her reality was fading when she was laid upon her side, her body covered in sweat and secretions. Sir Alec was deep inside her, fucking her slowly, one hand in her hair to hold her head back while he stared into her face, his other upon a breast which he mauled gently.

The young man lay behind her, his prick sliding in the wet valley between her buttocks, stroking her flesh and kissing her neck.

Sir Alec looked into her eyes and said: 'Are you ready to accept Father Michael's third virginity?'

Her heart leapt with both desire and the fear of the unknown.

'Yes. Oh, yes,' she said.

Father Michael parted her buttocks and the head of his prick stirred the wetness in her most secret of places and she pushed against him.

Sir Alec said: 'Do not contract. Relax and push as if to open yourself, to allow him entry.'

Amy did as she was bid and his finger slipped inside to test the tight passage. She contracted around it in delight.

When she let it go, he replaced the finger with the head of his penis, swirling it in the juices to create a slow whirlpool of feelings. She relaxed and pushed as she had been told and it slipped inside.

She cried out for it was large and the passage was small. Tears were in her eyes.

'Relax,' Sir Alec said, kissing her face. His prick inside her vagina was the fulcrum upon which her body seemed to rotate.

Amy relaxed and Father Michael eased inside another inch. She cried out and he rested, and then another inch, and she cried out again. Tears ran down her cheeks and Sir Alec licked them away.

'Do you want it, Amy?' he said.

'Oh yes. Please, please. Fuck me, Michael. Fuck me.'

The young cleric pushed again and this time was not deterred by her cries, as his weapon was fully consumed in her anus.

Amy was limp between them, her head lying back against Father Michael's shoulder, her arms still stretched above her, her wrists tied with silken cord. She was impaled front and rear between two strong, hard bodies.

They began to fuck her.

Her name was sex and at last she could wallow as she had longed to wallow all those wasted years before. Her body was a soft altar upon which she wanted men and women to lavish sensual attention and transport her to that highest state of physical pleasure that humanity could attain.

Fuck me! Fuck me! her mind screamed.

Use me! Use me!

Make me lose my very being in orgasm!

The smells and sounds, the feelings and sensations and the delicious helplessness of the double impaling, all combined to confuse reality. Her existence became one long orgasm.

Amy could never have imagined there could be so much sensation in the world.

Sir Alec reached up, as the timed thrusts at front and rear began to gain momentum, and untied her wrists. She understood the symbolic gesture. She had attained freedom from her fears and prejudices and her senses had been gloriously released.

She put one arm around her father-in-law's head and reached behind her to stroke Father Michael's hips, encouraging his assault as she squirmed softly between them, no longer able to tell where one orgasm finished and another began.

Father Michael began to come for a third time and Sir Alec held her steady upon his steadfast weapon as the young man bucked and heaved upon her bottom.

When he had finished, Sir Alec touched his arm gently and said: 'Stay there.'

The cleric's penis was still a handsome size, even though the steel edge had left it, and he kept it inside her anus as Sir Alec now assaulted her more purposefully from the front. He drove her back upon the slumbering weapon, so that her body was flattened against the muscular sweating maleness behind her, as he pressed against her breasts and stomach.

Amy was coming again when, at last, he tensed within her and his head fell back and his loins discharged with force into her vagina.

Their bodies slid apart and Amy slipped into an exhausted sleep.

Chapter 25

Amy was carried, in her slumbering state, up to her bedroom. When she recovered she had a bath and a light snack.

Her body had a pleasurable afterglow and she was languid and content in the feeling that she was in control of her own destiny for the first time in her life.

Even Tarquin's unexpected arrival from Spain that evening did not disrupt her composure.

She relaxed on the terrace with Sir Alec and Michael, who had discarded his cassock for jeans and a casual shirt, and listened while her husband enthused about the exhibition he was mounting in Barcelona.

They listened and drank coffee and asked all the right questions. Amy watched Tarquin's gestures and his body language and wondered if her suspicions might, perhaps, be partially correct.

In his excitement, he had either forgotten or forgiven the way Amy had misused his teddy bear. He no longer avoided eye contact or direct speech.

When it was time to prepare for dinner, she allowed

Tarquin to go up to the bathroom first, giving him sufficient time to bathe and dress before she followed.

He wore and elegant and well-fitting cream suit. With his tan and white linen shirt and long dark hair, he looked foppishly handsome.

On the pillows of the bed he had sat Bongo the bear.

'He didn't like Spain,' Tarquin said.

'Why did you come back so soon?' she said.

He shrugged helplessly.

'I missed you.'

'The exhibition?'

'The arrangements are going well.' He smiled ruefully. 'No doubt my father is one reason they are going as well as they are.'

'But you missed me?'

'Yes.' He looked at the floor for a moment and cast a sheepish glance at the mirror. 'I may not be able to demonstrate my love as fervently as you may wish, Amy, but I do love you and I will try, as best I can.'

'And so will I,' said Amy. She gave him a sisterly kiss on the cheek and retired to the bathroom. 'Don't wait for me. You go down. I will follow when I am ready.'

Her preparations took longer than she anticipated.

Amy sent for Greta and a pair of scissors and solicited the maid's help in cutting her long blonde hair as short as possible.

It now lay close to her head, accentuating even more her fine features, but also adding a mysteriously boyish look that she could dispel, if she so desire, with one pout of her angel mouth.

For the first time in months she wore trousers. They were in black silk and tailored with pin fronts to hang with elegance rather than display her curves. On her feet she wore flat black shoes.

Amy put on a black silk blouse, enjoying the feel of the material against her skin and nipples that were still sore and aroused from her experiences earlier in the day. To complete the outfit, she wore a double-breasted silk jacket that matched the trousers.

She appraised herself in the full-length mirror and blew a kiss to the hidden camera.

'What do you think, Greta?'

'You look outstanding, madam. Very different, very stylish.'

'Yes, I do look different, don't I? Now, just one thing more.'

Amy's entrance downstairs silence the conversation of the three men.

Sir Alec said: 'Absolutely stunning, my dear.'

Michael nodded his agreement.

'You look beautiful, Amy.'

Tarquin's eyes were wide as he admired his wife.

'Exquisite,' he said.

They dined and, afterwards, Tarquin and Amy walked on the terrace in the moonlight.

He said: 'I have never seen you looking so attractive.'

'Thank you.' She took his hand. 'You are very handsome.'

They stood by the balustrade and looked through

the dusk towards the lake. Amy stood in front of her husband and wrapped his arms around her so that she could feel his body pressing against hers.

He said: 'I really did miss you. I kept thinking you might get bored with this house and my father and go to London and discover someone else.'

'No,' she said. 'I did not go to London and I was not bored. I am not interested in marriage with anyone else.'

'When I return to Spain, will you come with me?'

'I think not.' She lay her head back against his shoulder and pushed gently with her bottom against the stiffening in his trousers. 'But we shall have weekends. Abstinence is an aphrodisiac. We shall have marvellous weekends.'

His erection was hard and lay between the crease of her buttocks. He moved gently against her.

'Come,' she said. 'Let's go to bed.'

Amy led him through the house and up the stairs to their bedroom, but did not switch on the light when she closed the door and they were alone together.

They kissed in the dark, his hands stroking her short hair before sliding down her back to gather the curves of her bottom in his palms.

As they broke apart, he noticed that a sheet had been fixed to the wall so that it completely covered the full-length mirror.

He looked at Amy and she smiled.

'We do not need anybody else tonight,' she whispered.

Then she turned and lay, fully dressed, face down

upon the bed. He approached slowly.

'Pull down my trousers, Tarquin.' Her voice was throaty with desire, almost masculine. 'Make love to me from behind.'

His fingers trembled as they unclipped and unbuttoned the trousers and he tugged them down until they lay around her knees. His hands touched the softness of her bottom and pulled down the black silk briefs to the same position.

Amy squirmed her derrière and raised it towards him. From the bedside table, she took a jar of medical jelly and smoothed a scoop over her buttocks and along the crevice between her cheeks.

'Do it to me this way, Tarquin. Do it to me now.'

Her husband hesitated before pulling off his clothes. As he did so, she worked the jelly deep into the crevice and into the orifice of the third virginity. Her bottom squirmed around her fingers.

'Hurry, Tarquin. Hurry.'

He climbed upon the bed, kneeling behind her, and lowered himself upon her buttocks. His penis was stiffer than she had ever known it. He lay it upon her flesh and moaned, before moving to probe between her legs with its bulbous head. Her hand, which she had pushed beneath her, was waiting to guide it to the correct entrance.

'Oh, that feels so good, Tarquin. There, right there. Do it, Tarquin. Push into me and do it.'

Her husband gasped, pushed tentatively and gained entry. He waited for her to adjust and pushed again. She sighed with sheer delight at the sensation.

'All the way, Tarquin. Fuck me!'

The word was a release and he sank upon her and his penis penetrated her to its entire length. He buried his head in her neck and licked and kissed at her skin, his hands held her hips, and he fucked her with slow and intense passion.

Amy gave herself up to his enjoyment and her hand reached across the pillow to Bongo the bear. She pulled the creature down the bed until it was between her thighs, took hold of the smoothly polished wooden leg and inserted it into her vagina. She groaned and fucked.

Bongo did not complain – and neither did her husband.